It's October in South Cove, California, and the locals in the quaint resort seem to be happily pairing off in the lull before the holidays. Everyone, that is, except for Jill Gardner's elderly aunt, who just dumped her besotted fiancé—and she won't say why.

When Jill hosts a talk at Coffee, Books, and More on the topic of elder abuse, all that's really on her mind is lunch. But the topic hits close to home when she discovers Aunt Jackie has been getting mysterious calls. Jill's certain the caller is a con artist, of course, but her feisty aunt claims to understand this, though she's still shaken—and Harrold's still heartbroken. Who's behind the scam and why was her aunt targeted? When a volunteer from the Senior Project is found murdered, Jill's detective boyfriend is on the case—and it soon becomes clear no one is safe when a caller from beyond becomes a killer in their midst.

Also by Lynn Cahoon

The Tourist Trap Mysteries
Killer Party
Hospitality and Homicide
Tea Cups and Carnage
Murder on Wheels
Killer Run
Dressed to Kill
If the Shoe Kills
Mission to Murder
Guidebook to Murder

The Cat Latimer Mysteries
Sconed to Death
Slay in Character
Of Murder and Men
Fatality by Firelight
A Story to Kill

The Farm-to-Fork Mysteries
One Potato, Two Potato, Dead
Killer Green Tomatoes
Who Moved My Goat Cheese?

Memories and Murder

A Tourist Trap Mystery

Lynn Cahoon

LYRICAL UNDERGROUND
Kensington Publishing Corp.
www.kensingtonbooks.com

LYRICAL UNDERGROUND BOOKS are published by

Kensington Publishing Corp.
119 West 40th Street
New York, NY 10018

All Kensington titles, imprints, and distributed lines are available at special quantity discounts for bulk purchases for sales promotion, premiums, fund-raising, educational, or institutional use.

Special book excerpts or customized printings can also be created to fit specific needs. For details, write or phone the office of the Kensington Sales Manager: Kensington Publishing Corp., 119 West 40th Street, New York, NY 10018. Attn. Sales Department. Phone: 1-800-221-2647.

Lyrical Underground and Lyrical Underground logo Reg. US Pat. & TM Off.

First Electronic Edition: November 2019
ISBN-13: 978-1-5161-0304-1 (ebook)
ISBN-10: 1-5161-0304-1 (ebook)

First Print Edition: November 2019
ISBN-13: 978-1-5161-0307-2
ISBN-10: 1-5161-0307-6

Printed in the United States of America

Dedication to the crew at IDHW—Region IV—Teresa, Roger, Gaylynne, Randy, Loretta, Shirley—Thanks for teaching me that the most important factor in caring for people is not the rules but the implementation and delivery of the news.

Acknowledgments

Memories and Murder brought me back to my time working in social services agencies serving the poor, elderly, and people with disabilities. I have strong feelings about making sure we care for others, but being my Libra self, I see both sides of the political discussion. Even if we don't always agree, I love people like Paula, Sadie Michaels, and Pastor Bill. I've worked all sides: the state/federal agencies, the nonprofits, and the long-term care industry, but if I've gotten something wrong, it's my error, not my research assistants.

Finding myself in the publishing world, I've surrounded myself with caring and supportive team members to support my career as an author. Big thanks to Esi and the crew at Kensington for their attention to both me as their author and the books we develop together. And thanks to my amazing agent, Jill Marsal, for her help in developing my career.

Chapter 1

To everything, there is a season. This truth was given to us in the Bible as well as through the sacred music of the Byrds. Life goes in cycles. As I sat and listened to Paula Woods from the Senior Project talk to the business-to-business meeting, I pondered my own life and seasons. And, of course, the seasons of the ones I loved. As the South Cove city council liaison for the business community, it was my job to set up these monthly meetings. Most months we talked about upcoming marketing festivals or rules and regulations that the city council had taken up for discussion. This month, the topic was hitting closer to home.

I'm Jill Gardner. I set up the meeting and its agenda, but I also own Coffee, Books, and More, our regular meeting place. We are the only coffee-shop-slash-bookstore in our small coastal town.

In addition to the community business agenda items, we had a guest speaker. Paula was also a member of Sadie Michaels's church. Sadie had advocated for Paula to have a slot on this month's agenda.

October was a slow month for topics, with everyone getting back in gear from the holidays, so I'd scheduled her in for the last hour of our meeting. I could tell she was winding down and so was the attention span of our attending members. Me? I was checking my dark, curly hair for split ends.

"I just wanted to thank Jill again for inviting me to speak with you. Elder abuse is a serious topic that our country needs to address. And I hope all of you will think about the care and attention older people in your life need and deserve. Thank you." Paula looked my way, and I took that as my cue, jumping up to take the microphone before Mayor Baylor could even get out of his chair.

"Thank you, Paula, for your thoughtful presentation. I know a lot of us will be thinking about what you said for a while." That got me a glare from my aunt, who neither acted like nor admitted to being elderly. "I just wanted to remind everyone that our next meeting is after Octoberfest finishes, so I thought Darla might have some last-minute instructions for us. Darla, do you mind? I know I didn't have this on the agenda."

"Not a problem." Darla Taylor made her way to the front table. She'd been in charge of South Cove's festivals for as long as I'd owned my shop. Well, except for that one Christmas, but even then, she'd saved the day after the mayor's wife had messed up the planning. "I was going to jump in with some reminders before we closed anyway."

As Darla came up, the mayor glanced at his watch. I passed by his chair and he grabbed my arm, bringing me down to his level. He whispered in my ear, "I need to get back to my office."

"Go ahead and leave. You're not being held hostage." I turned toward him so my voice wouldn't carry over Darla's.

"You know I like to close the meeting. Besides, its election year and I need to remind people to register to vote." He cocked his head and studied me. "Your boyfriend isn't thinking about running for mayor this year, is he? Maybe this is a ploy to keep me from getting in front of the business owners?"

"I'm not Greg's campaign manager." I saw the fear my choice of words had caused. I pulled my arm free, certain everyone was pretending to listen to Darla but really focused on our little spat. "Anyway, he's not running. At least, not to my knowledge. Stop being paranoid. Go now or stay and talk. It's your call."

When I sat down, Aunt Jackie leaned over, unable to squelch her curiosity. She was dressed casually today in the blue Chanel suit that made her silver hair shine. She wore pearl earrings, but instead of the matching strand, she had on an old, silver heart necklace I hadn't seen her wear in years. "What did Mayor Bird want?"

I snorted at the nickname our mayor had been given, mostly because of his too-high voice. He glared at me across the table, like he knew what I was laughing about.

"He's afraid he won't have time to campaign with the group this morning. We're taking too much of his precious time." I glanced over at Deek Kerr, who was watching the proceedings with interest. Of course, the newest barista thought everything was interesting. He claimed to be a professional student, but at least with the barista job, he could convince his mom he was trying to be self-sufficient. He fit right in to the casual California lifestyle, with his blond dreadlocks and surfer-boy tan and looks, but the kid was scary smart. This month, his dreadlocks were tinged with electric blue. He saw my look and held up an empty coffee carafe. I shook my head. If we gave the group another round of coffee, they may never leave the shop. It was almost ten and time for Coffee, Books, and More to be serving actual customers.

"Well, maybe if he would actually do some mayor-type work, he wouldn't have to campaign so hard." Aunt Jackie checked her phone. It was a habit she'd picked up since she'd abruptly canceled her engagement with Harrold Snider a few months before. From what I could tell, Harrold, the owner of The Train Station, was my aunt's soul mate, so I had no clue why she'd taken such a drastic step. Soul mates were hard to find, and my aunt had gotten two in one lifetime. She'd loved her first husband without hesitation, and I wondered if her fear of losing that memory was what had made her run scared from Harrold. Whatever the reason, I was hoping for a quick reconciliation. My aunt was better when she was with Harrold. That wasn't just my opinion; it was a fact.

Fifteen minutes later, when the meeting closed—after the mayor had cheerfully reminded everyone to register to vote and that he would appreciate their support in the May primaries—I drew in a deep breath. I know these meetings only happened once a month, but they took a toll on me. I guess it was my nature to worry about things going horribly wrong with each meeting just because of my planning or lack of planning. Kind of like those dreams where I didn't study for the math test.

Sadie Michaels waved me over to where she stood talking to Paula. Sadie owned Pies on the Fly, which was my dessert supplier for the shop as well as being one of my best friends. Sadie looked like a baker out of a fairy tale. Her cotton dress and sweater had a fifties vibe, and she always seemed to have a bit of flour on her somewhere. She took Paula's arm and turned her toward me as I walked up. "Tell her she did awesome."

"It was a great talk. You gave out a lot of statistics I didn't know about." I had known Sadie would put me in this position, and because Paula's talk had been almost painful to listen to due to her shyness and lack of speaking skills, I had found at least one good thing to say.

Paula adjusted the purse strap on her shoulder. "You don't have to be nice. I know I'm not the most powerful speaker. But I am working on it. My boss tells me I need to practice more. She's always sending me out of town to talk to different groups. I keep telling her I'm not ready, but I still get sent. I'm part of a Toastmasters club that meets twice a month in Bakerstown. Your mayor attends our group, and man, can he talk."

That was probably an understatement, but apparently, Paula had a good impression of our mayor, so I'd leave her with that. "Sounds like you're really working on your career path. How long have you worked for the Senior Project?"

"Just over fifteen years. I started as an intern in college. My grandmother was dealing with some fraud issues, and when I went to talk to them, I decided to become part of the solution." She glanced outside, where a tall man with dark hair stood near the door. She waved at him, and I saw the come-to-me wave he gave her back. "I hate to cut this short, but I have to go. Ben, my boyfriend, is here. He's taking me to lunch today. He's such a sweetheart. I swear, he spends as much time volunteering at the center as I do working there."

As she walked away, Sadie watched her leave the shop before turning to me. Over Sadie's shoulder, I saw the couple through the window. Paula reached for the guy's hand, but he ignored it and started walking away. "He could have come in and heard her talk."

"It's probably a good thing for their relationship that he didn't." Sadie grimaced at the memory. "I owe you big-time for that one. I had no idea she was such a bad presenter. She'd told me she'd been in that speaking club for years."

"Yeah, but if Mayor Baylor is in the same club, she probably doesn't get a lot of practice time." I nodded to the coffee bar. "It's been forever since we talked. Do you have time for coffee and one of your brownies?"

I knew tempting Sadie with the treats she supplied us with for the shop wasn't the best incentive, but it was all I had. And her brownies were really good.

"I think I can squeeze out fifteen minutes for a friend. Amy and Justin are coming over Saturday afternoon to test cakes. I've already got fifteen sample cakes done, but I want to give her a few more choices." She walked with me to the bar, where she sat while I got the coffee and brownies.

"After fifteen cakes, I wouldn't know what I liked because I'd be on a sugar high." I filled cups and sat them in front of her, then went for the brownies. Amy Newman, my friend, worked at City Hall doing a little bit of everything. And a few months ago, she'd announced her engagement. Now, it was all about the wedding for her.

As Aunt Jackie moved behind me, she leaned close. "Don't forget to charge those to the marketing budget. We don't get those brownies for free, you know."

"Yes, ma'am." I dished up the brownies, then wrote out a receipt and put it in the till. When I heard the door at the top of the stairs shut, I walked over and sat down next to Sadie. "She's still in a funk. I keep trying to get her to tell me what Harrold did, but she insists he didn't do anything and this is none of my business."

"Well, she's right about that." Sadie put a comforting hand on my arm as I started to object. "It's not about you, Jill. This is her life, and if she called the wedding off, there has to be a good reason."

"I've talked to Harrold. He's as confused as I am. One minute Aunt Jackie's all bridezilla about the weight of the paper for the invitations. The next, she very calmly and politely dumps him the night of Amy's engagement party." I sipped my coffee. "It just doesn't make any sense."

"Have you thought about talking to her doctors? Or Mary?" Sadie bit into the brownie and groaned. "I know it's prideful to talk about your own cooking, but these are amazing."

"Mary's as confused as Harrold. And what's worse is Aunt Jackie won't talk to her. She's canceled three get-togethers at the last minute with very flimsy excuses." I broke off a piece of brownie and popped it into my mouth. Chocolate explosion. After I chased it down with a sip of coffee, I frowned. "That's not like her at all. Maybe I *should* call her doctor. She gave me a health power of attorney last year. That should get me around the doctor-patient confidentiality stuff."

"It might. If you need someone to get her out of her apartment so you can go snooping, let me know. We've been talking about visiting this restaurant supply place to get me new pans. She has connections." Sadie finished the brownie, then looked at the clock. "I better go. Three cakes today. Three tomorrow, and I'll be done. Then I'm helping Pastor Bill sort the food pantry. We got a ton of donations during the holidays. There's no way to figure out what we have to give away."

After Sadie left, Deek finished setting the dining room back up, then leaned over the bar, looking out the window. "Your friend is crushing on the preacher dude."

I smiled as I turned back around. Sadie was precisely crushing on Pastor Bill, but I had thought I was the only one who saw it. Deek was intuitive. His mom was a psychic and friends with South Cove's only fortune-teller and my neighbor, Esmeralda. "And why do you say that?"

"Don't play coy with me. She brightens up when she talks about spending time with him. And don't tell me it's because she loves serving God. I mean, yeah, there's some of that, but she wants that guy. I watch her every Sunday before, during, and after service. She's by his side, at his beck and call. Personally, I think it sets a bad example. She should be a little less available." He took Sadie's cup and plate and rinsed them to put into the dishwasher.

"You have good instincts, Deek." Of course, I agreed with him about Sadie and the preacher on all counts.

"Now, your aunt, on the other hand, plays it a little too cool. Man, that train guy is all bent out of shape." Deek held out his hands. "I can see their auras and they are both hurting."

"Is that true?"

Deek looked at me funny. "Is what true?"

"That you can see auras." He'd told me before that he didn't have any psychic ability, even though his mother was a practicing fortune-teller. And now he was throwing around words like auras?

"Don't overthink it. It's just a way of saying I can see they're both miserable without each other. Why did your aunt break it off?" He leaned closer, hoping to learn the answer.

The bell over the door rang and a couple came into the store. He beelined to the coffee bar, but she stopped and scanned the bookshelves.

"That is the million-dollar question. Can you handle them? I've got some paperwork I need to get done." I picked up my cup and plate and moved around to the back of the bar. As I refilled my cup with more caffeine than I knew was good for me, I heard Deek greet the man.

"So, what can I pour you while you're shopping for your next great read? I bet you enjoy international thrillers. You have the look of a spy."

Smiling, I left Deek to his magic skill of reading people to know just what they needed to hear to increase their purchases. He was so good at it that I caught myself being woven into his web when he wanted something and I knew I was being played. Maybe he did have a gift. I sat down at the desk and pulled out my aunt's calendar. Flipping to the back, I found what I'd been looking for. Her doctor's name and phone number. I just looked up my doctor online when I needed to call for an appointment. My aunt had a written name and phone number section in the back of a paper planner. And she'd had to paste pages she'd copied from an old address book she'd had for years.

Talk about old school. I dialed the number and when a receptionist answered, I asked for an appointment.

"What is this regarding?"

She didn't seem surprised when I said I needed to talk about Jackie Ekroth. "Tell Dr. Stevens that I'm her niece and I need to find out what is going on with her."

"You can come by tomorrow at one. He'll be on his lunch break, so he'll need to eat while you talk."

I was surprised at the speed of getting the appointment. And that the woman hadn't given me any grief about privacy laws. "I'll be there. Thank you."

"Don't thank me. Dr. Stevens told me to bring you in last week. I just haven't been able to find time to track down your number. As your aunt's next of kin, you really should keep that information updated." She paused. "Don't forget to bring a copy of your health care POA. We'll need to make a copy before you start talking."

I thanked her again for the appointment, then sat looking at the phone. Something bad was going on. I could feel it. Why would her doctor want to talk to me? I rubbed my face and then realized only one thing could make me feel better. I picked up my cell and dialed a number from memory.

"Hi. Do you want to meet at Diamond Lille's for lunch?"

Chapter 2

When I walked into Diamond Lille's ten minutes later, Amy Newman, surfer girl, city planner, and my best friend, sat at our favorite booth. We ate at Lille's so frequently, the booth should have our names and photos on the wall next to it. She was growing out her straight blond hair for her upcoming wedding, so instead of a short bob, it was already down to her shoulders. Amy waved me over, then leaned close as I scooted over on the red bench seat. "Did you see the new addition on Lille's wall?"

I angled my head to see the signed photograph of an actor who played the head of a very powerful motorcycle gang on an ongoing drama on one of the major networks. "How on earth did she get that?"

"Apparently, the guy believes in doing his research, so he was at a hog ride last weekend. Lille explained her wall of fame to him, and before you could say 'Lille's a big fat cheater,' she had the picture.

"He's so good-looking, isn't he?" Carrie sat down her notebook and pen on the table as she took a long look at the wall. "I touch it every time I walk by. I've heard that touching a picture can bring a spirit to talk to you. Maybe it works on live humans as well?"

"We couldn't be that lucky. The guy is probably already back out shooting his series. Why anyone that cute would stay in South Cove past the weekend is beyond me." Amy closed the menu. "Besides, I hear the show is shooting in Vancouver. Everything seems to shoot in Vancouver nowadays."

"You're probably right. What can I get you for lunch?" Carrie picked up her pen and notebook again. She looked at Amy, turning away from me. "You first. That one looks like she has the world weighing on her shoulders. She's screaming bad mojo voodoo vibes."

"Ewhhh. Stop. Now that image is in my head." I rubbed my face to get the bad mojo off me. "I'm going to have to order fish and chips because I've been traumatized."

"Like you were ever going to order anything else. Do you want a vanilla milkshake with that?" She waited for me to shake my head before turning her attention back to Amy. "And what about you, surfer queen?"

"Double-decker cheeseburger with fries. And a strawberry shake." Amy handed the menus to Carrie. "And if he does come in to the diner, call me first. You know I'm your favorite customer."

"You two might be my most-frequent customers, but you aren't my favorites. Your aunt's beau, Harrold, has been coming in a lot lately. He looks so sad. Can't you tell your aunt to get over whatever idiotic thing he did? Men are just stupid. We kind of have to forgive them for that."

As Carrie walked away, Amy watched me. "So, what has you so riled up? You seemed okay when I left the meeting."

"I'm not upset. Okay, well, I am upset, but I just needed to talk something through with you." I waited for Carrie to drop off glasses of water before I blurted out what I'd been thinking about for a while. "Look, do you think something bad is happening to Aunt Jackie?"

"Bad like...?"

I finished her thought. "Bad like sick bad."

Amy didn't speak for a while. She sipped her water. Set down the glass, then leaned back into the bench seat. "I have to say, I kind of thought the same thing. When I first heard about what she'd done, I thought she must have gotten some bad news from her doctors. It's the only reason I can think of that would cause her to cancel the wedding and break Harrold's heart."

I sank back into the bench seat, my appetite gone. Which never happens, by the way. "I have an appointment tomorrow with her primary doctor in Bakerstown. I don't know what I'm going to do..." I couldn't finish the sentence.

Amy reached for my hand and squeezed. "Whatever it is, we'll get through it. Jackie could just be being Jackie. You know how stubborn she can be."

"Like the time she didn't talk to me for a month because I told that magazine salesman that she was up in her apartment and she definitely needed new cookware?" I apparently hadn't gotten my sense of humor from my aunt.

"Or the time she told me that all that sun and surfing was going to turn me into an old woman before I knew it?" Amy flipped back her hair. "Then she pointed out a few wrinkles on my face and handed me a jar of her face cream. She had to have been planning that one for a while. Who carries that size of moisturizer in her purse?"

"My aunt does." I smiled at the image. "I always told her she needed to go on that show where they ask for something random from your purse. Like an airline napkin or a child's report card."

"*Let's Make a Deal.* I think." Amy smiled at Carrie, who dropped off our food. "That was fast."

"You too looked like you needed cheering up." Carrie refilled our water glasses. "The shakes will be right out. I hope I didn't say anything wrong earlier."

I shook my head. "No. You were fine. I've just been having a bad day."

"Well, I'm going to go hurry along those shakes." Carrie patted my hand. "I'm sure this is just a phase and everything will be all right."

Amy watched the waitress walk away. "Now that's optimism. She'd have to be an optimist. She's worked here for Lille for like ever. She deserves a medal. And maybe a retirement plan."

As we finished eating, I noticed Paula, the morning speaker at the business meeting, sitting alone at a table. I tried to catch her gaze, but she was focused on her phone.

"Who are you looking at?" Amy turned around to see the section of the diner behind her. "Oh, her. What a mess, right? I can't believe she's even trying to talk for the Senior Project. She can't be very effective in bringing in money."

"That's not very nice." I watched as Paula glanced out the window and followed her gaze. Ben was in the parking lot, on the phone. And from his body language, the call wasn't going in his favor. "I wonder what her boyfriend does for a living."

"Why?" Now Amy was as engrossed in watching the drama unfold as me.

"She said he spent a lot of time volunteering. And it's Tuesday afternoon. Shouldn't he be getting back to some job if he has one?" I watched as Ben put away the phone in his pocket, and instead of coming back into the restaurant, banged on the window for Paula's attention.

All eyes turned to him. Red-faced, Paula quickly grabbed her wallet from her purse, threw some bills on the table, and ran out of the dining room to meet him. When she got close, he opened the driver's side door to his car, not even waiting for her. The guy didn't seem very warm and cuddly to me.

"Now that's a first-class jerk. You see all kinds in here." Carrie had returned with my vanilla shake. "I don't understand why women put up with being treated like that. I bet he didn't say two words to her the entire time they were here eating. Then, when he got that call, he just jumped up and went right outside. He's been out there for a good half hour and she's been trying to act like it didn't bother her."

Not everyone had a good relationship with their significant other. But it kind of broke my heart to remember how excited she was to see him in the window of the shop. The girl had it bad for the wrong type. Even if he liked to volunteer.

"Look, I've got to get back to work. Fred, Mayor Baylor's campaign manager, is coming in at two and they'll want me to keep them stocked up on lattes and muffins. I'll probably be making two trips over to the shop. Are you going back or heading home?" Amy nodded to my milkshake. "You could get a to-go cup."

"I'm heading home, so I'll just finish it here." I stood and gave Amy a quick hug. "Sadie said you and Justin are choosing a cake on Saturday. I'm sorry I took up all our time with my concerns."

"No big. I'll give you all the details on Sunday. We are still on for brunch, right?" Amy laid out money for her meal.

"I'll be right here at nine and ready to hear all about the wedding planning." I watched my friend leave the diner and head back to City Hall. Then I pulled a novel out of my tote and got lost in the small-town romance series I loved. This was the last one of the series, and it was breaking my heart that I'd have to leave this Oregon coast town and all my fictional friends in less than one hundred pages. If I ran the publishing world, series like these would never stop.

I'd finished the book about the same time as I finished the milkshake. Most of the lunch crowd had left, and Carrie came over to clear off the rest of our table. I pulled out money for the meal and tip. "Sorry, I know you're probably off-shift soon."

"Colleen would have taken care of you if I needed to leave." Carrie picked up my check and money and slipped it into her apron pocket. "I started reading the first in that series about a week ago. I love the setting."

"Me too." I handed her the book. "Here. You've got five more before you get to this one, but you might as well have the last one."

"That's kind of you." Carrie took the book like it was a huge cash tip. "I think you're a sweet girl, no matter what Lille says."

Then she walked off with my book, leaving me wondering what I'd done to tick off Lille recently.

When I got home, I had two options: clean the bathroom—which had been on my to-do list since the weekend or take Emma for a run. Being a responsible pet owner, I chose the latter. The bathroom would wait until tomorrow. Or Saturday.

For three o'clock on a nice October day, the beach was eerily empty. I glanced up and down as far as I could see and there were no walkers or sea lions or even other dogs. I unsnapped Emma's leash and we started running. She liked playing in the waves. I kept farther up from the water's edge, where the sand was hard-packed and dry. As I ran, I emptied my mind of all the things that had worried me. Aunt Jackie. Amy's upcoming wedding and the dress I'd have to look amazing in. The ten pounds I wanted to lose before the wedding so I would look amazing. Greg and me as a couple.

When we reached the rock where we turned around, I fell onto the sand and watched Emma continue to play. I'd have to leave her outside until she dried, then brush all the sand out of her before I let her back into the house, but it was worth it. She exuded joy.

As I watched, I realized I'd been thinking about couples and relationships for a while now. We were all at different spots in our relationships. A few months ago, I was worried that Greg and I were the only ones not talking about marriage. Now, we were right where we needed to be. Aunt Jackie had gone from planning her forever wedding to not even talking to the guy I knew she still loved. Only Amy and Justin seemed to be enjoying the planning process.

Maybe it was because they worked out their stress by surfing together. I'd be so worried about falling off the board, I wouldn't be able to think about anything else.

When we got back to the house, Harrold's small electric car sat in my driveway. He was sitting in the driver's seat, looking at his phone. I let Emma in the backyard and shut the gate before I walked over and knocked on his window.

He hadn't seen me walk up and the sound of the knock made him jump. Which made me smile. I know it wasn't funny, but he looked shocked as he rolled down the window.

"You did come to see me, right?" I waved him out of the car. "Come inside and we'll have some coffee and cheesecake."

"I don't mean to interrupt your day." Harrold put his phone in a compartment next to the seat. "I was trying to find your number and was just going to give you a call and leave a message."

"Harrold, this is silly. Come inside and let's talk." I opened his car door and held out a hand. "I can spare a few moments for the nicest man in South Cove."

"Even if your aunt hates me?" He shook his head. "That's not right. I don't think she hates me at all. I see her watching me and the love is still in her. Why is she acting like this?"

I was afraid the tears forming in his eyes would start falling before I could get him inside or I started crying myself. I repeated my invitation. "Let's go inside. I just ran and I'd really like a slice of that cheesecake." He smiled and climbed out of the car. "You are such a sweet girl. Your aunt is lucky to have such a strong family system." "I don't know about that. It's been just the two of us for a long time." I slowed my pace to stay by Harrold's side. "I have to admit, I was looking forward to adding one to the party."

"And I would be honored to be called family by you, but you've done a great job of making everyone around you that you love not only your friends but your family." He took the rail in his hand and slowly stepped up the few stairs to the porch. I hadn't realized how stiff Harrold was due to his arthritis. My aunt had always been pushing vitamins on him, and they'd walked the beach trail daily. Apparently, he hadn't been doing that since the breakup.

Emma sat on the back porch. I opened the door and checked to see if the screen door was locked. Then I leaned down to talk to my dog. "You're staying out until you dry off, missy."

Harrold stood uncomfortably at the edge of the kitchen. He'd been over here for meals a million times since he'd started dating my aunt, but now, I guess he felt out of place. I waved him to a chair. "Come, sit down. I'll start the coffee."

I grabbed two cups and set up a pot to brew. Then I took out the cheesecake and cut a large slice for Harrold and a smaller one for me. Setting the plates on the table, I grabbed forks before I sat down.

"You're too kind." Harrold picked up his fork, then set it back down. "Look, I probably shouldn't be here. I'm putting you in a bad position, but I need your help."

"Eat and we'll talk. I'm worried about you. Are you eating enough?" He smiled and picked up the fork. "Actually, I've had several women from the church come over with a casserole for the last few weeks. I guess they believe I'm back on the market."

"I hear you've been at Lille's a lot." I took a bite of the chocolate cheesecake Typically, I tried to over order at least one full cheesecake a week. My aunt hadn't caught on yet, or if she did, she hadn't said anything about it to me.

"Lille's a good girl. If I don't show up, she sends food over. I'm blessed to have such wonderful friends in my life." He took a bite of the cheesecake. "This is amazing. Sadie Michaels has a gift with food."

"That she does." I wondered how long we'd be tiptoeing around the reason he was here. The coffee was finished brewing, so I jumped up to fill the cups. Harrold took his coffee like me, black and hot. I set the cups on the table. "Why don't you tell me what you need? You know I'll help any way I can."

He sipped his coffee, took another bite of the dessert, and then took another sip. "I am going to win your aunt back. To prove my intentions, I'd like to fix up her porch."

"At the apartment?" The back door was used less as a real door and more as a minigarden and sitting area by my aunt. She used the front door, which dropped down into the back room of the shop, to go in and out of her place.

"Yes. I bought a new bench, along with a few shelving units. Kyle is painting them, and when he's done, I'll be filling it with more plants. The porch will be an oasis, and a place for her to sit and watch the ocean." He sighed and then absently took another bite. That was the magic of Sadie's cheesecake. You couldn't stop eating it once you started. "I don't have much hope that it will change her mind, but we'd been talking about doing it for a while. The least I can do is make her dream come true for the area."

"Let me know when you want to get it set up and I'll make sure she's out of the building." I wasn't sure how I'd get that done, but with Mary's help, maybe I could set up a girls' day in the city for the two of them. Whatever was going to happen between Harrold and my aunt, she needed to get back to living her life. And that meant spending time with her best friend.

"I appreciate your help." He looked down at his empty plate in surprise. "I didn't really feel hungry when I came, but I guess I haven't eaten since last night."

"The power of food. It can help to heal." I stood and held out the coffeepot. "Do you want more coffee? Maybe another slice of cake?"

He drained his cup and stood, putting his dishes in the sink. "I've taken enough of your time. I'm so glad you're letting me do this for your aunt."

"Harrold, if I could figure out why she broke up with you and fix it, I would." Now I felt the tears behind my eyes.

He reached out and gave me a hug. Rubbing the top of my head like I was a child. "I know you would. I would do anything to make things right. I just don't know what I did."

Chapter 3

I hadn't slept well. After Harrold left, I'd cleaned not only the bathroom but the entire downstairs. And then I gave Emma a bath, which meant I needed to clean the laundry/mudroom, where I'd set up a large counter and sink for the grooming process. If I sold the house, the new owners would think I really loved to do laundry. But the room worked great as a place to get Emma clean and smelling good.

Even with all the activity, my mind wouldn't shut down. Or it might have been the fact that I'd finished the pot of coffee that Harrold and I had shared. It felt wrong pouring coffee down the drain. So I drank the last cup at about eight last night, when I turned on the television and snuggled with Emma on the couch.

Greg had been busy at work, so, for the last few days, he'd left early and come home late. We were supposed to have a date night on Friday. I was looking forward to the evening, and not only for the food at the restaurant where we had reservations.

I just had to get through two more days and it would be date night. I needed some me time. Especially after I talked to Aunt Jackie's doctor later today.

I'd called Deek and asked him to come in an hour early so I could get into Bakerstown on time. Instead of walking into town, I drove my Jeep. Walking would have helped me wake up. At least a little better than the caffeine from yet another pot of coffee I'd made that morning. If work was slow, I was going to be jumpy by the time I left. It was inventory week, so at least I could go through the books while I was waiting for the time to pass. Books always seemed to relax me, even if I was just going through the stack to see what I needed to order.

Deek showed up a little before eleven, and I grabbed my tote and headed out to the back parking lot, where I'd left my Jeep. Emma had looked sad when I left, but I'd promised her a run as soon as I got back from Bakerstown. I figured after I found out what Aunt Jackie's doctor had to say, I would need the distraction anyway.

The drive up the Pacific Coast Highway typically relaxed me, but today, I didn't find enjoyment in the scenery or the fresh ocean breeze that filled my vehicle. I got to the office fifteen minutes early and sat skimming all the magazines that were scattered through the almost-empty waiting room. Once I'd finished that, I checked the shopping list I kept on my phone. I might as well stop at the store while I was in town. I added a few items, and when I was finished, a nurse stood in front of me.

"Miss Gardner? Dr. Stevens will see you now." She led me back past the exam rooms and an alcove where a chair sat next to a scale and a blood pressure machine. She knocked on a door before she opened it. "Doctor? This is Jill Gardner. Jackie Ekroth's niece."

The room looked like what I imagined a doctor's office should look like. The top of the desk was clean and sparse, with only a laptop open on top, along with a simple spiral notebook and a pen. The guy must be old school in some ways. It made me like him just a little more, because I liked to plan using paper. Writing it down felt more substantial than keying it into my computer.

"Miss Gardner, I'm so glad you could come in. I know you're busy, but I wanted to talk to you about your aunt." He glanced at the chart, then back at me. "Has she appeared distracted lately? Maybe making abrupt decisions that don't seem like her?"

"Yes. Can you tell me what's going on?" I leaned closer, trying to read the chart upside down. But the type was too small.

"Actually, I'm not sure. She's said some things to me that seemed strange, but I can't get her to submit to testing. She says she's fine." He glanced at the chart. "And physically, she's in great shape. But she has me worried."

"What did she say? Did she tell you about canceling her engagement?" This wasn't going the way I'd planned. I thought I'd come in, he'd tell me that Jackie needed medicine or, at worst, surgery. But from the way he was talking, there was nothing physically wrong with my aunt. "Oh, God. She doesn't have Alzheimer's, does she?"

"Not as far as I can tell." He shut the file. "Look, your aunt is in better shape than most forty-year-olds I treat. I can't see any reason to be alarmed. She's not showing signs of dementia or loss of cognitive ability. She just asked me something weird."

I could tell he was winding down, that soon I'd be driving back to South Cove as confused as I was driving here. I needed to know why he was concerned. "What did she ask you?"

He squirmed uncomfortably in his chair. "It's probably nothing. But if you'd let me know if anything happens that you think is unlike her?"

"No, I want to know. What did she ask you that has you worried about her? If you need to see this again—" I dug in my purse for the copy of the health care power of attorney, but he waved me down when I tried to hand it to him.

"I don't need to see that. We have a copy of your aunt's wishes on file." He tapped his pen on the desk, then leaned back. "She asked me what the signs of a brain tumor would be."

"A brain tumor?" Now my stomach clenched. "Aunt Jackie has a brain tumor?"

"No, your aunt has none of the signs of a brain tumor, but once I listed them off, she asked one more question." He paused, waiting for me to calm down a bit. A knock on his door sounded, and a nurse poked her head in.

"Your next patient is ready in room two." The woman disappeared as quickly as she'd appeared.

He stood and walked around the desk. My time was apparently over.

As I stood, I took two deep breaths and pushed out the fear. "So what was her question?"

He paused at the door, concern filling his face. "She asked if there was any medical reason someone might be hearing voices from the past."

* * * *

I thought about the question all the way home. And then some more on my run with Emma. Finally, I decided to go and talk directly with Aunt Jackie. She was worried about something and I needed to know what it was. This guessing game was driving me crazy. I glanced at the clock and saw I had just enough time to catch her at the apartment before her shift started.

I hurried into town and went through the coffee shop to the back staircase. Deek watched me rush through the room, but he was talking with a customer, so I got by with only a "Hey, Boss."

Now I stood at the door to my aunt's apartment. I had a key for emergencies, but I didn't use it. I knocked on the door.

"Just a minute," my aunt called out. She sounded fine. Maybe I was worried for nothing. But when she answered the door, I saw the lack of sleep on her face. "Oh, Jill, am I late for my shift?"

"No, you aren't late for your shift." I didn't wait to be let in. Instead, I moved around her and went to sit on her couch.

She closed the door and shook her head. "I'm sure I raised you with more manners than that. But come on in and have a seat, even though you're already in."

"We need to talk."

Her eyes widened and she came over and sat beside me. "Do you need coffee? I have a pot going. Are you okay? What's wrong?"

Leave it to my aunt to think *I* was the problem. "I don't need coffee. I need to know what's going on with you. Mary's worried. Harrold's worried. Even Dr. Stevens is worried."

I saw the iron in her spine tighten, and she was about to tell me it was no one's business when I held up a hand. "Don't give me that pat answer. It's been long enough; you need to talk to someone."

And as if I'd popped a balloon, I saw the fight go out of her. She reached for her cup, but it was empty. "Do you mind getting me some more? I don't think I can even start saying this without some fortification."

"Just coffee?" I picked up the cup and went into her kitchen. The apartment used to be mine, before I moved out to the house that my friend, Miss Emily, had left me. And Aunt Jackie moved in.

I heard the smile in her voice. "Yes, just coffee. I do have a shift in twenty minutes."

I delivered the coffee, then sat and waited. She'd talk when she was ready.

"I guess I should start at the beginning. About the time Greg's friend was killed, I started getting strange calls. Hang ups, really. I was annoyed." She glanced at the cell phone that sat on the coffee table. "They were all from the same number. So, finally, I got tired of them, and when they called again and hung up, I called back."

"You know there are a lot of spam calls. I thought I put your phone on the no-call list, but I'll check and register it again. You shouldn't be getting them." I relaxed just a little. Had these calls been what had upset her?

"I'm not done with the story, dear." Now she got up and paced the living room. "So I called back, and a man answered. He called me by name. Said he knew it was wrong for him to reach out after all this time, but he'd heard about my upcoming nuptials with Harrold and he needed to at least try."

"This is all about an old boyfriend?" Now I did relax and took a sip of my coffee. "You know Harrold is perfect for you. I haven't seen you this happy since before Uncle Ted passed away. You and Harrold make an amazing couple."

"I agree. Harrold and I did seem to be a perfect match." She sighed and picked up her cup again. "But it wasn't an old boyfriend who was calling."

"I'm confused. Then why would you call off the engagement? Who was it who called?"

She leaned back in her chair and looked pained. She shook her head. "You're going to think I'm crazy. Heck, *I* think I'm crazy."

"Aunt Jackie, just tell me. We can fix this."

At that comment, she laughed, but there wasn't humor in her voice. "This can't be fixed. Jill, it was your Uncle Ted who called me. He's alive."

The first thing I did after I pushed my jaw up from the floor was to call Greg and have him come over. How in the world could she even think the calls were from my long-dead uncle? It wasn't like he'd just taken off one night. The guy had died. Funeral and everything. I pushed off my worry about my aunt so I could deal with getting this fixed. I'd fall apart later. The second thing was to drop down to the shop and make sure Deek could stay a while longer.

"Sure, Boss Lady. I'm free and clear today." He nodded to the upstairs, concern showing on his face. "Everything all right with your aunt? She's been down in the dumps for a while now."

"She's fine. But if Greg comes in the front, send him upstairs. We'll be waiting for him." I started toward the back room. Deek moved into my path.

"Look, I know it's not my business, but if there was something wrong, you'd tell me, right?"

I blew out a breath and paused, thinking about what I wanted to say. "Honestly, I don't know what's going on, really, but I think she's all right. Or she will be now. As soon as I can, I'll tell you what I can."

He stepped out of my way. "Thank you. I know I'm new to your world, but I think Jackie is the bomb and I'd do anything to help."

How did someone help when your dead husband started calling you? No wonder Aunt Jackie had been out of sorts and secretive. It sounded crazy. I impulsively gave Deek a quick hug. "You're a good guy, you know?"

His face turned beet red and he nodded when I let him go. He stammered, "You too." Then his eyes widened and he took a step away from me, staring at the doorway.

I turned back and followed his gaze. Greg had stepped into the dining room, in full detective uniform, including the gun on his hip. He narrowed his eyes and strolled toward us. "What's going on?"

Deek stammered, "Nothing."

I met Greg and took his arm. "You have to talk to Aunt Jackie. You are not going to believe this."

With one last glare toward Deek, Greg followed me up the stairs to Aunt Jackie's apartment. I glanced back at him. "Why do you mess with Deek so much?"

"Mostly because it's fun." He grinned as he met me on the landing. "He's going to be avoiding me for months now."

"You're mean." I held open the door. "Aunt Jackie? Greg's here."

"I told you not to call him. I know what I'm doing." She snapped at me, but I could see her heart wasn't in it. "Besides, I've got to go relieve Deek. It's time for my shift."

"I've already talked to him, and he's staying while you tell Greg what you told me." I sat down on the couch and took my aunt's hand. "Look, we need to find out the truth about this, and Greg can help."

She shook off my grip and picked up her coffee. As she stood, she pointed Greg to a chair. "Might as well sit and get comfortable. You want a cup?"

"That would be nice." Greg looked at me and I shrugged. This was Aunt Jackie's story and, apparently, she needed some space to tell it.

When she came back into the living room, she handed Greg his cup. Then she looked at me. "Go into the kitchen and grab that plate of cookies I set out. A man needs a late-afternoon treat."

"Yes, ma'am." I didn't mention that she hadn't offered me a cookie, but I needed more coffee anyway.

When I returned, Greg set down his cup and focused on Jackie. "Do you want to tell me what's going on?"

"My niece seems to think you can help with this problem I'm having." She picked up her cell, opened the contents, and then played a voice mail.

A man's voice filled the room. "Jackie, I know this is upsetting and I don't blame you if you hate me. But call me back; I need your help."

Greg waited for her to set down the phone. "When did this call come in?"

"Yesterday at about five." She sipped her coffee. "I've been avoiding his calls for the last week. I wanted to figure out what I felt about this whole development."

"Do you know the caller?" Greg had his notebook out now and was scribbling notes.

Aunt Jackie paused long enough that he looked up from what he'd been writing.

Greg repeated the question, but more softly this time. "Jackie, I need to know what's going on. Do you know the caller?"

She nodded and glanced at me. "I don't think Jill remembers much about him, but I remember everything. When you're married for a long time, you know things. Things that other people may not hold as close as I do. I've thought about this a lot. And I've come to the conclusion that it's my husband Ted's voice."

Greg frowned. "I don't understand. I thought Ted..."

"Was dead? Yeah, so did I." She picked up a cookie and took a bite. Then she set it down. "I've gone through three dozen of these in the last two weeks. I'm going to gain two dress sizes before this is over."

Greg reached for the phone, then wrote down the number. "Don't answer again. In fact, can I take this into the station? I'd like to have someone else listen to the voice mail. Did he leave any more?"

"You believe me? You think its Ted calling?" Aunt Jackie handed Greg the phone. "I don't have it pass coded."

"Honestly? I think it's someone pretending to be Ted." He tucked the phone in his front shirt pocket. "Now, Jackie, tell me you haven't sent this guy any money."

Her eyes flashed heat. "I'm not an idiot. When someone calls and tells me he's my deceased husband, I don't send him the codes to all my bank accounts. Besides, I'd already lost a lot of my money to that financial scammer years ago. There's not much more to share."

"That's the Jackie I know." Greg stood and patted her on the shoulder. "We'll get to the bottom of who's calling you, but I would lay money on it that it's not Ted."

She glanced at the point on his shirt where she knew the phone rested. "I'm not quite as sure."

I followed Greg to the door and pulled it shut behind me as we talked in the hallway. "What do you think? Is she being scammed?"

"If she's not, Esmeralda's going to be out of business." When I looked confused, he laughed. "No one will pay for her talent for delivering messages from the dead if they can just use the cell phone frequencies now."

"Come on, be serious." I glanced back at the door, like I could actually see inside to watch my aunt.

"I am being serious. At least we caught it before she sent this guy any money." He saw the question in my eyes. "Oh, crap. You think she actually sent him money?"

"She was too defensive when you asked. I didn't push, but I saw the look on her face. She sent him some, I'm just not sure how much."

Greg tapped the phone. "Well, as long as I have this, she shouldn't be bothered again. I'd like to wring this guy's neck. Is this why she canceled the engagement with Harrold?"

"Wouldn't you, if your dead wife called you out of the blue?"

"One, Sherry's not dead, and no, I wouldn't. Sherry had her chance with me." He grimaced. "But I could see Jim doing something stupid like this. Let's see if we can find out who was doing this before they move on to their next target."

He kissed me and then headed downstairs.

"Tell Deek we'll be right down."

"Will do. Right after I give him grief about hugging my girlfriend," he called back up the stairs.

"Technically, I hugged him," I called after him.

"Doesn't matter. I'm still giving him grief." Greg waved from the bottom of the stairs, then disappeared into the office.

I returned to the apartment to find Aunt Jackie had cleaned up our coffee cups and was heading to the door. "Where are you going?"

"It's time for my shift. We don't want to be paying overtime to anyone just because you want to talk." She tried to move around me, but I blocked her.

"I do want to talk." I waited for her to go sit back down, but she didn't move. "Fine, we can do this here. You really don't believe that's Uncle Ted on the phone, right?"

I saw that the shot had hit as soon as my words were out of my mouth. She tightened her hands around her tote. "Yes, Jill. I do think it's your uncle. Although why he would do something like this to me, I can't begin to guess."

"So you broke your engagement."

She didn't meet my eyes. "I can't marry someone else if I'm still married, now can I?"

"Look, this guy isn't Uncle Ted. He's a scammer. You have to know that."

She looked defeated. "All I know is, he knew way too much about Ted and me to be some random outsider. If he's not Ted, he has a heck of a lot of information about me and my life."

I let her go downstairs and smiled a bit when she started ordering Deek around. She was feeling a little less alone in this problem. Even if she didn't want to admit it.

Two hours later, I hadn't heard from Greg and I was beginning to get antsy. So I dialed his number to invite him to dinner. That would give me lots of time to grill him about what he'd found.

"Hey, Jill. Sorry, this is a bad time."

I jumped in before he could hang up. "Come over for dinner and you can tell me what you found."

"I haven't been able to look in to it. I'm sorry." He called out an order to someone else.

"Where are you?" I was kind of mad he hadn't even tried to find out about who was impersonating Uncle Ted. I know Jackie had been dealing with this for a while, but geez, the guy had promised.

"I'm at a murder scene." He paused. "Some guy got shot in his house just after I left the shop. Sorry, I really have to go."

I realized he'd already hung up on me. I knew Greg's commitment. If he hadn't been able to help Aunt Jackie yet, he would. I just hoped it wouldn't take too much longer. I didn't know if she could stand not knowing if her husband was really dead or just a jerk.

Chapter 4

Early the next morning, Greg sat at the counter in the shop, drinking his second cup of coffee and eating a big slice of cherry cheesecake. "Sorry I didn't call you back last night. I didn't get back to the station until after midnight, so I crashed on the couch. I'm heading home for a quick shower and change of clothes before the circus begins again today."

"Let Emma out when you get there. When her routine is changed, she gets nervous." I glanced toward the stairs. "I take it you didn't get anywhere with Aunt Jackie's phone?"

"Actually, I had Tim take it to the crime lab this morning. They have a tech who's pretty good with electronics. I told them I had the victim's permission. You don't think she'd give me that in writing?" He looked at me with pleading eyes. "I'd ask, but I've got a lot on my plate this morning, especially with the murder."

"Sure, throw that in the mix." I refilled his coffee. "I'll write out something and have her sign it before I leave for home. You want it at the station or home?"

"The station." He finished off his cheesecake. "I don't think I'll be home much for a while."

"Who was killed? Do I know them?" I was treading carefully, knowing that Greg didn't want me involved in investigations. But maybe, just maybe, he might be tired enough to let this one pass.

"A man who lived just at the edge of town. His girlfriend said she'd lived there for five years, but I'd never even seen them in town." He covered a yawn with his hand. "I've got to shower. The coffee isn't even keeping me awake."

"Why don't you take an hour or so?" In my opinion, Greg always pushed himself too hard, especially during an investigation. "Emma would probably take a nap with you."

He chuckled. "I bet she would. Okay, you win. I've got a briefing with the mayor at three. If I'm still asleep when you get home from your shift, wake me up. I don't need Marvin any madder at me that he is already. I swear, every election he gets more paranoid."

He gave me a quick kiss and then walked out. I remembered I was going to tell him about my conversation with Harrold, but it would have to wait. I took my coffee over to the couch and booted up my laptop again. I'd decided late last night when I couldn't sleep that there was one way to handle my aunt's problems. I had to prove to her that my uncle was really dead.

By the time Deek arrived for his shift, I'd run into a brick wall. I had some old clippings of Uncle Ted as he ran his café. Had I known that Aunt Jackie had helped him with the café for years? Probably, but by the time I went to live with her, Uncle Ted was gone and she'd sold their business. Back then, she waitressed at the diner she used to own. Mostly to keep me in school and fed. I'd never asked about family finances, because she'd always said Uncle Ted had provided for her. I guess he just hadn't counted on a teenage girl moving into the house after he'd died.

"You look down, Boss Lady. What can Deek do to cheer you up?" Deek sat on the chair across from me, and not for the first time, I wondered how he'd melted into my life, our lives, so seamlessly.

"Tell me where I'd find records of deaths for over twenty years ago." I laid my arm across my eyes. I was burned out. Time to call it a day.

"That's easy." Deek turned my laptop and hit a few keystrokes. "So, who's the dead dude you want to find?"

"Ted Ekroth. He died in early May." I sat up, watching him. I thought about my childhood with my aunt and felt my lips turning into a smile. "I know it was in May because Aunt Jackie made me go with her to visit his grave twice every May. By the time I was a teenager, I started complaining about it to my friends. But never to my aunt."

"Twenty years ago?" Deek used his fingers to count back the years.

"Somewhere around that time. I moved in with Aunt Jackie the summer before my freshman year." I drank down the rest of the cold coffee and glanced at my watch. I needed to go home to make sure Greg was up.

"Here it is. Theodore W. Ekroth, survived by his wife, Jacqueline." Deek frowned at the website. "But that's all that's listed. There should be a lot more information here. Maybe your dead guy isn't dead."

"What?" I couldn't believe this was happening. Had Uncle Ted really faked his own death? There was no doubt in my mind that Aunt Jackie had believed she'd buried her husband. But now, finding proof seemed to be a bigger issue than I'd expected. "That can't be."

"I'm just playing with you." He took out his phone and started keying. "I'm emailing the information to Trina. She works at the county records department. She's in my marketing seminar this semester. The girl is crazy good with computers. If there's a record to be found, she'll find it."

"Thanks, Deek." I stood and tucked my laptop and notebook into my tote. "If you hear something from her, would you call me? Or email?"

"Sure thing, Boss." He tucked his phone into his pocket and followed me to the coffee bar. "You okay?"

"I'm fine. Just worried about Jackie." I rested my hands on the coffee bar and waited for him to pour his coffee. "Look, can you not discuss this with my aunt? Just keep the search and results between us?"

"Of course. Deek's lock is on full security mode." He glanced toward the door leading into the back and to the stairwell up to Jackie's apartment. "I'll keep an eye out on her too. You know, just in case. She's not acting normal. I haven't gotten reamed for not doing my job for more than a month."

"Thanks. I appreciate it." Thinking of something else, I turned back toward the coffee bar. "And don't let any strangers talk to her. Not unless you have vetted them with me."

"This is serious stuff, then?" Deek's question echoed in the empty shop.

"I'm afraid so."

* * * *

Emma greeted me when I got to the house. She was out in the backyard and sat by the gate, her fluffy tail cleaning the sidewalk of any dirt or debris as she wagged it so hard while I walked up. I loved having a dog to welcome me home. Especially when I'd lived alone. It made me feel warm and safe. Now, I had Greg to welcome me home, but with his hours and schedule, a lot of the time it was still me and Emma.

"Hey, girl." I let myself in through the gate so I could take Emma into the house with me. "Is our boy awake? Or have you been out here for a while?"

"I resent that remark," Greg said from the back porch. He was sitting in my porch swing watching us. "I wouldn't let my best girl hang out in the backyard while I slept. Besides, she's my nap buddy."

"Hey, you're awake. I wondered if I was going to get to throw ice at you."

He patted the swing. "Come sit with me a bit before I go back in. I know this murder case is going to keep me working twenty-four-seven, so this might be the last you see of me for a while."

"You have to eat and shower sometimes. Maybe I'll bring over a picnic dinner tonight."

He shook his head. "The county sheriff's coming over to go over the case. Dinner is being catered. Apparently, he's doing a favor for Marvin."

"Isn't it a little early in the investigation to get outside assistance from other law enforcement agencies? Or is this guy a big shot?" Emma brought me her ball and I threw it out into the yard. Then I wiped the slobber off my hand onto Greg's jeans.

"Unemployed loser, from what I can see. I guess he lived off his girlfriend." Greg lifted my hand off his jeans. "The guy's a friend of the mayor. Marvin's just trying to keep me on my toes. He thinks if he keeps me busy, I won't have time to start my campaign to run against him in the primary."

That made me shoot up to my feet. "Don't tell me you're actually thinking about running? I told the mayor you weren't even considering it."

"I'm not. But it doesn't hurt to keep the guy on his toes. He's been unopposed for too many elections. He needs to remember why he wanted to be elected in the first place. It needs to be about the citizens again." He pulled me back down to sit beside him. "I can't even imagine doing all the campaigning and baby kissing."

"And yet, you sound like the perfect candidate. No wonder our mayor is nervous." I leaned back and curled into his side. "I don't want to share you any more than I already have to. I missed you last night."

He kissed the top of my head. "I missed you too. But now I've got to go. I'll text you if I'm not coming home tonight."

He stood and I grabbed his hand. "I hate to ask, but..."

"I'll put Esmeralda on the search. If there is anything that proves your uncle is alive or dead, we'll track it down. Then I'll go with you to tell your aunt. Can you find out if she really did give the guy money? And if so, how much? We might be able to track down a bank transmission." He squeezed my arm. "Don't worry about it. Now that we know what's been going on, we can fix this."

"I hope so." I watched as he went out to the driveway and backed his truck out to the main road. I knew my aunt's problems weren't as high on the list as a murder, but I wished Greg had real time to put toward finding out who was scamming her. It seemed like older people should be off limits for this type of crime.

I smacked my hand on my forehead. Elder crime. I should call Paula to see what she knew about this type of scam. Maybe there was already an investigation going that I could get information from. I dug my phone out of my tote and dialed the number from the card she'd given me.

"This is Tessa from the Senior Project. How can I help you today?" a chipper receptionist answered the phone.

"Hi, Tessa, I'm looking for Paula Wood. Is she in yet today?" From what Paula had said, she worked more hours than she was paid for, so my chances of catching her were good.

A silence fell over the line. I'd thought maybe I'd been cut off or put on hold. I glanced down at the phone, but I was still connected. "Hello? Tessa?"

"I'm sorry, Paula isn't in today. She had a family emergency."

"Oh? What happened?" From what I'd heard, the only family Paula had was that less-than-stellar boyfriend of hers. What was his name? I tried to think, but then I heard the click. This time, I *had* been hung up on. I went into the house and found my paper day planner. Then I wrote myself a note to remember to call back tomorrow. I should have thought about this as soon as Jackie told me about the caller.

Emma had followed me inside and looked at the couch. I didn't have anything else to do and I really hadn't been spending enough time with my dog. So I grabbed a soda from the fridge, turned the television on to a music station, and then curled up on the couch with a book I'd brought home from the shop.

I could worry later.

I'd just gotten to the middle of the book where the killer was stalking the heroine when I heard a knock on my door. I had a dilemma. I could set the book down and answer the door. It was probably some true believers in water vacuums trying to get me to buy. If I ignored the knock, I could avoid the face-to-face denial of entry and not see the disappointed look on the salesman's face. And I could keep reading.

I chose option number two and focused on the page in front of me.

The knocking got louder and more insistent. Emma nudged my foot with her nose, staring at the door.

"It's probably no one we want to talk to anyway." I said to my concerned dog. "Just ignore it."

Emma laid her head on my foot, but the look in her eyes told me she didn't believe me.

"Jill, I know you're there. I just saw Greg as I was walking down here," Amy called through the closed door.

I jumped up and ran to the door, Emma at my heels. When I opened the door, Amy pushed her way inside, a box in her arms. "Whoa, that looks heavy. Sorry, I thought you were a door-to-door salesman."

"Do I look like a salesman?" Amy asked as she walked into the kitchen with the box.

I didn't want to tell her that, yes, she kind of did. Following her, I studied her digging what looked like random items out of the box. "I thought you were at work."

"Marvin sent me home. He's meeting with his campaign manager and worried I'd eavesdrop and tell Greg what they're planning." Amy grinned as she took out the last item from the box, a roll of mint-green ribbon. "Score for me. Now you can help me decide on the table decorations for the reception."

Great, craft projects. Not my favorite activity, but Amy was my best friend. I guess this was the price of being a maid of honor. I went over to the coffeepot. "Coffee or iced tea?"

"Coffee. I didn't sleep last night. I've been so worried about the reception. I've been trying to set up seating charts, and there's no one I can sit at the mayor and Tina's table."

"I'd throw some of Justin's coworkers there. You don't want to make his family suffer that kind of evening." I started the coffee, then sat down, looking at the pile of ribbons. "What are you making out of these?"

"Hold on." Amy moved piles around the table. "I know I had the directions here somewhere. I printed them off when I was at work. Then I laid them near my phone when I got a call..." Amy backtracked her steps while still digging into her purse. She dropped the purse on the floor. "Crap, I must have left them at work. I guess I'll have to go back. This is the only time I have to figure this out until next month. And by then, it will be too late."

Amy looked like she was about to cry, and I wasn't sure she'd make it back to City Hall without beating herself up with every step. "It's okay. Let me call Esmeralda and she can grab it and fax it to us. I have a printer in my office."

Of course I never used the home office, but I had it all set up. In fact, Greg used it more than I ever had. Amy seemed to be calming down. "Why don't you get us coffee while I deal with this?"

She went to the coffeepot and I stepped into the living room, dialing the police station's nonemergency line. I was surprised when Greg picked up instead of Esmeralda. "You filling in for dispatch now?"

"She ran to get some lunch at Diamond Lille's. I'm keeping her here late today, so I told her I would watch the phones. What's up?"

I explained Amy's dilemma with the instructions. "So can you fax that page to me?"

"Sure. Give me a minute and I'll walk over to her desk. What do the instructions look like?"

"How should I know?"

He chuckled. "So you're helping her with a craft project? Has she ever met you?"

"Are you going to help or not?" I hated to admit it, but Greg was right. I'd tried and failed at a lot of different craft activities over the years, but at least I'd tried.

"You're going to owe me. I'm putting you on hold and going to her desk now."

I heard the canned music come over the line, with the mechanical voice telling me how important my call was and someone would be right back on the line. I didn't believe the sentiment, but I heard the click as Greg picked up the line.

"I don't see anything...Wait, here it is." I could hear his laughter. "Are you sure you want the instructions? I don't think you're going to be able to help."

"Just fax them to me." I was about to tell him to hurry when I heard other voices.

"I knew it; you're spying on me." Mayor Baylor's high-pitched voice came over the speaker easily.

"I'm not spying on you. I came to get something for Amy." He must have realized I was still on the line because he spoke into the phone now. "Jill, I've got to go. I'll fax this to you as soon as I get back to Esmeralda's desk."

The phone disconnected and I went back into the kitchen to get my coffee. "Your boss is crazy."

"Yeah, so what else is new? Did you get ahold of Esmeralda?" She handed me a cup of coffee.

"No, but Greg is faxing the instructions to me. Let me go boot up my computer and wait for the transmission." I looked at the pile on my table in fear. This was not going to be a fun afternoon. Not fun at all.

Chapter 5

Walking into work the next morning, my fingers still hurt from where I'd burned myself—and not just once or twice—with the glue gun. Finally, Amy had mercy on me and changed my assignment. But for some reason, when we finished the first fifty near six o'clock, I'd offered to take on the rest of the decorations on my own. Two hundred and fifty more. As long as Amy didn't get married for five or so years, I might be ready.

As I got closer to the shop, I saw a shape sitting at one of the outdoor tables. I glanced at my watch, thinking I must be later than I thought, but no, I still had thirty minutes before I had to open the shop. Whoever was waiting was just early. Really early.

Reaching the shop, I realized it was Paula sitting in front of my shop. Her hair looked like a rat was still sleeping in its nest, and I swore her shirt was inside out. "Looks like someone really needs coffee this morning. Come on in while I get everything set up."

"I'm sorry to be here so early, but they won't let me back in the house, and I didn't want to go to the lobby of the motel where I stayed last night to get coffee. Silly, right?" Paula followed me into the shop.

As I turned on the lights and started coffee, I realized what she'd said. I took a piece of peanut butter cheesecake out of the display case and handed it to her. "Why are you not allowed in your house?"

Tears filled her eyes, and for a second, I thought she was going to break down in front of me. Instead, she grabbed a napkin from the counter and wiped them away. "Funny, after all the tears I've cried since I heard, you'd think my well would be dry."

"Paula, what's wrong? What's going on?" I was afraid I already knew.

She threw away that napkin and stuffed more in her purse. "When I went home on Wednesday, Ben was dead. Someone killed him in our living room." This had to be the case Greg was working on. I hadn't realized Ben and Paula even lived in South Cove. I poured her coffee and put it in front of her. "Oh, no. Are you all right?"

"I'm alive." She poured sugar into the cup, then stirred it, watching the spoon circle the china. "The police officer, he said that had I come home when I was supposed to, I would be dead too. But I had to take one more call. Help one more person."

"You're lucky you did." I took my coffee and sat next to her. "Eat the cheesecake. You probably haven't eaten since you heard."

She stared at the fork like she didn't know how to use it. Finally, she took a sip of her coffee. "Am I lucky? Or should I be dead like Ben?"

This wasn't going well and I was way out of my depth. I grabbed my phone. I was going to bring in the expert. "Paula, I'm calling Sadie, if that's all right. I think you need someone to talk to and she's better at this than I am."

"If you think that's for the best. I don't know what to think anymore. Ben always made the decisions. I didn't even know what shirt to put on today, so I put on the same one from yesterday. Isn't that funny? I should know how to dress myself."

"You've had a big shock. Hold on a minute while I call Sadie." I walked into the back office and stood where I could see Paula sitting. I didn't want her going anywhere. Sadie would know what to do.

"Hey, girl, you caught me just before I was heading to take a nap. The baking's done, and this afternoon I've got to help Pastor Bill at the food pantry," Sadie chatted brightly, especially for someone who was just about to go to sleep.

"Hey, I hate to ask, but can you come down to the shop?" I went on to tell her what had happened. "I'm not really good at this; can you help?"

"Of course. I'll be there in just a few minutes. Let me change clothes and lock up."

I exhaled a sigh of relief. My brand of comforting circled around food. If Paula didn't even want to take a bite of the problem solver that was called cheesecake, I was out of ideas. "Thanks, I appreciate this."

"No problem. And Jill, you *are* good at this. You just don't give yourself enough credit."

I started to disagree and realized I was talking to dead air. I glanced at the back stairs. I'd call in Aunt Jackie, but she had enough on her plate.

No, this time, I was going to have to deal with Paula on my own. At least until Sadie changed and got over here. I prayed she was a fast dresser.

"Well, that's done. Sadie will be here in a few."

Paula just looked at me.

I glanced at her cup and picked it up. "Looks like you need more coffee. I love coffee. It's the perfect drink. It's warm and comforting at the same time." I continued to chatter as I refilled her cup and then sat next to her with my own.

"Ben didn't like coffee. He said it was a stimulant and against God's teachings." Paula sipped more coffee. "I drank it at the office when he wasn't there. Hiding something like that is probably more of a sin than actually drinking coffee, don't you think?"

Now, see, this is why I wanted Sadie here. My religious upbringing was spotty at best. My mom had sent me to vacation bible school, mostly because it got me out of the house. And unlike horse camp, it didn't cost money. "Honestly, I'm not sure. I guess because I run a coffee shop, I can't believe that drinking coffee is a sin."

Paula seemed happy with that statement. She looked around the dining room. "It's a good shop."

Before I had to respond, the bell over the door rang, and I looked up to see South Cove's Methodist preacher striding into the shop. Thank God for Sadie. Not only had she promised to come, she had reached out to someone to come save me in the meantime. I was going to owe her big-time.

"Jill, so nice to see you today." He turned toward Paula, holding out his hand. "I'm Pastor Bill. Sadie asked me to come talk to you. I understand you've had a rough few days."

Paula nodded silently as she shook his hand.

"Do you want to come over and sit on the couch with me and we can talk?" Now, he covered her hand with his other one, a comforting gesture that made me misty-eyed. The guy was good.

"That would be fine." Paula looked at me. "Don't you think it would be okay?"

"Yes, Paula, I think it would be perfectly fine." I wondered if the shock was still running through her, or if she'd taken some sedatives. She acted like she was drugged. I caught Pastor Bill's gaze. "Can I bring you over some coffee? Black or..."

"Black is perfect. Thank you, Jill, that's very kind of you." He smiled at me, and for just a second, I could see the man behind the collar. The man Sadie saw and had fallen in love with, even if she hadn't admitted it to herself.

I set up a tray with a carafe and three fresh coffee mugs. Sadie should be here soon. Then I added cream and sugar to the tray, along with a plate of cookies. I'd throw it all on the marketing budget. My aunt seemed to know when I ate a cookie and didn't write it down. I was still betting she had installed security cameras in the shop and just hadn't told me about them. I took the tray over to where they were talking. Or at least Pastor Bill was quietly talking to Paula. I'd brought more napkins and set one on Paula's lap before going back to the coffee bar.

When Sadie arrived, she paused at the bar to get her own cup of coffee. "Thanks for calling me. I'm so glad William got here quickly. I called him as soon as we hung up."

"Thanks for sending him over. I didn't know what to do. She looks so wrecked." I snuck a glance over toward the couch. I'd lost a friend to a tragic death, but I'd never lost someone I was building a life with. Sadie, on the other hand, had lost her husband. If anyone could understand Paula's grief, she could. "Can I do anything?"

Sadie smiled and patted my hand. "You did exactly what you needed to do. Go on and run your day. I'm going to see if we can move this conversation over to the church. The counseling office has a lot of material she'll need. You've got a good heart, Jill."

As I watched Sadie join the group on the couch, I doubted her words. I'd called her because I knew I was out of my depth, not because I had a good heart. But the end result was the same; Paula now had people to talk to and to get her to the next step.

Long after they'd left the shop to go to the church, I thought about what Paula had said. That she didn't know what to do because Ben made the decisions. Decisions that apparently had her sneaking a cup of coffee at the office every now and then. Relationships were hard, and they were worse when one person was on a power trip.

* * * *

Toby Killian came in at noon for his shift. The barista/deputy looked like an alpha male from one of the romance novels from the shelves. And if his muscular body, dark hair, and piercing eyes weren't enough, the guy had a sharp wit and was kind as a puppy. Toby worked full-time on the weekends for Greg as a deputy, so he only picked up a few midday shifts at the coffee shop during the week for extra money. And because I was renting him the shed apartment in the backyard, his expenses were pretty low. Last I'd heard, he was saving money for a down payment on a house. But that was before he and Sasha had broken off their relationship. "Hey, Jill. I used my key and let Emma out for a bit this morning when I did my laundry." He slipped on the CBM apron and washed his hands at the sink. "Thanks again for letting me use your machines. I could go to the laundromat in Bakerstown if you get tired of me."

"Doesn't bother me. Besides, Emma gets some attention while I'm working." I tucked a new book into my tote. With Greg on an investigation, I knew I'd have plenty of time to read this week, especially because I was stalled on this Aunt Jackie thing. "I'll talk to you later. I'm going to Lille's for lunch."

"Oh, I almost forgot. Esmeralda stopped by on her way into the station. She said she had some information about your aunt." He adjusted the coffee cups to the other side of the espresso machine. Aunt Jackie would move them back when she came on shift. I think he liked knowing he was messing with my aunt's process. "What's going on that I don't know about?"

"Nothing I can share right now." Aunt Jackie was already upset that I'd brought Greg into the mystery of the man posing as Uncle Ted. It would all come out, but I didn't want my aunt to feel foolish when it did. "I wonder why Esmeralda didn't come here. She knows I work the morning shift."

"Yeah, and being a fortune-teller and all, she should have known, right?" Toby laughed as he leaned over the counter, his dark hair framing a too-good-looking face and deep blue eyes that were sparkling with humor. "Anyway, she seemed surprised when I answered the door. I guess she saw Emma out in the yard and thought you'd stayed home for some reason."

"Well, I guess I'm going to the police station on the way to lunch now." My stomach growled in protest, but the side trip wouldn't take long. Or shouldn't. Maybe she'd traced the guy's number and we could actually finish this up today. "Have a great shift and thanks for letting Emma out."

"No problem." He nodded to the door. "I got here just in time. My girls are here." He stood and started making coffee drinks as ten women who went to class at the cosmetology school in Bakerstown piled through the door.

I hated to break it to Toby, but the women had started to come on days Deek was handling the midday shift as well. Hiring two good-looking guys had been good for my business. Especially when one was a total alpha hero and one a classic, hot nerd hero. I shook my head. I'd been reading too many romance novels in the last few weeks. But as I left, I saw several of the women pause at the bookshelves before going to the coffee bar. Maybe they were reading about finding true love too.

My good mood stayed with me as I made my way down Main Street to City Hall and entered on the north side, where the police station took almost half of the building. It was an efficient set-up, but one that Mayor Baylor hated. Luckily, the council liked the lower cost of having one city building that met both needs.

Esmeralda was at the desk and, from what I heard, on a call. Today, her black, curly hair was pulled up into a messy bun, and she was dressed in a short-sleeved polo with South Cove Police Department on the pocket. She looked completely normal. Not like when she wore her gypsy outfit when clients came to her in her home studio across the street from my house. She waved me closer. "Okay, Mr. Adams. I'll have Tim come over as soon as he gets on shift this afternoon and take a report. Hope your day gets better."

She hung up the call and made a second one. "Amy, would you handle the phones for an hour? I'm taking a lunch with Jill. Thanks a lot."

Confusion must have shown on my face because she laughed as she grabbed her tote and came around the desk.

"I didn't know we were doing lunch." I followed her out of the building, trying to keep up with her long strides.

She turned back, realized I was falling behind, and slowed her pace. "I need to talk to you and I don't really want to do it in public. I've got potato soup and a quiche at my house, if that's okay."

"That's fine." I tried to keep the shock from showing, but Esmeralda had never invited me over for more than a cup of tea in all the years we'd been neighbors. I didn't even know she cooked. "So what do you need to tell me?"

Esmeralda looked around the empty street before crossing over on the other side from Diamond Lille's. "I think I can shed some light about what's happening with your aunt."

Chapter 6

We walked in silence to her house. Every time I'd try to say anything or even ask a question, she'd shake her head. Whatever Esmeralda wanted to tell me, it must be a doozy of a story. Finally, we reached her house, and as she let me inside, her cat jumped on my legs, asking to be picked up.

"She likes you. She's always staring over at your house. Maybe she should have been your cat." Esmeralda nodded to the kitchen. "We can eat in there."

I reached down and scratched Maggie behind the ears. "Hey there, girl. What's been happening in your world?"

The cat leaned into my hand, then followed me into the kitchen, meowing all the way, like she was telling me a story. Unfortunately, I didn't understand cat language.

"Soda or iced tea?" Esmeralda picked up a glass from the already set table. She must have done it that morning.

"Iced tea is fine." I glanced around the sunny kitchen. It had been painted a bright orange. Not my favorite color, but somehow, it looked right for Esmeralda. I put a hand on one of her ladder-back chairs. "Can I help with anything?"

"That's kind of you to offer, but I have it. I woke up early today and couldn't get back to sleep. It happens, but for some reason, you and your aunt were on my mind. Then I realized the similarities." She set a glass of tea down at both places. "Sit, I'll get lunch going, then we can talk."

I glanced around the kitchen. All the appliances were upgraded, like in my own kitchen. The houses had been built in the 1930s, but they were sturdy and, with a fresh coat of paint and new flooring, better put together than the new ones they were building now. The china was one of my favorite patterns, an English rose. Very feminine and fancy. I had colorful Fiestaware, but someday, this was the formal china I wanted. Of course, that seemed like something out of the past. Probably by the time I decided to buy new china, everyone would be eating off paper plates all the time. The soup was in a Crock-Pot and already warm. I could smell the creamy goodness as I waited. Esmeralda cut two large slices of quiche, filled the bowls with soup, then brought it all to the table. When she finally sat, I watched as she closed her eyes and whispered something.

She caught me watching and laughed. "A bit of gratitude to the goddess. It's not much different from what you would consider a prayer, just more nondenominational."

"I wasn't..." I stopped talking. I *had* been questioning her actions. "Sorry. I didn't mean to be rude and intrusive."

"You were neither. Just curious. And that's not a problem—well, except for cats." She picked up a spoon and tasted the soup. "Let me know if you want the soup hotter or the quiche warmed up. We can pop it in the microwave for a few minutes."

I tasted the soup, which was perfect. "No, this will be great. Thank you for lunch. You didn't have to do this."

Esmeralda sipped another spoonful of soup, watching me. "You're right, I didn't have to; I just wanted you to see me as normal. Like a regular neighbor, you know."

"You are a regular neighbor, but I'm not sure normal fits your style." I smiled as I took another bite. "Not in a bad way, but no one would ever call you boring."

"You're honest; that's what I like about you. I guess it's silly, but I want you to like me. Not to think I'm just the crazy woman who lives next door."

I started to speak, but she shook her head.

"Don't. This isn't about you or how you see me. I just haven't told anyone here in South Cove much about my past. And I'm scared, just a little." She smiled and leaned back against the chair.

"I know a little more now that Jake told us about your childhood." Esmeralda and her friend Jake had been part of a Halloween weekend Greg and I had attended. One where a real-life ghost had shown its powers. Or at least that's what I thought. Greg still thought it had been one of the other people staying there, or the crazy handyman who'd been tasked with caring for the house. "You grew up in New Orleans and were a foster kid in a big, loving family that took in a lot of kids."

"And taught them the art of the scam."

Not knowing what to say, I reverted to my comfort zone. I took a bite of the quiche. "This is really good."

"You are a mystery, Jill Gardner." Esmeralda sipped her tea. "So anyway, I learned about scams at a young age. That was what funded the household, but my foster parents had the gift of prophecy too. So when they saw my natural talent in what you call fortune-telling, I was given more training in developing my power."

"You're telling me they taught you to be a psychic? And to scam people out of money?" I wasn't sure I wanted to know this, because if Greg found out, he might have to fire her from her police dispatch job.

"I never stole or did anything illegal. Probably skimmed that edge a few times, but nothing that would jeopardize my job." She sipped her tea again, clearly nervous about my reaction to what she was saying. "Anyway, I knew the scams, even though I didn't participate. I think that's what's happening with your aunt. I believe someone is running a con on her."

"I agree." I had almost finished my soup, so I set down my spoon and focused on Esmeralda. "Look, I'm not going to give you grief over what happened in your childhood. But if you know who's doing this, I really need a name."

"I don't know who's doing it, but I recognize the con. Usually, it happens closer to when the guy dies. And it's always played on grieving widows. I guess they don't think a man would be as willing to push away reality for a good story." Esmeralda stared at something over my shoulder. "My foster father was really good at manipulating people's emotions, especially around death. Your aunt wants to believe. Her head is telling her that it's not true, but in her heart, she feels a need to find out."

"Even if it means throwing away a new love with a good man?" Pushing away the now empty bowl, I could feel my aunt's pain. She probably hurt every time someone asked her why she'd broken off the engagement. I knew she had kept the wedding planning book. I'd seen it in her closet one day when I ran upstairs to grab her a sweater. "You don't think it's your father who's doing this, do you?"

"Foster father, and no. He's been gone for many years now. And his son is running the family business. Nic, he's not the type to hurt people." A soft smile creased her face.

I decided not to push that button, but even I could see that Esmeralda was soft on the guy. "So we find out who's been posing as my uncle. What did you find when you traced the calls?"

"The phone company hasn't sent back the records yet. We probably won't get them until the first of the week." Esmeralda picked up her half-eaten soup and poured it down the drain. "I'm sorry I had to tell you this."

"Well, at least I know my aunt isn't crazy now. I didn't realize this was such a common scam. Paula talked about how the elderly were targeted, but you never think it's going to hit so close. My aunt is smarter than that." At least I'd thought so when I heard about the different fraud scams. Which reminded me, I needed to find out if she'd actually given the guy any money yet. It looked like I was going back into town this afternoon to talk to her again.

"Well, I'll let you know if any of my leads come up with something. I reached out to some of the old family. If someone is doing this con full time, they'll know about it." She picked up my plate and bowl. "You must have liked my cooking."

"Are you kidding? You're a great cook. No wonder I don't see you much in Diamond Lille's." I could feel my invitation was drawing to an end.

"I like cooking. It helps me think. And the spirits leave me alone when I'm in the kitchen. I think they are afraid they'll scare me and I'll hurt myself." She set the dishes in the sink. "I guess I'd better get back. The station is swamped now with this murder. Can you believe someone just walked into a house and shot the guy?"

"Greg doesn't have any leads?" I wondered who would want to see Ben dead, except anyone who liked Paula at all. Which was a lot of people.

"He doesn't, and that bothers me. The spirits are too quiet on this subject. I think there's some darkness around this guy." We walked out to the porch, where she locked the door.

"I don't think he was a good guy either." I could believe Esmeralda's insight into Ben after talking to Paula today. But there was no way the woman had the spine to kill him. She wouldn't know how and would have had to ask for permission. At least that was my take.

"Just make sure you keep your doors locked. We're too isolated out here by the highway." Esmeralda started jogging toward town and back to work.

I crossed the street and went to my back door to let Emma out. While she explored the fence line around the yard, I sat in the swing and thought about everything. Aunt Jackie, Greg and the murder, Paula, and even Amy and her upcoming wedding. The thoughts were swirling together and mixing up, so I grabbed my notebook out of my tote. For the next twenty minutes, I wrote down everything people had told me and things I'd thought about. One page per person.

Then I read through what I'd written. It looked like a mixture of *The Guide to a Perfect Wedding* and a *Guidebook to Murder—How to Kill the One You Love*. Books: I always related problems to books. And this was no exception. I put Emma in the house and walked back into town. I needed to talk to my aunt.

When I got there, I was surprised to see Toby still working the coffee bar. Then I glanced at my watch. It was only two. My aunt didn't come on shift until five. He was busy with someone, so I just waved as I walked by and went into the back. Then I headed up the inside stairs and hoped I wouldn't wake her from a nap. Grumpy Aunt Jackie was hard enough to deal with. Tired and grumpy Aunt Jackie was impossible.

I listened at the door and heard the television. A good sign. I lifted my hand to knock and the door flew open.

"Oh, it's you. What are you doing, skulking around my hallway?" My aunt held what appeared to be a baseball bat. And by the way she held it, I was apparently the ball.

"Whoa, slugger." I raised my hand and lowered the bat. I'd known she'd bought a bat for the shop, but I didn't know about the one in her apartment. "Are you feeling threatened? Maybe we need to talk about home security rather than hand weapons."

"I don't need security. Although I believe someone has been on my back porch recently. One of my pots was knocked over. They cleaned up the mess, but I could tell." My aunt let me take the bat and motioned to the umbrella stand where, apparently, it resided. She turned and walked into the small kitchen to the left of the apartment. "What are you doing here anyway? I thought you went off-shift a few hours ago. Don't tell me Toby bailed on us."

I knew who had been on the porch, so I wasn't as worried as I had been when she answered the door with the baseball bat. "Toby's working. I was talking to Esmeralda about your situation and..."

She pushed a cup of coffee at me. "First you tell your boyfriend, now the town fortune-teller? I guess I can't have any secrets in this town."

"I didn't tell her. Greg had her looking into the calls. So she knew." I climbed onto one of the stools and sipped my coffee. "She said there's a con out there that mirrors what's been happening to you."

"And how did she come by this piece of information?" Jackie eased herself onto one of the stools next to me. She winced, and I could see the activity had aggravated her pain. "Or did the spirits tell her?"

"You think you've been talking to my dead uncle, so I'm not sure you have the moral high ground here." My aunt turned red and I knew I'd crossed that invisible line. "Don't get mad. I'm here to help, not to argue." Aunt Jackie started to speak, but took a sip of coffee first. "I'm sorry about that. I'm edgy and feeling like a silly old woman. If it's Ted calling, he got away with disappearing right under my nose. If it's not, then I'm the gullible, grieving widow, searching for one speck of hope. Neither of the roles fits my personality."

"I don't think its Uncle Ted, and I don't believe you do either." I leaned back on the stool. "How much money did you give him?"

She stared holes through me. Finally, she spoke. "I didn't. I probably would have, if you hadn't gotten involved and made me question everything. I'd taken the money out of my portfolio and had it in my checking account. I was planning on sending it this week."

"Don't get me wrong, it's your money and you can do what you want with it. But I just don't want someone skimming it off you. Not," I paused, then continued, "not unless you understand what is really happening."

"You were going to say 'not again.'" My aunt looked older than I'd seen her in years. "I know I messed up before. I trusted the wrong person. That's not going to happen again. And I have you to thank for that. If you hadn't stuck your nose in this, I would have been taken again."

"Let's not think about that." I pulled my notebook out of my tote. "So tell me everything that happened."

She sipped her coffee. "Are you sure? Greg doesn't like you sniffing around his cases."

"Greg's busy with the murder of that guy. He's not going to mind. Especially because it will keep me out of his investigation, where he'll constantly have to worry." I opened to a blank page. "Are you ready?"

"I think your logic is a little flawed, but I want to know what's going on just as much as you seem to want to investigate." My aunt sipped her coffee, looking at me. "I guess I'm going to have to trust you on this."

"I'll keep you in the loop on every step I take." I held my pen over the page. "So, are you ready to tell me what happened?"

"Might as well." My aunt set down her cup and traced a circle with her finger. "The first call came in the day before Amy's engagement party. He told me he'd been moved out of state, that his death had been faked and he was in witness protection."

As she talked, I wrote down everything. Some things word for word. I had to know the whole story before I could look for patterns. Finally, my aunt stopped talking. I made a few more notes, then looked up. "Tell me about the voice. Besides Uncle Ted, are you sure you'd never heard the voice before? In person, I mean?"

Aunt Jackie shook her head. "Actually, now that I think about it, I can't even say if it sounded like Ted or not. I guess I wanted it to be true for so long, I thought I might have wished it into being. This is why I didn't want to tell you. I do sound like a silly old woman."

"You don't. You sound like someone who's always dealt with problems head-on." I patted her hand. "I'm checking into Uncle Ted's death certificate. Did you get a copy after the funeral?"

"I must have. I had to transfer accounts from joint to single. And I had to send one to that sleazy broker I had who stole my money." My aunt brightened. "Do you think this might be the same guy? We couldn't press charges then because he'd taken off for some island, but if he's back, maybe I can get some of the other money back. He'd know enough about Ted and me to do it."

"Give me his name and I'll have Greg check him out." I knew I was making promises for my boyfriend that he might not be able to keep. At least not until he solved the murder investigation on his desk. But I had to start somewhere. I put down my pen and finished off the coffee. "So about Harrold…"

Aunt Jackie cut me off like I'd said a swear word. "I'm not putting Harrold through this. I made my decision and I'll stand by it, even if my reasons were not so solid in hindsight. A girl can't just break, then unbreak an engagement. It's all about trust. He'd never trust me again."

Chapter 7

Harrold stopped by the shop at about eight thirty Friday morning. He slipped off his light jacket and draped it across the stool. He glanced around the shop. "Looks like the place is clear. Jackie must still be upstairs?"

"If I know her, she's just getting ready to sit down and start watching her shows. She really likes her talk shows." I picked up a coffee cup. "What can I get you?"

"Just decaf. Black." He patted his stomach. "I have to stay in shape in case your aunt comes to her senses. She likes my body."

"TMI." I laughed as I poured the coffee. "Please don't talk about you and my aunt."

"Now, Jill, you have to know that older people have needs too." His eyes twinkled as he watched my reaction. "Anyway, I didn't come in to tease you about how sexy I think your aunt is. I came in to see if you had gotten any farther on getting her out of the apartment. I think I can have everything ready by next weekend. Maybe she and Mary could have a girls' day in the city?"

"I'll see what I can do. She knows someone's been out there. I guess you knocked over a plant?" I sat next to him with my own cup of coffee. "You're going to have to be more careful if you have to take measurements."

Harrold set down his cup and stared at me. "I haven't been up on the porch since your aunt dumped me. I had this project planned as an engagement present, so I already had all the measurements."

I saw the concern flash in his eyes. "I'm sure it's the neighborhood cat, then. We have a problem with feral cats running around the neighborhood. But every time I call the pound, they just disappear. They're smart."

"You're right, it's probably one of the cats. I think Jackie was feeding them, which is why they keep hanging around." He took a sip of his coffee, but even I could see I hadn't convinced him with my answer.

"I hear you've been eating a lot at Diamond Lille's. I can't believe your friends with Lille. What is she like when she's not being a raving witch?" Changing the subject was one of my specialties, especially when the conversation got too deep.

He laughed and took another sip. "You remind me a lot of her. She's strong, determined, and willing to do anything for people she loves. Which works in my favor. The girl was a godsend after Agnes passed away. I definitely will never starve with her in my camp. But, then again, I may have to buy the next-size pants. I'm too well fed, I'm afraid."

I squeezed his arm. "You're just right. Besides, you deserve to be pampered." I didn't add *after what my aunt had done to him*, but I think he got the point.

"Well, I'd better get out of here before your aunt pops in and finds me here." He pulled a sheet of paper out of his pocket. "Would you be a dear and order these books for me? I have a lot more time to read now, and I'm afraid I'm running out of material."

"Of course. Do you want me to call when they're in?" I glanced down at the list of mostly historical fiction and nonfiction.

"That would be nice. And I'll come in the morning again to avoid any unpleasantness." He stood and kissed me on the cheek. "Thank you. I have to admit, I was looking forward to having a new niece in my life."

I wanted to say it might still happen, but I didn't want to give him false hope. Especially because my aunt was as stubborn as a bull not wanting to leave the barn. That might not be the right analogy, but it kind of fit. "You're still a part of my life, no matter what my crazy aunt does. I don't think Greg would mind me sneaking around with an older man."

Laughing, he put his jacket back on. "You are a lot like your aunt, even if you don't want to admit it."

I watched him leave and thought about what he had said. I wasn't at all like my aunt. She was all business and brusque. Me, I'd rather be lost in a book than worrying about customers not coming into the shop. To prove I was not like my aunt at all, I grabbed my coffee and the book I'd been pretending to read all morning and headed to the couch.

Deek found me still there when he came in for his shift. He dropped down across from me. "Whoa, Boss. What has you down in the dumps?"

"What are you talking about? I'm in my happy place." Which I was, but I'd been reading the same page for over an hour now. I kept thinking about Aunt Jackie. And Harrold. And Paula.

"I don't think so, but I won't push. Besides, I got something for you yesterday when I was at class in Bakerstown." He pulled out a piece of paper. "Ta-da. Here's the death certificate for your uncle. Trina, the girl I know, said it was filed wrong."

"Filed wrong?" I unfolded the paper and read the details of Uncle Ted's death. All of the facts, but none of the feelings. Like how he used to buy me books on his business trips and bring them back to me when they visited. He was probably the reason I read so widely. He was always finding weird stuff he thought I might like.

"Well, classified wrong. I guess it was more of a computer issue than an actual filing error. The weird thing is, the change happened earlier this summer. The guy has been dead for years and just a few months ago, someone changed the spelling on his last name so it didn't come up when you search."

I stared at my newest barista. "You're kidding, right?"

"I swear on my well-loved copy of *Eats, Shoots and Leaves*." He grinned. "Speaking of writing, I wanted to see if I could pull together a writers' group to meet here one weeknight evening. They wouldn't be a bother and they'd definitely buy coffee and food. And probably some books."

"Sounds like a good idea, but you need to bring it up to Jackie. She handles the late shift."

He sighed and leaned back in his chair so his hair fell over his eyes. "I was afraid you'd say that."

"Why? Because you're afraid of Jackie?"

Now he flipped back his head and met my gaze. "You're exactly right. I am afraid. Maybe you could..."

Instead of answering, I picked up my book and stuffed the paper with Uncle Ted's death certificate inside. "See you tomorrow."

"You're a tough one," he called after me.

Smiling, I left the shop. Maybe I was just like my aunt after all. I looked toward the police station. I hadn't heard from Greg for days. I knew he'd been home sometime during the night because I'd felt his presence in our bedroom. Or I'd dreamed it, because he hadn't been there when I'd gone to bed, and when I'd awoken, the other side of the bed was cool to the touch. When Greg worked a case, he rarely slept. Too much on his mind.

I needed to talk to him about Aunt Jackie and her stalker. At least that's what I'd come to call the guy. And let him know about the death certificate. And maybe talk him in to having lunch with me. A girl could hope.

Esmeralda was on a call when I walked in, but she pointed to Greg's office. Apparently, the path was clear for me to talk to him. When I walked in the room, he had his head back in his chair with his eyes closed. Files were spread out on his desk. I walked over and picked one up. Ben Penn's face looked up at me. It had to be a driver's license shot. I don't believe I'd heard his last name before. Penn. Maybe he'd shortened it?

"You need to stay out of this one." Greg's muffled voice shocked me and I almost dropped the file.

"Why are driver's license photos so bad? I mean, can you really tell who it is when you pull them over?" I set down the file and pointed to Ben's picture. "I met the guy this week and he didn't look a bit like this."

"You're stressed when a cop pulls you over. It's easier to match a solemn shot than one where you're grinning into the camera. Unless, of course, you like interacting with the police, which no one does." He walked around the desk and kissed me. "Sorry I missed you last night. I was working on a lead."

"And this morning." I ran my fingers down his cheek and could feel the stubble coming on from his beard. Either he'd forgotten to shave, which was unlikely, or he'd been up and out of the house really, really early.

"I'm talking to the girlfriend this afternoon. I needed to know as much as possible before I interviewed her."

"She's freaked out." I hurried to add what I wanted to say before I got more of the lecture about staying out of the investigation. "She came into the shop this morning. I called Sadie to ask her to come talk to her. You know Sadie can calm down anyone."

He nodded. "She's got a knack for working with people."

"Yeah, you're right. So I called Sadie, because Paula was scaring me. And then she called Pastor Bill, and he came and they all talked. Then they went to the church, so if you're looking for Paula, she's probably there. Or Sadie knows where she is." I watched as Greg left my side and went back to his desk.

He picked up the phone and told Esmeralda what I'd just said. "Would you set up a meeting with Paula at two? Jill and I are going to Diamond Lille's for lunch. I'll have my phone on if you need me."

He stood and looked at me. "Are you ready?"

"I didn't ask if you had time for lunch." It was creepy, his ability to read my mind.

He pulled me out of my chair. "You're kidding, right?"

"No. I mean, I was coming to ask you that, but how did you know?"

He pointed to the clock. "It's noon. You were probably on your way to Lille's and stopped to report on what you'd found out. You're a creature of habit."

"Oh, yeah." I didn't like being told I was so predictable, but because this was Friday and Lille's would have clam chowder along with a fish and scallops lunch, I figured it couldn't hurt—at least not this time. "I need to talk to you about Aunt Jackie. Someone's been on her porch."

As we walked, I told him everything I'd found out about her predicament. Including the fact that someone had been on the porch and it hadn't been Harrold.

"Make sure she locks that door. And maybe you could put a chair or something against it. We could put a gate at the bottom of the stairwell too. But that's more of a long-term solution. I really don't like that the entrance goes right back to the alley way." He held the diner door open and I went inside. "Just block it for now. I'll spend some time on trying to figure out what's going on with her this afternoon."

As we settled into a booth, I watched him. "I didn't think you'd have time to work on this until after the murder was solved."

He broke eye contact and studied the menu. "The special looks good."

"You have a suspect." I pushed down the menu. "Don't tell me you're thinking about charging Paula?"

"Jill, it isn't just based on a feeling. Someone had means, motive and opportunity. And all those things point to his girlfriend." He leaned forward. "They were seen fighting the day the guy died. And I've already talked to the other woman in the relationship. She says Ben was planning on leaving Paula."

"He was cheating? Wow, I didn't see that coming. Paula was hooked on the guy." I thought about watching him talk to someone at the diner that first and last day I'd seen him. "Are you sure the other woman didn't kill him? She probably had all the same reasons Paula would."

"I agree, but the woman has an ironclad alibi. She was at work at a residential care facility. She works the night shift as a nurse and has several people who can alibi her for the time of death."

Carrie stopped by the table. "I'm always walking into the most interesting discussions with you two. What are you having, Detective? I'm pretty sure I can guess Jill's order."

Predictability. I really had to switch up my lifestyle and my choices. Except I liked my choices. I handed Carrie the menu. "Have at it."

Greg laughed. "You are a trusting soul. What if she gets Tiny to cook you up liver and onions?"

"Then I'll just have to send it back." I smiled at Carrie. "Besides, she likes me. Lille, on the other hand…"

"She'd make you do your own ordering." Greg handed Carrie his menu. "I'm having the pork chop plate. And bring me some apple pie. I may not get dinner."

"Do you want a chocolate milkshake to go with Jill's vanilla one?" Carrie took the menu and jotted down Greg's order.

"Why not." He waited for Carrie to leave. "So that's my afternoon and evening. I'll have to stay while the prosecutors decide on charges. But I should be able to work on your aunt's case while I'm waiting."

"I don't believe Paula did this. She's too passive."

Carrie dropped off the milkshakes and quickly left the table.

"What we think and what we know are two different things." He took a sip of his shake. "There just aren't a lot of other options in this case."

"Greg, I've never told you that you're wrong before, but you are looking at the case wrong." I took a small sip of my shake. I didn't really feel hungry now that Greg had spilled his news. I pushed away the shake.

"Look, I don't want to argue about this. If there was any other possible suspect, you know I'd look into it." He took my hand. "Jill, you know me. I promise."

"I guess that will have to do." I couldn't point him in the direction of another option because I had no idea who or why someone would kill Ben. I just knew it wasn't Paula. No way, no how. I thought about what she'd said about him spending time volunteering. "He spent a lot of time at the Senior Project. Maybe someone there didn't like him."

"I interviewed the staff this morning. They said he was the best. He worked on their computers and saved them a lot of money in tech fees. He built their website and set up a client intake form for recordkeeping." He squeezed my hand. "I know you're looking for unicorns, but this one is just a plain old horse."

"I never understood that phrase." I leaned back as Carrie delivered our meals. A fish-and-scallop basket for me and Greg's pork chop plate. The smell of food made my stomach growl. So apparently, I was hungry again. I just felt sad for Paula.

Greg changed the subject, and for a while, we talked about bits and pieces of our lives. Because we were now living together, we had bills to talk about as well as vacation plans we needed to make. I kind of liked sharing my life with someone. It made the day-to-day decision-making less stressful because there was another viewpoint besides my own.

When his phone rang, he was just finishing up his meal. "Sorry," he said to me as he picked up the call. "Greg King."

I half-listened while I ate the last French fry and drank the rest of my shake. Comfort food was my go-to drug. And yet, my favorite meal hadn't pulled me out of the slump I felt over Paula's pending arrest.

Greg finished his call, then took out his wallet. "Look, I've got to go. Apparently, the Senior Project is getting some complaints about someone having their clients' information. They think that maybe Paula leaked some confidential information."

I shook my head. "I don't think it was Paula. Who was the guy working on their computer programs? Who had access to their systems? And who's dead right now?"

"I know, I thought of that too. Maybe your gut is spot-on with this one." He threw some bills on the table and stood and kissed me on the head. "I'll call if I can."

I sat there and watched him leave. Then I grabbed his overflow container of shake and poured it into my glass. I might have to waddle home, but I was going to push away this bad mood before I left the table. And because the Senior Project staff had just given Greg another avenue to investigate, this last cup of chocolaty shake might just do the trick.

Of course, this break in the case made Jackie's stalker go to the back of the list. I decided I'd try to do some Google investigating when I got home.

Chapter 8

After two hours of searching the internet, all I had to show for it were rumors and scam warnings. This scam was often played on elderly victims. They'd get a call from, usually, a living relative in trouble. And then they'd send out money. I think my aunt would have seen this version of the scam coming. She didn't take to being asked for money from anyone. Especially someone who had been stupid or careless in their actions.

She'd told me several times when I was away at college that if I found myself in a police cell, I might as well use my one call for a bail bondsman because she wasn't going to help me out of the situation. My aunt had invented the phrase tough love.

But having her deceased husband call with an explanation of his being in witness protection? She'd fallen for that scam in a heartbeat. Not because she didn't love Harrold. She'd just loved Uncle Ted first.

I had proof that my uncle was dead. And I'd learned that someone had messed with the record just before this scam had started. Had they been trying to use the lack of official death confirmation as a way to convince Jackie it had been a hoax? I realized I'd forgotten to tell Greg that piece, so I shot him a quick email, not expecting to hear from him until tomorrow.

My phone rang just a few minutes after I hit Send. "Hey, I figured you were busy."

"I am. But I was taking a break to clear out my email and make sure there wasn't anything I had to handle. So I saw your message when it came in."

"Lucky me. Was there anything important?" I snuggled back into the couch. Sometimes just hearing his voice was enough.

"Besides ten emails from the mayor about my responsibility to clean up the streets from these murders? Not much." He sounded tired, but I had a feeling his fed-up meter wasn't going off because of the current case. "I don't have a lot of time, but I thought the fact you found out about the death certificate was interesting. I'm having Esmeralda call over to the records department to see if they were having computer problems around that time."

"Seems like a lot of computer problems going around. Did you find out more about the Senior Project's issues?" I doodled in my notebook, making a dotted line between the county records department and the Senior Project. Would there be any employees in common?

"Not yet, but I'm heading out now to go talk to some of the key people over at the project. Did your aunt ever go there for help?"

The question hadn't occurred to me. But then again, I hadn't known Aunt Jackie was taking yoga until her best friend ratted her out. She knew everything about my life, but my life was pretty vanilla. As long as I wasn't tied up in one of Greg's investigations and trying to hide my interest. "I don't know. I'll call her. She should be at the shop now."

"Let me know. If the scammer's information is coming from there, maybe we can get this problem solved while I'm figuring out who killed this guy." He paused. "I'll probably be late tonight."

"I figured. Wake me up when you get in. I'd like to say I saw you twice today." I smiled as Greg's picture came up on my laptop. Yes, I was that goofy girl who had her boyfriend's picture as her wallpaper. But sometimes he was so busy, that was the only way I got to see his face. Life with a law enforcement officer. Of course, he'd probably say the same thing about me, because I was always busy with something about the coffee shop. We were two of a kind, which was why our life together worked.

"Maybe we can get away for a week when I get this put to bed." Greg chuckled. "I guess I'm always saying that, aren't I?"

"The good thing is, I get a lot of guilt attention after you get your work done. It's fine. If you want to plan something, I'm in. Toby's trip to Yosemite has me craving some mountain cabin time."

"I was thinking more backpacking and tents, but we can negotiate." He mumbled something to someone else, and I realized he had covered the microphone on his phone.

"Sounds like you have to go," I said, trying to break into his other conversation. I didn't want to be the clingy girlfriend who kept him from his job.

"Yeah, Tim just got here. We're heading out. Make sure you eat something for dinner besides that quart of vanilla bean in the freezer."

He knew me too well. "You too."

"When the city is picking up my meals, I make sure I eat." His tone softened. "Talk soon, okay?"

"Later. Emma loves you."

"Tell Emma I love her back."

I set the phone on the table and scratched Emma behind the ears. We'd fallen into a code of telling each other the dog loved them. For me, it was easier to say than "I love you." Greg just thought it was funny. Besides, he knew how I felt. Even if the word was hard to get out sometimes. And I saw this as practice.

I glanced at the clock. Aunt Jackie should be at the shop by now. I dialed CBM's number and was surprised to hear Deek's voice.

"Hey, what are you doing there still? Did a tour bus stop in?" I opened my calendar but didn't see any notice of scheduled arrivals, though that didn't mean anything. Sometimes they just showed up.

"Actually, no. Your aunt told me she needed her shift covered. She said she was going out with some friend." He paused. "Is she okay? I don't think I've ever covered one of her shifts before, especially on such short notice."

"I'm sure it's nothing," I lied easily, even though my heart was racing. Where was my aunt? "Call me if you have any problems."

"Sure thing, Boss."

Now my aunt was missing? Emma licked my arm and I looked down into her brown eyes, which showed concern. "Aunt Jackie didn't go to work today. Let's see if we can find her, okay, girl?"

Emma laid her head on my leg in comfort. That was one of the reasons I loved my dog. She seemed to sense when I was going off the rails. Which, today, was every five minutes. I punched in the numbers for South Cove Bed and Breakfast. When Bill answered, I let my shoulders droop. My aunt and Mary could have taken an unscheduled trip into the city.

"Hey, Bill. I guess Mary's already left?" I went to the email program on my laptop to see if I'd gotten any new emails in the last ten minutes. Yes, I was an overchecker.

"No, she's right here. Hold on, Jill." He handed the phone over to Mary and asked her where she was going. I loved listening in on conversations, but when Mary just took the phone, I felt my gut tighten.

"Jill, is everything okay?" The concern in Mary's voice told me that my aunt hadn't made plans for a girls' night out. "Is Jackie okay?"

"Honestly, I'm not sure. Are you two doing something today? She asked Deek to cover her shift."

"No. In fact, I called her this morning and she said she couldn't get away this weekend. Something about inventory at the store? I was trying to get her out of the house. Harrold talked to me and told me his plans."

My aunt had lied to her best friend. We'd done inventory last weekend. Something was definitely up. "Thanks. I guess I'll give her a call to see what time I'm supposed to be at the shop."

"Don't lie to me. I knew she was making up a story when I heard it. My bullcrap meter isn't broke and it's going off now just like it did when I talked to Jackie. What is going on?"

I set my laptop on the coffee table and leaned back into the sofa. "I don't know. But I'm going to find out. I'll call you when I find her, okay?"

Mary didn't respond, but I heard sniffles on the other end of the line.

"You're not crying, are you? We don't know anything yet." I tried to sound soothing, but deep down, I was ready to bawl as well.

"Find her, Jill. She's been acting strange since she broke it off with Harrold. I think something's really wrong."

I knew something was really wrong, but I'd let my aunt tell Mary the whole story. "I'll call you as soon as I know something."

When I got off the phone, I grabbed my tote and my keys. Emma stood at the door, looking at her leash. "Sorry, girl, you need to stay home for this trip. I'm going to find Aunt Jackie, and I might have to go somewhere they don't allow dogs."

Emma eyed me like I was making up these imaginary places where dogs wouldn't be allowed. She went to her bed, made three circles, and plopped down, her head turned away, not looking at me. She thought I was lying as well.

"We'll run tomorrow." I went out the back door and locked it. My dog still didn't look up. I was in big trouble and I wondered, as I crossed over to my Jeep, if I'd put away the sofa pillows. If not, I wouldn't have any by the time I got home. Tearing up the decorative pillows was her way of paying me back. And yet I kept buying new ones, thinking she'd grow out of the phase. Hope springs eternal.

The first place I stopped was at the bookstore. I parked in the back and noticed that Jackie's car wasn't in its spot. I parked the Jeep there. If she was just out getting groceries, I'd be in the dog house, but it was superclose and convenient. Besides, I didn't think my aunt was shopping. She'd never skip a shift for something that trivial.

I ran upstairs to the balcony that Harrold wanted to turn into a deck garden. Right now, it had one planter of geraniums that were just starting to bloom out for the fall. The view of the ocean from this spot was breathtaking, and there were two folding chairs. One chair was folded up, the other faced west, and I knew my aunt spent nights she wasn't closing the store sitting here, watching the sunset.

I knocked on the door. "Aunt Jackie? Are you in there?"

No answer. I pulled out my key and, with a slight hesitation, opened the door. A chain stopped me from opening the door all the way. All I could see through the crack was a neat-as-a-pin kitchen sink cabinet. I called again. "Aunt Jackie?"

No response. If I was going to get inside, I'd have to go through the office. I shut the door and relocked it. There were scratches on the silver keyhole, as if someone had tried to pick the lock. I glanced around the patio one more time. Convincing myself that nothing else looked out of place, I slipped the key back into my pocket and headed downstairs. Instead of coming in through the back, I moved around the building and came in through the front door. The coffee shop looked busy, with several couples and a few teens sitting at tables, drinking and eating. Deek was finishing up an order but caught my eye when I entered. There were a smattering of people browsing the shelves. It looked like a typical date night for our small town. People either went to Diamond Lille's for a full dinner or came here for a drink and a treat. Or went to the bar across the street.

I greeted several of my regulars and had more than one stop me to tell me that my book recommendation had been spot-on. That was one of the joys of running a bookstore, when you could share a great story with other people. I finally made it to the counter. Deek had just finished with the last order and leaned against the counter, watching me.

"You're busy tonight." I smiled as I glanced around the shop once more.

He nodded. "I like this shift. The customers are more relaxed, wanting to enjoy their time here, not just a quick in and out for coffee or their next read in between errands."

My aunt had said the same thing. We had good traffic and great numbers in the evening shift, but she always said she didn't need help. Deek's observation was probably why.

He picked up a travel mug. "Can I pour you a coffee while you run upstairs?"

"How can you read me so easily?" I shook my head, amazed at my most recently hired barista. He had been with us less than a year; he shouldn't be able to guess my actions so quickly.

"You forget about my mother. I guess I've learned a few tricks from her." He glanced at me. "I'll pack a half-dozen cookies too for your drive."

"I don't know if I'm driving anywhere yet." But of course I was. If my aunt wasn't in her apartment—and I knew she wasn't—I was going to drive through South Cove, then head north to Bakerstown and drive to her favorite restaurants and stores. Maybe I'd get lucky. Most likely I'd burn a tank of gas and not have anything to show for it. "Never mind. Coffee and cookies would be great. I'll be right back."

I went into the office and headed straight up the stairs. Knocking again on my aunt's door, I was afraid of what I might find. "Aunt Jackie? Are you there?"

I was stalling. I knew it. My aunt wasn't in the apartment.

I opened the door and took a deep breath. Then I went inside. The apartment, like the peek at the kitchen, was spotless. I could smell the lemon cleaner Aunt Jackie used. Her morning must have been spent cleaning every inch of the apartment. Her bed was made, and as I touched the soft quilt, I could tell she'd changed out her linens as well. The bathroom shone and clean towels hung on the rods.

There was one habit both my aunt and I shared: when we were trying to work out a problem, we cleaned. My house didn't get this deep clean often, but if I was worried or concerned about something, it shone. Like my aunt's apartment did.

I stopped by the coffee table, where she'd left a notebook. I'd learned my habit of writing down everything I had to get done from my aunt. I opened it to the last page. An address was written in the notes after *Make sure Deek understands how to close.* I recognized the address. It was a park in Bakerstown. I'd gone there with Greg just last month for a joint police family day and picnic event.

What business would my aunt have at a place like this? The answer was clear. She'd gotten a message from the spammer to meet him. And because Greg had her phone, it had been before we'd talked. She hadn't told us.

I hurried out of the apartment. I was halfway down the stairs before I realized I'd forgotten to lock the door. Hurrying back, I quickly relocked the apartment and then hurried down to the shop. I paused at the coffee counter and scribbled a note. Then I handed it to Deek. "Look, if I don't call you in an hour, call Greg and give him this address."

"You shouldn't go alone." Deek held up his hands like I was trying to give him the hot potato. "And you know the man is going to kill me if something happens to you."

"Greg isn't going to kill you. And nothing is going to happen to me." I put down the piece of paper on the counter. "This is just insurance. I'm not such a total idiot that I'd go running off without at least some insurance. Trust me."

He picked up the sheet of paper and held it, seeming to consider my request. Then he nodded. "The energy around this adventure is clear. I'm not going to have to use this; I know it."

"So your 'spirits' are telling me I'm safe?" I shook my head. "Between you and Esmeralda, I'm beginning to fall for your fortune-telling."

"Dude, I don't talk to spirits. I just get vibes." He did something with his watch. "I've set an alarm. If I don't hear from you, I'll call first. If you don't answer, I'll call the dude and he'll yell at me. And I don't have to have the sight to foretell that scene happening."

I picked up my coffee and cookies. "Thanks, Deek."

When I got onto the highway, I put the Jeep on cruise control exactly four miles over the speed limit. I didn't trust myself to regulate my own speed. I wanted to get to Bakerstown now to make sure Aunt Jackie was okay. Even with Deek's positive vibes, I was worried.

Twenty minutes later, I found Jackie's car in the front row of the parking lot for the small city park. I parked next to it, and as I left the car, I threw away the now-empty cup and bag that had held the cookies. I started down the path and saw her sitting on a park bench a few feet into the park. She was reading.

I slipped onto the bench next to her. My heart was pounding, probably from the caffeine and sugar. "You drove all this way to read?"

"You drove all this way to check up on me?" Aunt Jackie didn't look up from the book.

"No. Well, kind of. You never skip a shift. I had something to ask you for Greg for the investigation, and then you weren't there and I got worried." Now that I was saying the words, I sounded totally paranoid. Or I would have, if I didn't know that my aunt had been getting those calls.

She closed the book, tucked it in her large Coach purse; finally, she turned to me. She'd been crying. "There's no need for me to lie now. I was meeting the caller, but as you can see, he stood me up."

Chapter 9

"What were you thinking?" As the words came out of my mouth, I thought about all the times Aunt Jackie had asked me the same thing when she became my guardian during my high school years. And it was always about a guy. The answer then had been, I hadn't been thinking at all. Just going with the flow. If the current guy I'd been dating had suggested something like driving up to the ski lodge and biking down the mountain, I'd said yes. Even if the adventure had sent me to the emergency room with a broken arm.

My aunt's smile confirmed the fact that she too was remembering one of the times, though maybe not the broken-arm one. She pulled out a tissue and wiped the side of my mouth. "You were eating cookies in the car, I see."

I wiped my mouth with my hand. "Stop changing the subject. Why are you here?"

"Just before you and Greg held your intervention, the man calling himself your Uncle Ted had set a meeting with me today. Here in this park. We used to come here on Sundays before his death." She pointed to the fountain that hadn't run for over six years. "We'd buy chicken and come out here to sit and talk."

"This guy knew about that?" Now, I was wondering if all my investigating was giving me the wrong answers.

Aunt Jackie shook her head. "No. He just called it by the park name. I suggested the fountain, and it was like he'd never known one was here. That's probably why I told you and Greg about the calls. That's when I suspected it wasn't Ted after all. He would have never forgotten our Sunday place."

Now I was totally confused. "And yet you came here. Why?"

"Just in case. I couldn't give up on him if he was real, now could I? I was his wife for over thirty years. You can't just walk away from something like that." She wiped at her eyes and pulled out a compact. "I look like a silly old woman."

"You look like a strong, sensible woman." I watched as she patted on powder. "Why didn't you tell me? I would have come with you."

"I wasn't going to come. Then I had the strangest dream last night. A dream I couldn't shake. When it was my shift time, I called Deek. If he had said no, I wasn't going to go. I was going to call Greg with the information. When he said he could take my shift, I took it as an omen."

I pulled out my phone. "Speaking of Deek, I need to call him to let him know I'm all right."

"You really shouldn't use our employees as a message machine for your little adventures." My aunt slipped her compact into her purse. "I guess I should return home and go back to the world where my husband is dead."

"I'm sorry." I could smell fresh-cut grass. Happy voices from kids on the nearby playground echoed around us. It wasn't a place to talk about pain and death, but I needed to push on. We needed to finish this.

I waited a few minutes, letting the park's happy feel surround us. To protect us from the pain. Then I asked what might tie this all up. "Have you ever worked with someone over at the Senior Project?"

"No, at least, I don't think so. There was a woman from some financial assistance agency who came and interviewed me when that awful man took my savings. I was living in the city then. And I don't remember what state agency she was with. Maybe something to do with aging?" My aunt tapped her fingers on her purse. "I probably have the paperwork at home in my files. I might have her card still. She was very understanding."

"If you could find it, Greg's looking at an information breach at the Senior Project. Like he doesn't have enough on his plate." I glanced around the park. "This must have been a lovely place to spend time."

My aunt smiled and tapped my forearm. "You're a sweet girl. It *was* beautiful, and sitting here has brought back fond memories. I still miss him, you know."

"I do." I stood. "There's an ice cream shop right over there by the edge of the parking lot. Do you want to get a scoop and walk around for a while?"

Smiling, she stood and took my arm. "That would be lovely too. Did you bring Emma?"

"She stayed at home. I'm pretty sure I'll have torn-up pillows when I get home." We strolled toward the small purple hut.

"I don't know why you even buy those pillows. You know she has an addiction."

* * * *

I followed my aunt's car until we hit the South Cove turnoff on Highway 1. Then I pulled into my driveway and watched as she continued into town. Esmeralda was standing on her porch and waved before going inside. She was dressed in the full fortune-telling costume, so I figured she must have a client arriving soon. And as if I'd predicted it, a Range Rover pulled off the highway and turned into my neighbor's driveway. I wasn't sure why she continued working as a police dispatcher. I was sure she was raking in the money in her side hustle. But maybe the police gig was her actual side hustle, and I knew she got her benefits from her job with Greg.

Of course, that didn't come from him. Greg was tight-lipped when it came to his employees. The good news was, Amy let some things slip when we were eating lunch.

Small towns took care of their own. At least, that's the way it happened in South Cove. Which was one of the 101 reasons I loved living here. I just hoped that when we found the man who'd been hurting my aunt by pretending to be my uncle that he was out of the country and not down the street. I wanted to hurt him. Bad.

I went inside and, remembering my promise to Greg, looked in the fridge for something to eat besides the ice cream in the freezer. I pulled out a chicken breast and seasoned it, then put some water on to boil. I was going to make my favorite spaghetti salad to go with it. Not wanting to mess with the grill, I grabbed my grill pan and seared the chicken on both sides before tucking it into the oven to finish. The pasta was cooked and timers were set, so I grabbed a glass of wine and went out to the porch to sit on my swing.

What would it be like to live with the same man for thirty years? Greg and I had been dating for close to five. And now we were living together, which hadn't been as much of a life change as I'd thought it would be. Of course, at the end of our dating period, I saw him every day, so living together just meant he came home and stayed with me instead of going back to his apartment.

I'd been thinking about weddings, but with both Amy and my aunt getting married, I'd pushed the idea aside. I figured I was just getting antsy with all the marriage talk. But now that Aunt Jackie had canceled the engagement, I couldn't blame my random thoughts about being Mrs. Greg King on anything but our relationship's next big step.

While dinner cooked, I pulled out the notebook I'd started on my aunt's mystery. There wasn't much there except questions. And I had a few to add today. First off, who had been trying to open Aunt Jackie's apartment door? Why were there scratches on the lock? And why hadn't the scammer shown up? Had he been in the wings, watching my aunt? Which was a supercreepy thought. Or had he never planned on showing up in the first place? Was this meet just a way to see if she would follow his directions?

I wrote a quick note about the mislabeled death certificate and took the copy out of my tote and taped it to a page in the notebook. Now who was being creepy? I glanced over the bare facts of my uncle's life. His full name, Theodore Walter Ekroth. No wonder he'd gone by Ted. He'd been born in South Dakota. Had I known that? Aunt Jackie and Uncle Ted had lived in California all the time I knew them.

I turned the page and made a quick to-do list. Tomorrow I'd call Esmeralda to see if she'd found anything. Then I'd go to the Senior Project to see if my aunt had been a client. She told me she would look for her records, but if she'd never worked with them, I could cross off the center as a potential information leak. Happy with my plan, I closed the notebook and finished up my dinner. Tonight, I was going to binge-watch one of the many shows I'd wanted to see forever. Maybe with a glass of wine.

* * * *

Saturday morning, I woke before my alarm. I'd had a restless night, dreaming about my aunt. Jackie would be there one minute and gone the next. I'd spent all night following her in my dreams. Typically, when I have stress dreams, I'm running after cute little puppies, trying to keep them safe. This time, the stakes were higher, and even I knew what the dream meant. I didn't need Esmeralda to interpret.

I rolled over to find the other side of the bed empty. And if Greg had come home, I'd bet he slept on the couch so he wouldn't disturb me. Emma was sitting on the floor watching me. That was my second clue that we were alone. Emma would have been downstairs, sleeping with Greg. The dog knew I moved around too much in my sleep, so she preferred Greg's more still night moves. Or nonmoves.

I glanced at the clock. If we made it short, we could get in a run before I had to be at the shop. Running in the morning was cool and gave me time to wake up and think about things that were bothering me. Today, I needed both. I grabbed my running gear, and in less than five minutes, Emma and I were out the door.

The sun was just beginning to come up over the mountains and the beach had that prelight morning glow about it. No one seemed to be on the beach, so I unhooked Emma's leash as soon as we hit the sand. She ran to the waves to chase off the seagulls that were looking for their breakfast in the wake and I started running.

By the time we were running back to the parking lot, we were not alone on the beach. An older couple walked near the shoreline, stopping every so often to pick up and sometimes discard a washed-up shell. But they were headed away from us, so I didn't worry about Emma with them. A man stepped off the parking lot steps and headed straight toward us. He was dressed in a Hawaiian shirt and cargo shorts, and as we got closer, I noticed Emma's excitement. I reached down to hook up her leash.

"Leave her off." Harrold called to me. "I haven't seen my girl for a while."

With that, Emma took off to meet up with Harrold. When she reached him, she sat with a wide grin on her face, her tail making sweeping motions on the sand. I caught up with them and put a hand on her back, hoping she wouldn't jump on him and knock him over. The man was old enough that I worried about him falling. "Hey. You're out early."

"I stopped by your house for coffee, but I didn't get an answer, so I thought I'd take a chance you might be here." He reached over and kissed my cheek. "How are you?"

"I'm good," I lied. It didn't do any good to share with him my concerns about my aunt. Not until she figured out that Harrold was the best thing that had ever happened to her. Or, at least, the best thing after my uncle died. "We thought we'd get a run in before I headed in to open the shop."

"I don't think you're telling me the whole truth." He studied my face, concern showing in his eyes. "I don't remember the last time I saw those dark circles under your eyes, but I'll let your statement stand. At least for now. I was wondering if you'd gotten a date set for your aunt to be out of the apartment. Well, out of South Cove would be better. The woman does have a knack of showing up right at the wrong time."

I laughed. Harrold did know my aunt well. But I'd forgotten about his request yesterday when I'd talked to Mary. My aunt owed me for worrying me to death. "Sorry, I haven't gotten that done yet. I will this weekend."

He stroked Emma's head, then straightened and locked his gaze with mine. "You would tell me if something was going on, right?"

"Right now, I'm just trying to figure out what is going on." I placed my hand on his arm. "You know Aunt Jackie. She always wants to handle things on her own. I promise, as soon as I can, I'll fill you in."

He sighed and looked out over the ocean. "I guess that will have to do. I love your aunt. She needs to know that there isn't anything I wouldn't do for her. Or you, for that matter."

I put my arm around his waist as we walked back to the parking lot, where his little electric car was parked. "We'll get through this. I know she loves you, Harrold. We just have to get her to understand that we're here to help, not to get in her way."

"Hopefully, the patio remodel will help. At least if it doesn't, she'll have to think about me every evening as she watches the sun set."

I paused at the car. "You're tricky, you know that?"

"I have to be. I'm trying to woo back your cynical aunt." He rubbed Emma's head one more time, then got into the car. "Try for next Saturday. I've got all the parts ready, and my son is coming in that weekend to help."

"I'll try." I wasn't convinced that I could convince my aunt to take a girls' day with Mary, even though I knew she needed one. She wanted to figure out who had been impersonating my uncle just as badly as I did. Maybe even more. I just hoped Greg or I figured it out before she did. My aunt didn't take being tricked very well. "I'll call you as soon as it's set up."

"I'm counting on you." He started up the car and headed back to his shop, The Train Station.

As I watched him disappear, I looked at Emma. "I think we're in over our heads with this one, don't you?"

Emma woofed, but I think she was talking about the rabbit on the edge of the parking lot and not my dilemma. But I could have been wrong. We headed back to the house so I could get ready for work. With today being Saturday, I didn't think the Senior Project would be open, so I wasn't sure how much of my snooping list I could get done before Monday. But I could put a bug in Mary's ear about the girls' day next weekend.

Deek showed up two hours early and set up a computer on one of the tables. "Hope you don't mind. I have a paper due Monday and I'm not getting anything done at Mom's. She's having back-to-back readings until after Halloween. Some of those people are so weird."

"You could get your own place, you know." I poured him a coffee and walked it over to the table. "You're a working man now."

"With what you pay? I'd be lucky if I could afford a tent site at one of the RV campgrounds. Besides, Mom's is usually okay. It's just during the fall that it gets really too much. Well, and the holidays. People come out of the woodwork to talk to their loved ones during any holiday." He opened his computer. "Besides, I have first dibs on Kyle's apartment when he marries that girl of his. Apparently, her grandmother left her a house up above Bakerstown within walking distance of the beach. I'm watching her too, just in case Kyle gets stupid and she dumps him."

"You are such a good friend," I said with a laugh as I watched a pair of teenagers enter and run toward the bookshelves. "You may want to work in the back. Some of your book club members are here."

"No probs. They know if I have my computer up, I'm off-limits. We are very clear on the boundaries. Besides, they just want to be early to get the good seats for book club. We're talking about a fantasy/time-travel book this month. They were the ones to choose the book." He glanced down at the Word document that just came up.

"Work. Sorry to have bothered you."

He held up the coffee. "You didn't. You brought sustenance. Besides, I wanted to ask if your aunt was okay. She came down last night and helped me close. I told her I had it, but she seemed like she needed something to do, so I let her tell me what to do."

"That's her favorite pastime." I leaned on one of the chairs, getting closer. "She's fine. Someone has been playing pranks on her and we're trying to find out who."

Deek held up his hands. "Don't look at me. I like a practical joke as much as the next guy, but your aunt is too classy for me to even attempt one. Besides, I wouldn't want to get payback from her."

I laughed and started to step away. "Work hard. If you need more time, I can stay late and watch the shop."

He reached out for my arm and stopped me from leaving. "Does this have anything to do with the death certificate you had me get? That's cold. You shouldn't mess with a person's grief."

Since this was coming from the kid of a woman who made a living talking to the dead, I had to assume that Deek at least thought his mom's power or talent was real. Even if I didn't. "Yes, someone has been calling, saying he's her dead husband." A thought occurred to me. "Hey, your mom doesn't know of any scammers who would do something like that, does she?"

His eyes darted away from looking directly at me. "Not that I know of, but I can ask. She knew some people when she was a kid."

"Were she and Esmeralda friends back then?" I didn't want to call Esmeralda out, but if there was another source for this information, maybe this was a path to an answer?

He shrugged. "Look, she doesn't like to talk about those times. And the two of them never talk about the past. The only thing I know is Mom refused to pay a dime of my college costs if I went to a Louisiana school. Not just one in New Orleans. That's weird, right?"

Because I knew Esmeralda grew up there, maybe that wasn't as weird as Deek thought. "Don't worry about it. But if you could ask her, I'd appreciate it."

"Of course." He sipped his coffee, and I could feel his gaze on my back as I walked over to the bookshelves to check on the new customers. But Deek had been right. They were just browsing and waiting for the book club meeting at three.

My aunt came down just before I left. She was Deek's backup when he started the meeting. I hadn't expected to see her, but it was a good time to ask her about next Saturday.

"Jill, you really need to refill the dessert case before you leave on Saturdays. Deek has enough on his plate with the book clubs to have to bother about making sure we have enough food displayed." She started counting the desserts.

"If you would notice, I'm still here and have thirty minutes before my shift ends." I pointed to the clock. "That's more than enough time for me to refill the dessert case."

She set down the pen and paper. "Sorry, you're right. I've been off my game for months. Last night I almost forgot to reset the coffee for this morning, but Deek handled it nicely. Maybe I'm just getting too old for this job."

Not looking at her, I laughed. "The day you retire is the day I'm going to have to close the store. You know more about this place than anyone else, including me. By the way, Mary said something about calling you for a day in the city next week. Do you need me to cover your shift?"

I felt the stare on my back, but I refused to turn to look at her. That would show weakness, and that was the worst thing you could do in front of my aunt. I counted out the brownies on the bottom shelf and waited.

"I don't think we made plans yet."

I shrugged and took my pad, heading to the back office. "Well, let me know. Greg's busy with this murder, so I don't have anything else to do anyway."

I hoped she'd take the bait, but I couldn't be sure. Not for a few days.

Chapter 10

Sundays were typically really laid-back at the shop. Regulars didn't show up until nine, if they were on their way to church, or ten, if they were skipping the service. Today, I was glad about the slowness because it gave me time to think about the Aunt Jackie issue. Deek had asked me to cover the early shift, so I'd canceled brunch with Amy. Besides, I didn't want to report on how many of the table decorations I'd finished. Especially because the answer was none.

Darla came in right after I opened. She sat at the counter and, after ordering her favorite large mocha with whipped cream, took out her notebook. "So tell me what you've found out about the crime."

Shock registered on my face, but I quickly turned away and poured myself a cup of coffee. I didn't think anyone would know about this, well, except the police and Esmeralda and now Deek. How had Darla found out?

"Come on, sit down and spill. You know something about the murder. I can see it in your reaction." Darla patted the stool next to her. "Your boyfriend has been unusually quiet on this one."

"Oh, the murder." My shoulders drooped and I went around the counter, glad the shop was empty. I sat and sipped before answering her. "It was Paula's boyfriend. Paula was the woman who came to talk to us about keeping seniors safe at the last business-to-business meeting. Remember?"

"I knew that much." Darla stared at me. "Why did you seem relieved when you realized I was talking about the murder? What else is going on?"

I shrugged. I'd already given away too much. Darla could have been a top-ranked journalist if her folks hadn't died and left her the winery to run. Now, she treated the roving-reporter job for the *South Cove Gazette* as a fun hobby. "Nothing that I know."

"I doubt that, but one investigation at a time. I already knew Ben was the victim. From what I've learned about him, the guy was a saint. He volunteered a lot of time at the Senior Project." Darla flipped back through her notes. "Everyone loved him."

"I thought he was a jerk to Paula. I saw him on his phone at Diamond Lille's and he'd just left her at the table to pay the bill. Of course, she didn't leave the diner until he'd finished his call. I tend to give Greg space for his phone calls, but at least he comes back in to get me. Ben just rapped on the window." I watched as a lone customer walked past the shop and wondered if my "Open" sign was plugged in.

"Wow, you're the first one to say he was a jerk. Even his girlfriend, Paula, sang his praises. Maybe you misunderstood what was going on?"

"Maybe." But after working with abused women for way too long when I was an attorney, I'd seen the signs before. Paula was too aware of his location at all times. Even when she was trying to eat. And I hadn't imagined the tears in her eyes when she sat alone at the table. "So, what else did you need to know?"

"That's all you've got?" Darla lifted her hand to my forehead. "I can't believe it; are you sick?"

"No, I'm fine. Why are you being so weird?" I pushed her hand away.

Darla closed her notebook. "It's been over two days. I'd figured you would have a suspect in mind and already be working on a way to get him to confess."

"Not my job." I held out my hand and circled it toward the shop. "I'm busy keeping the lights on here. Greg's the one you want to talk to."

Now Darla just looked confused. "You're going to sit right there and tell me to my face that you have no idea what happened to Ben Penn?"

"Not a clue." My gaze went outside the front door, where two people were staring into the shop. They saw my attention, and with a sheepish grin, pushed the door open. "And here's my first customer."

"Second."

"What?" I looked down at her and saw her own grin.

"I'm your first customer; they are your second." She drained the cup and then stood. "Don't think I'm going to forget this. I'll be back as soon as I get my story filed. Then you can tell me what has you so distracted."

Darn it, Darla was right. I'd been so busy with what was happening to my aunt, I hadn't even thought about Ben. Had Greg really questioned Paula about the murder? That girl wouldn't hurt a fly, especially when the fly was her boyfriend. She'd been head over heels for the guy, even if I couldn't figure out why. After getting the few customers who'd walked in after Darla left situated, I pulled out my laptop.

Deek would be in at two to run the Baby Boomer Bibliophiles book group he'd developed. It was my aunt's women's fiction idea, but amped up, and the women loved Deek. As well as his choices. This month they were reading a book about women serial killers. Next month was a trilogy of cozy mysteries focused around Halloween. The subjects seemed to change with the season and the whims of their leader. He'd given me a list of the next six months' book choices for all his groups and I was pleasantly surprised at the variety.

Starting in November, they'd have to move their book club meeting to Tuesday night. We closed down the store on Sundays and Mondays for the winter. Even though we never got a true winter here, like in the northern states, tourist traffic started slowing after October. I didn't mind an off day, but my aunt had tracked our sales over three years and her numbers had convinced me we should take advantage of winter hours. I cut back my own hours during the winter as well, so my staff could still get the hours they needed. What can I say? I'm generous. Cutting hours also gave me a lot of time to travel and read. Which might seem selfish, but really, it's all for the shop. At least that's my story.

Setting down my coffee cup, I started researching Mr. Ben Penn, formerly of South Cove. After a few unsuccessful searches, I went into the listing of local residents the city had provided to businesses for marketing purposes. The resident had to agree to receive the materials, but most did because they were part of the business community too. A lot of our business owners lived in our little town. I looked up the address I'd gotten from Greg when he'd mentioned that Paula and Ben had lived in town. But from what I could see, Paula was the only one on the lease.

Why had Ben been so invisible? I would bet that Paula had all the utilities in her name, just like on the lease. Residents got parking stickers for their cars so the police wouldn't tow or ticket them for parking too long in a residential area. When the beach parking lot filled up, I had a line of cars parked down the narrow street in front of my house. Even with the "No Parking" signs. Toby and Tim loved handing out tickets on weekends because it was so easy to pick up one violation after another.

I emailed Amy at her work account and asked what the parking records showed for Paula's address. Hopefully, she wouldn't mention the question to Greg. He must have been happy to have me working on something else and out of his investigation. And I really wasn't involved. I was just researching.

Tomorrow was going to be a busy day. I had to go to the Senior Project, and talk to Amy. Good thing I didn't have to work my shift at the coffee shop; we were out of dog food, so I was going to have to make a trip into Bakerstown for groceries.

I closed my laptop and started making a shopping list. But then I turned the page and started making a Ben list. I could stop by the funeral home to see if Doc Ames had anything from the autopsy. I mean, I could stop by to give Doc some treats because I hadn't seen him in quite a while. And maybe I could talk to him about what was happening with Aunt Jackie and see if he'd heard any gossip about that kind of scam. As he mentioned to me often, people told their funeral director a whole lot of things they should probably be telling a therapist.

I still had three hours to go before I got to go home. While Deek would be in at two, I worked the first hour and Aunt Jackie came down to cover Deek's second hour. I could call Mary and convince her to talk my aunt into a girls' trip next week. I went over to the coffee bar to grab some coffee and Aunt Jackie pushed through the door, talking on her newly returned cell.

"Of course I'm not implying you stood me up, but I was there and you weren't. What else would you call it?" My aunt pointed to the phone, mouthing the words, *trace this.*

I grabbed my cell and called 911. It was Sunday, so only the deputy on shift would be answering the emergency line.

"South Cove Police, how may I help you?" Toby's voice came over the speaker and I stepped away from my aunt.

"Toby," I whispered, "can you track a call coming into my aunt's cell?"

"Jill? Why on earth do you want me to do that? Is Jackie finally calling Harrold?"

"Listen, Greg already knows about this, and there's some sort of program on Jackie's cell. He gave it back to her yesterday. Can you figure out how to track it?"

I heard voices on the other side of the line, and then Greg came on. "Toby's running the trace now. I forgot to tell him about it. I told Tim, but, well, it's been busy. Can she keep the guy on the line?"

I made a rolling motion with my hand at my aunt and she shrugged. "She says she'll try. I thought maybe this was all over."

"Why, because the guy didn't show up yesterday? Yes, your aunt told me all about your little excursion into Bakerstown when I dropped off the phone. I guess she didn't mention that when she called you."

"I didn't take her to see him. I just followed her." I could hear the ice in Greg's voice. Fighting with my boyfriend had not been one of the things on my to-do list today, but you had to make room for impromptu items. "You don't expect me to just stay out of this, do you?"

"Darn it." My aunt had set down the phone. She looked over at me with tired eyes. "He hung up."

"Don't answer my last question. Aunt Jackie says the guy ended the call. Was that long enough for the trace to work?" I motioned my aunt to sit at one of the tables. Then I went to the coffee bar and poured her a cup while I waited for Greg to respond.

"I'll be over in a couple of minutes." Then Greg hung up on me.

I supposed I wasn't totally out of the doghouse, but like I'd told him, I hadn't gone off trying to find the guy, just my aunt. Deek walked toward the coffee bar. He stopped about halfway.

"Whoa; the energy in here is totally chaotic. Is this a bad time? I finished my report." His gaze moved from Jackie to me, then back to Jackie. "You're having issues again, right?"

"I don't know what you mean." My aunt threw me a look that told me she knew exactly what Deek meant and blamed me for the fact that he knew about her gentleman caller who wasn't a gentleman at all.

"Sorry, I had to ask him for a favor. He doesn't know much, just that you are having issues." I shrugged. "It's not my fault that in order to figure out this situation, I needed help. Deek's the one who had the friend who got us Uncle Ted's death certificate."

Deek nodded and set his backpack on a table near a wall socket. "And she called me this morning and told me more."

We watched as he went to pour a cup of coffee and then sit down and started unpacking his computer.

"Do you want to tell us the new information?" *Or should I beat it out of you?* I figured saying the second part in my head was positive human resource protocol. Besides, I wouldn't have a chance; my aunt was surprisingly quick when she wanted something.

Deek looked up, confused. "Oh, yeah, I didn't finish that statement, did I?"

"No, you didn't." I saw my aunt move around the counter and figured I could grab her before she reached Deek's table. Or at least I hoped I could. "You might want to hurry up."

He glanced over at Aunt Jackie, and something he saw in her face must have alerted him. "Okay, then. Trina called earlier and said it wasn't just your uncle's file that got mislabeled. It was a bunch of them. Trina said they think a computer hacker got into their systems, made copies, and then messed with the files to throw the IT geeks off the trail. A guy from the FBI came by and talked to the big bosses on Friday."

"They opened an investigation on this?" Greg would know if that was true. I didn't think county death certificates were that big a deal. But maybe I wasn't seeing the whole picture.

"No investigation. They just wanted to let the county guys know that their security systems were way out of date and needed to be upgraded. The bosses weren't very happy because of the cost. At least that's what Trina says. She's looking for another job, just in case she gets canned in a budget-cut process." Deek shook his head. "I'd been thinking about applying at the county for the job security, but I guess there's no such thing nowadays."

"Do a good job, you'll have job security." Greg pushed open the door. "Are you thinking about finally firing this pain in the butt?"

Deek's eyes widened and he stared at me.

"No, I'm not firing Deek. Besides, that's not what we're talking about. Did you know that the county records department had a security breech?" I walked around the coffee bar. "Can I get you something to drink?"

"Sure. Coffee would be great. And yeah, I talked to the agent in charge on Friday. He thinks it's probably a prank, but he drove down from the city to talk with us anyway." Greg sat at the counter and held out his hand to my aunt. "Can I see your phone?"

She nodded toward the cash register, where she'd left it. "If this doesn't stop soon, I'm going to take the battery out and throw it away in the ocean. That way, no one can find me."

"And that's the rub. No one can find you if you do that. Not me, or Mary, or Harrold." I almost grinned at the baleful look my aunt gave me at my mention of Harrold's name. "Look, maybe you should take a day off next week. Like Saturday? Deek and I can handle the shop. You take Mary and go have a girls' day. Stop at the spa, visit some art galleries, maybe stay over a night and take in a show. That should relax you."

My aunt moved toward the back door and the stairs leading to her apartment. "That's a surprisingly good idea coming from you. Thoughtful. But if you think you can handle the shop, I guess I'll give Mary a call."

I started laughing as Greg looked surprised. My aunt was nothing if not direct. "So glad you finally see how valuable I can be."

"Now, Jill..." My aunt started, but Greg interrupted her.

"I'm switching out the card on this phone. Don't give anyone the number, okay? Have your friends reach you through the shop." Greg put the cover back on the phone and handed it to her. "And don't make an arrangement to meet this guy without talking to me first."

She reached for the phone, but Greg didn't release it. She held up her hands. "Fine, I'll be a good girl. You know I took care of myself for more years than you've been alive, Greg King."

She was pulling out the full-name trick. I bet if she'd known his middle name, that would have been tucked into the warning as well. My aunt didn't like it when people tried to take care of her. The problem was, since she and I had moved to South Cove, we had a lot of friends who tried to do just that. Like family would. I smiled as Greg released the phone.

"Miss Jackie, I'm just trying to keep you around for when Jill realizes the error in her ways and begs me to marry her and sire a boatload of children."

Deek snorted, which earned him a glare from all of us.

"Well, I'm going to have to take better care of myself so I can live long enough to see that happen." My aunt tapped her hand over Greg's. "Thank you."

And then she left the shop and headed up to the apartment. Greg slipped the extra SIM card into his pocket. "I gave her one of the phone numbers we use for undercover work. I don't want this guy reaching out and getting her again. You need to make sure you screen the shop phone."

"I'll send shop calls to my cell during her shifts." I glanced at Deek. "You just need to make sure she doesn't beat you to the phone when you're working together. Can you let Toby know too?"

Greg nodded and stood. "I've got to get back to the station. I'm going to set up this number in a cell I'll have monitored twenty-four seven. Hopefully, the guy will be stupid enough to call back and talk long enough to get the trace. All we got today was he's in Bakerstown."

"Do you think he was watching her yesterday?"

He kissed the top of my head as he passed by on his way out the door. "I'd bet money on it."

Deek whistled as he watched Greg leave. "Man, you have him really angry. What did you do?"

The usual. That was the real answer. Greg was mad because I was investigating. But instead, I nodded to Deek's computer. "You better get busy. You have a book club to run in a couple of hours."

Chapter 11

Instead of spending Sunday night with Greg, I ate alone at the house. I heard him come in and Emma run down to greet him, but I fell asleep before he came upstairs. I know going to bed angry was against the couple rules, but I wasn't going to apologize for trying to find my aunt. He hadn't even asked for my side of the story before he got all preachy on me. So he could apologize first.

Toby had my early morning shift, so I was off all of Monday. When I awoke, Emma was staring at me and Greg's side of the bed was empty. So much for his apology. I went downstairs to let Emma out and get a cup of coffee. I had my laptop on the kitchen table where I'd left it, so I booted it up to check my email.

Surprisingly, I had an email from the Senior Project. I quickly opened it and realized it was a marketing letter aimed at people caring for their elderly loved ones. Aunt Jackie would flip if she knew I was getting mail like this. I read through the list of services and realized they had just given me my opening to go talk to them. The email said I should call Denyse Lindt to set up an appointment. I glanced at the clock. They should be open by eight. Which gave Emma and me just enough time to get our run in before the beach got crowded.

I quickly made a short list of what I needed to do for the day, including hitting the grocery store and the pet store for dog food. I'd brought home a dozen cookies for Doc Ames, so I wrote his name on the list. Then I ran upstairs to change into my running gear. The day was looking up.

By the time we'd finished our run, it was close to eight. Emma and I went into the house through the back door, and as I hung up Emma's leash, I saw a note on the table next to a Diamond Lille's box. I picked up the note and read it aloud.

"Sorry about being grumpy yesterday. I brought you a peace offering. I thought I might catch you before you left to run, but I couldn't wait. See you tonight for dinner? I'll grill if you pick up steaks at the market."

I set down the note and opened the box. Greg knew my weaknesses. Six maple bars and five blueberry cake doughnuts were inside. There was an empty spot that had probably held an apple fritter, but my boyfriend had left me all the rest. I programmed another cup of coffee and went upstairs to shower and change.

Back in the kitchen a few minutes later, I texted Greg a thank-you note. Then I took out a plate and set one of both types of doughnuts on the plate. I booted up the laptop again and studied the book order Deek had put together yesterday at the end of his shift. The guy was a natural at running a bookstore. He could spot a trend faster than either Jackie or I, and he knew what the kids were reading.

If I didn't own the store, I'd peg him for the town's book geek. I was starting to put the puzzle pieces together. I'd put a bug in Aunt Jackie's ear about getting out of town next Saturday. I'd call Mary in a few days to confirm the date and time. Operation Harrold Wins Jackie Back was on track. Today, I'd figure out if that guy who stole my aunt's money a few years ago had also sold her information to a new scammer. Or at least that was the plan. I might be optimistic, thinking that this Denyse from the Senior Project would be up on this type of thing, but Paula had spoken about it just last week. You'd think most of the counselors would be savvy to the problem.

The first time I tried to call, I got an answering machine telling me the office didn't open until eight thirty. The second time, I actually got Denyse on the line, and we set an appointment for eleven. Which meant I had to leave by ten thirty to get to Bakerstown on time. I had two hours to kill.

Which meant laundry was back on today's list, as well as cleaning bathrooms. I put the first load into the washing machine and headed upstairs to clean the two upstairs bathrooms first. Always do the worst job first had been my mom's motto when it came to housecleaning and I agreed with her logic. The downstairs bath was just a half bath, so it would be quick. And I could start another load in the washer before leaving for Bakerstown and my appointments there.

By the time I left for Bakerstown, the house looked pretty good. I still needed to vacuum, but with a big dog in the house, that chore should have been on my daily to-do list. Humming along to the song playing on the radio, I made a list of all the things I was grateful for. My house. My dog. My car, which was the first brand-new, off-the-showroom-floor vehicle I'd ever owned.

I was grateful for my business and those who worked for me. And I was grateful for the people in my life. My aunt had been there for me when I was a kid, and now she'd stepped in to help me run my business. Although I'd only invited her for a few days, she wound up staying and loving South Cove as much as I did. I wouldn't let this scammer taint her feelings about this special seaside town.

I pulled up and parked in the Senior Project parking lot with fifteen minutes to spare. I sat back and looked at my notebook, writing out leading questions that might get me the information I needed without being blunt. I called it direct, but others were intimidated by my questioning style.

A knock on my window startled me, and I looked up to see Paula standing outside my car. I grabbed my tote and stuffed the notebook inside. Then I climbed out, locking the car as I greeted her. "How are you? I've been thinking about you."

"I'm as good as could be expected. I'm not sure what I'm supposed to be doing, but the director called me in today to get an update on all my files. I'm on administrative leave until this all shakes out." She pulled a tissue out of her purse. "I've lost Ben and I can't work. Good thing I don't have a dog, because with my luck, he'd be in danger right now."

She had her sense of humor still. I put my hand on her arm. "I'm sure everything will be okay. I've got a meeting with someone named Denyse. Do you know her?"

"She's technically my boss, so she's good. Just not as good as me." Now the smile on Paula's face looked real, not painted on. "But she'll be able to help you with your problems. Is this about your aunt?"

No secrets in a small town, but I wondered how much Paula really knew. "Actually, yes, I'm looking into things we need to get handled now. I hate to think about it, but since she's not getting married, I'm going to be the one to handle her affairs when the time comes. I just want to be aware of what I'm getting in to."

"You'd be surprised at how many people just stick their heads in the sand and don't deal with any of this." Paula nodded to the door, and we made our way to the lobby. "You're a good niece to educate yourself."

"Well, your presentation kind of scared me. I want to make sure there isn't any way for someone to just come in and walk away with all my aunt's money." Aunt Jackie really didn't have much anymore, but I was playing a role here.

"There are a lot of scams out there. We just have to be aware of what could happen to keep the wolves at bay." Paula studied me as we paused at the empty reception desk. "My talk really helped motivate you?"

"Darn right." The woman had been a horrible speaker, but her topic was interesting, and if I hadn't been investigating, I might have considered checking out my aunt's situation with these people. Or maybe not. Either way, Paula didn't need to know.

"Oh, I didn't know anyone was out here." A younger woman stepped out of an office. "Hi, Paula. Earl is waiting for you."

"Thanks." Paula smiled at me. "Good luck in your researching."

Apparently, investigating wasn't a bad habit in this world. I turned to the receptionist, who was watching me. "I've got an appointment with Denyse?"

"I thought you were with Paula." She glanced down at her clipboard. "I don't see anything on today's schedule."

A woman dressed in a coral dress with a matching jacket and stiletto heels came out of another office. "Sorry, that was my fault. I just made the appointment today."

Earl Hess stood outside his door. "Denyse? Do you have a moment? I'd like you to be here when Paula updates me on her caseload."

"I made an appointment this morning. I'll be doing an intake." She nodded toward me.

As we walked down the hall, I took in her professionally highlighted hair, which gave a touch of blond beach babe to the look. And if the woman didn't tan weekly, I'd eat my sun hat. Unlike Paula, who looked a little rumpled and off-kilter, this woman was well dressed and professional. The type you'd find in a law office, not in a small, community action agency. Glancing down at her left hand, I saw the rock. Yep, Denyse was a bored trophy wife who didn't need the money but wanted to get out of the house.

"Denyse, I'm Jill Gardner. Thanks for seeing me on such short notice." I followed the woman to a small kitchenette.

"No problem. I had an opening on my calendar today. I'm getting part of Paula's caseload for a few weeks later today, so this is perfect timing." She held out a coffee mug. "Can I pour you some?"

"Sure, I'd love some." I'd already had three cups at home. What would one more do? I took the filled cup and we walked into a nearby office. It was decorated in the same luxury style as its occupant.

Denyse set down her cup on a table by a wing chair and pointed to the couch. "Go ahead and sit. I need to get intake forms. This place is nothing if not a pile of information on our clients, but don't worry, I won't ask your weight or your bank account number. Although those are probably the only questions I won't ask. The interview can feel a little invasive."

"I'm not really sure I'm ready to act on anything for my aunt. She's very independent. And I'm in the dark about her finances." I wasn't completely ignorant on those subjects, but there was no way I was going to tell a complete stranger how much my aunt had in savings or what she earned at the shop. Especially because my end goal was to find the guy who was pretending to be Uncle Ted.

Denyse looked at the form, then set it aside. "Sometimes I think we expect people to jump into the role of caretaker way too fast. Let's just talk for a while, and if you decide you want our services, we can do the actual intake. How does that sound?"

Surprisingly perfect. I took my notebook out of my tote and grabbed a pen. "I appreciate your understanding. I have a few questions for you." I held back the story of my aunt's broker who'd taken off with a lot of her money. Instead, I painted the scene with broad strokes and focused on how vulnerable it had made her feel.

Denyse nodded and took a few notes, but actually seemed to be listening. "That must have been really hard on her."

"She barely asked me for help then. She's never asked for help before or after that day. But now, she's getting some calls we both think are scams. And I can't help but wonder if this is related to the other situation." I glanced down at my page, like I was looking for the question, but I had it ready. Life's a stage, right? "I wondered if there was a database where these people could store information about vulnerable people."

"You think your aunt was targeted now because someone was able to scam her before?" Denyse leaned back into her chair, appearing to be considering the question. "It's no secret that once someone falls for a scam, they seem to be hit over and over. We've always thought it was because they were easier targets and were susceptible to a good story. But if what you're implying is true..."

I nodded as the realization came over Denyse's face. "Then there is a way these scammers find their next target."

Denyse had another appointment scheduled at eleven twenty. Apparently, intake appointments were supposed to be brief, but she took my card and promised to call if she found out anything about this secret database. As I left the office, she leaned on her doorway. "You know, we could be grasping at straws with this. It could just be coincidence or a basic character flaw in the victims."

I thought about her parting statement during my shopping and as I drove up to the funeral home. Doc Ames was outside, working in the flower bed. I picked up the box of cookies and went to greet him.

He looked up at me, shading his eyes from the sun. "Well, aren't you the prettiest thing out here besides these mums?"

"Flatterer." I held out the cookies. "You got some iced tea to go with these?"

"I do, and we can eat in the kitchen. The afternoon light fills up that room and no one gets to enjoy it except the women from the churches who sponsor the gatherings after the funerals." He brushed the dirt off his knees. "From dirt we come, into dirt we go."

"I'm not sure that's the quote." I followed him around to the back door of the funeral home, where he put his gloves and garden hoe on a table.

Shrugging, he stopped by a sink in the mudroom. "Close enough. So, what has you here, as if I had to guess?"

"Actually, I might surprise you. I have two questions to ask you." I followed him into the kitchen and set the cookies on a table. "Can I help you with the tea?"

"You just sit down. Tell me what's on your mind. I'm curious. I figured you were here to talk about how Mr. Penn met his maker." He took two glasses out of the cabinet and put chipped ice from the ice maker into them. Then he took a gallon of sun tea out of the fridge and filled the glasses. He set one in front of me and then took a peanut butter cookie out of the box. "My favorite. You know I'll tell you almost anything for a homemade cookie."

"These are better than homemade. Sadie made them." I took a chocolate chip one and a sip of my tea. "I was wondering if you could tell me the process of filing a death certificate."

"Well, not the question I expected." He leaned back and looked at me. "But for you, I'll go through the boring details."

By the time he was done, I agreed that the process was boring. And I couldn't see a place where someone could change or destroy a record once it was filed. So the issue had to be at the county court office where they were stored.

"Did that answer your question?" He peered at me with faded blue eyes that held so much concern for everyone.

I pushed the box closer to him. "It did. So, one more question. How did Ben Penn die? I know it was murder, but was he shot? Stabbed? Poisoned?"

"Because I've already filed my report, I'll tell you what Darla has already gotten out of other people. The boy was shot. Not a professional job, so he lived for several painful minutes before he bled out. I think the owner of that house is going to have to replace that lovely, original wood flooring." He took a second cookie. "I would have thought that Greg would have told you this."

"I haven't seen him for a while." I didn't want to admit that we'd been fighting. Besides, Doc Ames knew Greg didn't like me involved in the murder investigations in South Cove if he could keep me out of them. "I've been working on another issue."

"The one that has you wondering about death certificates. What, has someone returned from the dead?" He grinned at his joke.

When I didn't respond, his eyes widened and the smile left his face.

"Well, we both know that's impossible, so I could look at the death certificate and see if I did the autopsy. If so, I'd know that the person was truly dead. Some of my peers, well, they aren't as upstanding as I am. Nor do they have as good a memory as mine." He tapped the top of his head. "I'm not bragging, but I have a very good recall of my guest lists."

"I bet you do." I wondered if Aunt Jackie would be any madder at me for blabbing if I told one more person. "I'd appreciate you keeping this between us. I mean, Greg knows, so he's okay, but if you could keep it close, I'd appreciate it."

"Who are you concerned about, Jill?" The concern in his voice made me feel better, even if I was betraying my aunt's trust once again.

"Theodore Ekroth." I waited for recognition to seep into his eyes. "Yep, my Uncle Ted. Did you do his autopsy?"

Chapter 12

I left Bakerstown with a promise that Doc Ames would look into my uncle's death. He hadn't done the autopsy, but he said he'd find the files, if there were any. Back when Uncle Ted died, there had been two mortuaries in Bakerstown. A rival one down the road hadn't survived long after the owner had been arrested. Doc had been hesitant to say any more, but I thought I could find the details on the internet. One more avenue of investigation that might just take me nowhere. I didn't know how Greg did this time and time again.

I hadn't told Doc why I was looking in to his death, but I'd bet he could figure it out. When I pulled into my driveway, Darla's little car followed and parked behind my Jeep. I opened the back and grabbed the grocery bags. I needed to get the ice cream I'd bought into the kitchen.

"Hey, girl, let me give you a hand with that." Darla rushed to my side, and after two trips, and letting Emma outside, we were in my kitchen.

"Sit down. Coffee, iced tea, or a soda?" I dug through the bags and got the ice cream out and put that away while I waited for Darla to decide.

"Do you have a Coke?" She sat at the table and took out her notebook. "I'd kill for one. Matt thinks I've given up soda, so I have to be careful and sneak one when he's not looking."

"Relationships die on lies." I grabbed two Cokes and set them on the table. I put the rest of the perishables away.

"I think that's considered the pot calling the kettle black." Darla opened the can and took a long drink. "Besides, I don't have these all the time, so I really appreciate it when I do."

I sat down and pointed to her notebook. "I'm sure you're not here just for your Coke fix. What's on your mind?"

"I told you I was going to come back to see what you knew about Ben's death. I was in Bakerstown this morning and saw your car at the Senior Project. They totally stonewalled me when I went in to ask questions. That guy who's the administrator is a total jerk. Did you meet with him, Earl something? I have his name in my notes. And that's about all I got. Did they tell you anything else?" She held her pen as she watched and waited.

"I wasn't there to talk about Ben." I ran my finger around the rim of the can. Telling Darla about the problems Aunt Jackie was facing changed the picture. She had a lot of contacts, but I wondered if I could really trust her not to say anything.

"I don't understand. If you weren't there to talk about Ben..." Realization filled her face. Sometimes I thought the woman was too good for her own sake. "Oh, no. Is Jackie all right? I figured there was something going on with her health after she broke it off with Harrold. She doesn't have dementia, does she? My uncle had what they called senility back then, but I really think it was Alzheimer's. Please tell me she hasn't been diagnosed."

Great, now my hesitation had Darla thinking the worst. "According to her doctor, she's fine. I talked to him last week. But someone has been calling her, and I think it's a scam. I went to the Senior Project to see what they knew about things like that."

Darla sipped her coffee. "She didn't give out her account information, right?"

"No, she says she hasn't given him any money, but I'm concerned. After I left, I did my shopping and then I went to give Doc Ames some cookies on my way home. I like to stop by when I'm in town; the guy doesn't get out and away from the funeral home much. I asked about the case and he said Ben was shot. Does that help your article?"

"I knew that the day after the murder. I really was hoping for some more specific details. I heard a rumor that the girlfriend was at the top of the suspect list." Darla set down her pen and sipped on her soda. "You and I know that they're always on the investigators' short list. At least until the evidence proves them innocent. Has Greg cleared her yet?"

"Not that I know of, but like I've said before, we really don't talk about cases. He's afraid I'm going to get my nose into something and the bad guys are going to cut it off."

"You know journalists have been killed during a juicy investigation. He's probably right. There might be people who'll want to kill you if you get too close to the truth."

I stood and grabbed a box of cookies from the sideboard. I ate one as I returned to the table. "Great, thanks for the encouragement. I guess I should just hide under my covers every time someone is killed in South Cove. Pretend like I don't care."

Darla reached out and took the box of cookies from me. I grabbed two out of the box before she moved them out of my reach. "I didn't mean that. And you need to do something about your stress eating. I don't know how you stay thin with being around all those treats all the time."

"I stress run too." I smiled at Emma, who was out on the porch looking in at us through the screen door. "Ben's murder seems off. The only thing I know about him is Paula adored him and he helped out around the Senior Project. Computer work, I believe. Is that what he did as a job? Freelance computer geek?"

"That's what people have told me. According to Paula, she paid the bills and he would give her money when he finished a contract. But most computer guys make better money than he was telling her. I got the feeling they were pretty strapped most of the time." Darla jotted down a note. "That's a good angle. I know a lot of couples keep their finances separate, especially when they aren't married, but you would think he'd be more upfront with what he really made. He could have a bank account with a hunk of change in it because he was making Paula pay all the bills."

"The bank isn't going to tell you if he had an account, much less how much he had in it." I sank back in my chair. "Seriously, Greg has his hands full with this one. If you take Paula off the suspect list, it could have been a random shooting."

"We don't get many drive-by shootings here in South Cove." Darla closed her notebook and tucked it in her tote. "Besides, who said Paula was off the list?"

I thought about what Darla had said long after she'd left. Was Paula really a suspect? She'd seemed so in love with the guy, I knew she couldn't have killed him. No way, no how. I pulled the cookie box closer, then reconsidered and picked up my phone instead. Dialing Greg's number, I expected to get voice mail, but instead, he answered.

"Hey, do you have time to eat? We have steaks, but if you don't have time to grill, I could meet you at Lille's." I held my breath. One, I hoped he'd say yes because I hadn't seen him for a while. And two, I was really hungry. I could go to Lille's on my own, but I could also make myself dinner here. Lille's just had more options and, bonus, I wouldn't have to cook or clean up.

"If we go now, I could get away." His voice seemed to calm me as it boomed through the speaker. "I needed to talk to you about Jackie anyway."

"Okay then, I'll get Emma settled and start walking." I wondered if he'd found out anything new.

"See you there." He clicked off.

Walking the few blocks up the hill and into town gave me time to form a casual question about Ben's murder. If I was too direct, Greg would shut me down, but I could put the blame on Darla; that angle he'd understand. Either way, I was getting a free meal out of the deal.

The place was almost empty because the diner rush hadn't started yet. Mondays at five didn't seem to be a popular time for the local diner. Although there were several couples in their golden years sitting and finishing their meals. Looking at them chatting and talking made me smile, until I thought about Harrold and Aunt Jackie. It wasn't fair that some creep had stolen their time together by playing with my aunt's emotions. I knew my uncle was dead. Now I just had to convince my aunt of that fact. Having Doc Ames's information would go a long way in doing that.

Greg hadn't arrived yet, but Carrie waved me over to our favorite booth. "You alone tonight, or is that man of yours joining you?"

"Greg should be here anytime. I bet he got hung up at the office. He's always trying to do one more thing." I sat down and took the menus. "How come you're still on shift? I would have thought you'd be gone by now."

"I work a split shift on Mondays. That way I can get some hours in when people are actually here." She glanced around the dining room. "Although this is usually the most people I get on the dinner shift. Everyone's home cooking for themselves at the first of the week."

I thought about Darla's comment about Paula paying the bills. "Hey, did you wait on Paula and Ben much? Do you know if they split the bill?"

"Ha. I don't think I ever saw him pick up a tab. That girl always paid. And she's a good tipper too. Always twenty percent, no matter what they ordered." Carrie peered at me. "You're not investigating again, are you?"

"Just thinking." I waved to Greg as he came into the restaurant. "Can you bring me an iced tea?"

"Sure thing." Carrie winked at me like we had a secret. I guess she knew I didn't want to continue the conversation with Greg at the table. "What can I get for you, hun?"

"Coffee and water. It's going to be a long night." He kissed me on the cheek as he sat across from me. When Carrie left, he glanced at the menu and quickly set it aside.

"You already know what you want?" I was surprised. Usually, he took a while to make his decision.

"Fried chicken dinner plate." He smiled and took my hand. "I'm really glad you called. Today has been brutal. I've been in more meetings than I usually do in a week. Everyone wants this Penn case closed and off the books."

"I didn't realize you even had a suspect." I had been considering a chef salad, but the chicken sounded much better. And I hadn't eaten another cookie. I set my menu on top of his and covered his hand with my own.

He frowned as he watched me. "I don't think you're going to like what I'm going to say, but yeah, Jill, I have a suspect. Ben was shot with a gun registered to Paula. It had her fingerprints on the grip. The only thing holding me back from jumping right now is that her hands didn't have GSR on them. But that could have been because of when we tested her."

"Paula didn't do it." I felt sick as I thought of how upset the woman had been while she talked to Sadie and Pastor Bill. "There is no way. She was heartbroken when she came into the shop."

"Facts are facts. And there's no other lead." He squeezed my hand. "Look, I know you liked the woman, but neighbors heard them arguing the night before the murder. Sometimes people kill people they love. It happens, Jill."

Carrie came back with our drinks. "Sounds like you're talking about the murder. That's all anyone here is talking about. You know, I wouldn't have known that they lived in town if it hadn't been in Darla's article. They weren't around much at all. I bet I can list off most of the townsfolk right here without batting an eyelash."

"Yeah, a lot of people have said that. In fact, one of their neighbors across the street said they didn't know who lived in the house. She left early to go to her job and he worked from home." Greg leaned back in his chair, but I could see questions forming in his eyes.

"It's just odd. I know we have our introverts, but it was like they didn't want to be part of the community. It's sad, that's all I've got to say." Carrie pulled out her order pad. "So what can I get you?"

Greg ordered first and I added, "Me too," which made both Greg and Carrie smile.

After she left the table, Greg held up his hand. "Before we get back into you trying to convince me that Paula couldn't have done it, I want to talk to you about your aunt's situation."

"Good, because I have some things to tell you too."

"Then you go first. I know you hate it when I steal your thunder." He sipped his coffee, and the challenge in his eyes made them sparkle.

"Fine, I will." I outlined what I'd done, including going to talk to Denyse at the Senior Project and my stop at Doc Ames's office. "You already know about what Deek's friend Trina said about the death certificate being misfiled. I didn't understand the process, and Doc was able to fill me in on what happens when someone dies and a death certificate is filed. I know he thought something was weird because he said he'd look in to it. Did you know there used to be two funeral homes in Bakerstown?"

"I've heard rumors. Apparently, the other home's owner was in to some shady practices and got shut down. You've seen the place. It's that plantation-looking building just off the highway. With those views, I'm surprised they haven't sold the property and torn the old place down."

Carrie dropped off our dinners. "You're not talking about Bakerstown Memorial Home, are you? That place is creepy with a capital C. Even when we were in high school, there were rumors about what the owner did with the bodies he had delivered."

"Like what?" Now I was curious, even though the aroma from the food was making my stomach growl.

"Nothing good, believe me. Kids always tried to sneak through the fence on Halloween to get pictures of the ghosts, but the cops usually had that place on their rounds, so they'd get rousted out of there." Carrie shivered and rubbed her arms. "I went in once and that was enough. I couldn't sleep for a week."

"Did you see something?" I leaned forward, watching her reaction.

"No, it was more of a feeling. And then we heard a noise coming from the basement, where the bodies were embalmed. We ran." She shook her head, like she was getting rid of a bad memory. "Anyway, definitely not dinner conversation. Enjoy your meal."

"I didn't know Bakerstown had a haunted house." I took a bite of the mashed potatoes and sighed. "Hold off until we're done eating and then you can fill me in on what you found out."

We spent the next little bit talking about nothing and enjoying our meal together. One thing I loved about Greg was, because he loved food almost as much as I did, he didn't tease me when I made that face because the meal was just that good.

By the time Carrie came back to take our plates, we were stuffed and happy. She refilled Greg's coffee. "Dessert?"

"Bring a piece of apple pie à la mode with two spoons." Greg looked over at me. "Unless you want something different?"

"No, that sounds perfect." Especially since I'd had way too many cookies today. "So tell me what you found out."

"I was at the Senior Project today too, but I was talking to the administrator, Earl Hess. He assured me that there is no way anyone could hack their system and get confidential information from their database. In fact, he was a little offended that I would ask." He sipped his coffee.

"Offended? That's an odd reaction." Now I was glad I hadn't filled out their intake paperwork.

"I thought so too. But I kind of switched gears on him and he wasn't ready for the question. He wanted to talk about Paula and how he knew she was troubled. He made it seem like she and Ben were having relationship issues. And that Ben had told him they were going to break up, but he'd still volunteer for the center."

I almost spit out the tea I'd just taken a sip of when I heard that. "Are you kidding me? Paula thought they were going to be married. That everything was fine."

"Yeah, she told me that too." He squirmed in his chair. "Look, I know you like her, but she might have been lying. What reason would the administrator have for telling me something that wasn't true?"

"I don't know. But it's weird, right?" I decided to get off the discussion of Ben and back on my aunt. I knew Greg was going to have to leave soon and it could be anytime if his phone rang. "I asked Aunt Jackie, but she hasn't worked with the Senior Project. She did have a social worker from the finance commission working with her when she lost that money to the financial planner guy. And this Denyse told me that they didn't share their information with any other agency."

"Yeah, that's what I heard too. But when I asked Earl to pull up your aunt's record, he found one. He wouldn't tell me what she'd contacted them for, but he said it was last year."

I sat back in the chair, stunned.

"I'll just drop this off with the check, then." Carrie said as she glanced back and forth from Greg to me. "You all okay on drinks?"

Greg assured her we were fine and then picked up his spoon. "Take a bite of this. It's really good."

I followed his motions and ate a few bites before setting my spoon on the table. "There are two possible reasons for my aunt's information to be in their database. One, she went down and met with them and either forgot, or she lied to me. I don't like either implication."

"And two?"

I took a sip of my tea, making sure I had my thoughts in order. "Or two, someone put my aunt's information into their system. And I know it wasn't me."

Chapter 13

By the time I got back home, my thoughts were jumbled. Paula and Ben were a perfect couple by one account. By another, Ben was leaving her and she was barely holding on to her job. As surprising as those inconsistencies were, clearing them up wasn't the first thing on my to-do list.

I checked my email, more out of habit than anything else. If someone had really needed something, they would have called. Scrolling through the mostly junk mail, I saw one from the Senior Project. The address wasn't the one Denyse had given me, but I opened it anyway.

"Good afternoon, I'm Tessa from the Senior Project and I am one of the team helping you and your loved one find help in their senior years. I noticed you didn't fill out your intake form, so I've attached an electronic copy for your convenience. No need to come back into the office to drop this off, just send it back to me when you finish. Looking forward to working with you."

Boy, they were persistent on their intake forms. I deleted the email and closed my laptop. I didn't feel like dealing with business, either work-related or personal right now.

I needed to find out how my aunt's information had gotten into their system and how much the Senior Project knew about her. It was almost seven. No one would be at the office. I'd forgotten to call Amy, and even if I called her now, she wouldn't have access to the parking permit information. It was time to do what I did best: curl up on the couch and read.

I made a quick call to my aunt to see if she was okay. Her curt response told me I'd interrupted one of her shows. We closed the shop early on Mondays, so neither of us worked. Tuesday was her second day off and I worked a little longer, and Toby would relieve me and close the shop at five.

I said my good nights and grabbed the book on my coffee table. At least I knew she was in for the evening and I'd done what I could for the day.

Tomorrow I'd do more research.

* * * *

The sun was bright and I could smell the ocean on the gentle breeze as I walked into town to open the shop. I'd already taken Emma for a short run that morning to help burn off some of the energy my dog had no matter what time of day.

Tuesday was a busy commuter day for the shop, so I didn't have time to open my laptop until after nine. But instead of getting lost in the research, I picked up my cell and called Amy as soon as I had a break between customers.

"South Cove City Hall, how may I direct your call?" Amy's voice rang professional in my ear. Apparently, she hadn't seen the number come up because I usually got a more personalized greeting.

"Hey, Amy, it's me. Do you have a second?"

"Good morning. Do you have a planning research question? I'll be glad to help you." Amy answered.

"So the mayor is standing at your desk and you don't have time to talk," I translated her code.

"That's exactly right. Give me the information and I'll do some research for you."

"I'm looking for information on parking permits for either Paula Woods or Ben Penn. Can you get me their application? Who owns their rental house?" Now, I knew I was grasping at straws, but after Greg had told me last night that he was probably going to have to charge Paula, I wanted to make sure there wasn't something, somewhere, that might at least give him another lead.

"I'll see what I can do. I should have this before lunchtime. Do you want me to mail you this information or will you contact me?" I could hear the mayor talking in the background about wrapping up the call.

"Lunch would be great. Lille's at noon?" That way, if she knew any gossip, she could give me all of it without worrying about the mayor eavesdropping.

"Perfect. I'll be expecting to hear from you. Thanks for calling South Cove City Hall and have a sun-filled day."

I almost gagged at the sugary-sweet sign-off, but Amy had already complained that the mayor was writing new scripts for everyone who answered the phones. I'd heard Esmeralda was planning a coup.

I grabbed my notebook where I'd listed off my to-dos for the day and scratched off "call Amy." Then I picked up the phone and glanced in the back room to make sure my aunt wasn't sitting at my desk as the call connected.

"South Cove Bed and Breakfast, this is Mary."

I walked away from the coffee bar and back into the book stacks, where I could still see the front door and the coffee bar. I kept my voice low, just in case. "Hey, Mary, this is Jill."

"Jill! Bill and I were just talking about you this morning. When are you going to stop by for a chat? I feel like I don't see you enough. And now that Jackie has become a recluse, I don't even get the secondhand gossip."

"Well, that's why I was calling. Can you convince her to go to the city next Saturday? I need to get her out of that apartment." I was hoping Mary wouldn't ask why. My plan fell under the theory of plausible deniability. "Maybe a trip to the city?"

"That sounds lovely, but I'm not sure she'll say yes. The last time she blew me off. Told me she had better things to do than go to a gallery opening. I'm pretty sure your aunt is sick. She loves attending openings."

"She told me this weekend that she really needs a girls' day out. I said I'd cover her shift Saturday, so you don't have to hurry back." I paused, knowing the next words would seal the deal. A white lie couldn't send you to hell, could it? "I think she feels bad about not going last time. You know how she gets when her arthritis is acting up."

"Oh, I hadn't considered that. You're right. She's probably embarrassed. I'll call her this morning. We have a light weekend and Bill can handle the guests. Besides, I really need a day out too. And don't tell her, but I miss spending time with your aunt."

I promised to keep it our secret, then hung up, hoping Mary's call would do the trick. I'd wait to make a call until after Aunt Jackie told me she was going. Operation Harrold Wins Jackie Back was looking good.

Then I opened the laptop and started researching Ben Penn. This time I found not only his Facebook page but also a Twitter page and a website. According to his website, he was a freelance computer expert, selling consulting time to set up your computer, stereo systems, and more. His most popular service seemed to be installing computer-run security systems in your house. Looking at his website, there was no way he shouldn't have been making money. So why was Paula paying all the bills? Greg and I had monthly budget meetings when we talked about the household expenses.

We had our own accounts because we were still single, but running the house was a mostly fifty-fifty deal. Because I owned the house free and clear, he set aside money he would have been paying for half that payment and put it in a joint travel fund.

But I knew Greg and I weren't like normal couples. Or maybe we were the normal ones, and people like Ben just liked to prey on the weak. Either way, it was interesting that Paula took on all the costs. I wondered if Greg had even looked at Ben's income and business accounts. It all followed the money, and from what I'd heard, Paula wasn't getting money from her live-in boyfriend, he was getting money from her. And she was still happy. That didn't sound like motive to me.

Toby came into the shop thirty minutes early for his shift. We'd tried having him work weekends, but now that he was getting more hours from his primary job being a detective with Greg, he worked early in the week as a barista, which left his weekends clear. From what I saw, the guy worked all the time. He was saving for his own place, and as much as I liked the extra income from renting him the shed behind my house, I would like to have that area back. Greg was making noises about turning it into a workout gym. I thought maybe it could have some ceiling-to-wall bookshelves so I could unpack the boxes I had upstairs in what we called the junk room. My home-office shelves were bulging, and I didn't want to just cull the collection before I knew what I had.

"Hey, Boss. I let your dog out before I left. She started barking when I went out to start my truck, so we played a few rounds of catch before I let her back inside." He went to the coffee bar and poured himself a cup. "I'm beat this morning. Greg had me on watch last night out at the crime scene."

"Why is he having you watch an empty house?" I knew Paula had been staying with Sadie. Which was another reason she couldn't be the killer. There was no way I'd feel okay with her staying there if she was. Sometimes my gut was more accurate about people than I could explain. Of course, Sadie was the one taking chances, not me. Maybe Paula should be staying at the local motel. I realized Toby had answered my question and I'd been lost in thought and had missed it. "I'm sorry, what did you say?"

"I knew you weren't listening. You get this look in your eyes when you're thinking about something else." He sipped his coffee. "What I said was, Greg wants to make sure there isn't any vandalism out at the house. You know, it's close to where the great gnome caper occurred."

"I thought he solved that case?" A group of local teenagers had thought it funny to steal gnomes from one of our local's yards. Then, one day, they all appeared in front of storefronts in South Cove. A lot of them were set up to appear to be drinking coffee out in front of my shop. "And I thought the ring leader was off to college this fall on the East Coast."

"Kids are always around." Toby shrugged; he appeared to not be saying something. "Look, Jill, you know how Greg gets when I tell you things about the case. He'll have my hide if he finds out."

"So there's more going on than just watching for kids. What did you find in the house?" If I didn't ask, he wouldn't tell me. He might not anyway, but it was worth the exercise. "Was Ben involved in something illegal?"

"Jill, stop browbeating Toby. You know he can't tell you anything but that the investigation is ongoing." Greg put his arm around me and kissed me. "I missed seeing you this morning. I was out early."

"I haven't seen much of you at all." I leaned into him as he put an arm around me. "And I wasn't browbeating Toby. We were just talking about why he was so tired this morning. So why are you watching an empty house?"

Greg squeezed me and laughed. "Sometimes you're like a dog with a bone. Because you were the one so adamant about Paula's innocence, I'll give you a little info. I've been looking into Ben's businesses. He had a lot of deposits in his account that seemed high for computer work or stereo installation. There wasn't anything on his personal laptop except for one or two jobs a month that couldn't account for those deposits. There's nothing on the laptop, so there needs to be somewhere else he was keeping his records. Neighbors reported someone going into the house the last two nights. Sadie gave Paula an alibi for both nights."

"So Ben had a partner in whatever he was doing?"

Greg nodded. "Paula confirms that he worked with someone he called Cash. I'm trying to find this guy so we can interview him, but so far, no luck."

"When I looked at his website, it appeared to be a small business. Maybe he had someone else who worked for him doing the actual installations." I tried to remember the language on the site. "He used 'we' a lot in the descriptors, but that might just be to make it look like a bigger company that a one-man shop. Sometimes people shy away from startups. How much were these deposits?"

"Now you're pushing it. That's all I've got for you, but I want to make sure you understand, if Paula didn't kill Ben, someone else did. And that someone else is still out there. So you need to stay out of this investigation. Okay?" Greg held my gaze until I nodded.

"Figuring out who has been messing with my aunt is taking up my time anyway." I stepped toward the coffee bar. "I'm just glad you're not arresting Paula. Do you want something to drink?"

"Large coffee would be great. And this doesn't mean Paula's off the hook. I'm just trying to tie up some loose ends here. Hopefully, one of them leads us to Ben's killer." He sat down next to Toby. "I saw your report. Nothing else to add?"

"No lights, no cars. Nothing." He sipped his coffee, then yawned. "I'll take a nap as soon as my shift's over if you want me to go back tonight."

"I think we should." Greg glanced over at me. "Jill's convinced that this time, the girlfriend didn't do it. And I'm beginning to agree with her."

"No problem, Boss." Toby stood and refilled his cup. "So, what's happening on the Jackie front? Have the calls stopped yet?"

I shook my head as I took Greg his coffee, then sat at the table next to him. "No, she got another one this weekend. After she went to a meet where he didn't show. It's like he's trying to keep her off-balance."

"A good con artist does that exact thing. I replaced her phone, so he shouldn't be able to reach her, but we have a tracker on the shop phone. So if she gets a call, she needs to call it in. Immediately." Greg stared at me.

"You tell her. She takes directions from me about as well as she takes my business suggestions."

"I'll remind her." Toby glanced at the clock and went to the coffee bar, where he put on his apron. "She likes me."

"Everyone likes you," Greg grumbled. He turned to me. "So what are your plans today? Do I need to be worried?"

"I'm meeting Amy for lunch. Then home to Emma. I think I'll do laundry today. Are you coming home for dinner?" It was better I didn't mention the fact that Amy was bringing copies of Paula and Ben's parking applications. The exercise probably wouldn't turn up anything anyway.

"Maybe. I have a meeting in Bakerstown this afternoon to tell the district attorney I don't feel I have enough to charge Paula. Which he's going to fight, because he wanted to get this closed and off the books before election next month."

"But you can't charge her if she didn't do it." I knew the district attorney liked closing cases, especially murder investigations in small tourist towns. Having killers wandering the streets was bad for business, and bad for donations to political campaigns.

He stood and paused at the table. "That's what I'm working toward. Do me a favor and be careful today. I don't want to be worrying about you with all this on the table."

"Believe me, I'm pretty well out of ideas on who could be conning Aunt Jackie. And besides my talk with Darla, I've stayed out of trying to get information on the murder."

Greg shook his head. "And visiting both the Senior Project and Doc Ames. And if I checked your history on the laptop, I bet I could list a few more stops."

"The visit to both of those spots was to help Aunt Jackie. I can't help it if Doc Ames likes to chat." I thought about my laptop and let Greg's comment go at that. He would find Ben's name in my searches.

We said our goodbyes, and with Toby already set up, I headed out to Diamond Lille's to meet up with Amy. She'd already arrived, so I weaved through the tables and plopped down in the other side of the booth. Amy was eating fried green tomatoes and had a chocolate shake sitting in front of her. A vanilla one sat at my side of the booth. "I take it you've had a bad day."

Amy looked up and wiped the grease from her mouth before speaking. "Good! You're here. I was worried about your shake."

"I can see that." I glanced at the menu. I should get a salad since this was my second visit to Diamond Lille's this week. But the French dip was calling my name. I compromised and got the sandwich with a side salad when a new waitress came and got our order.

"And for you? Are you good?" The girl's name tag said "Trixie," but I knew Trixie had left a few months ago. This woman was probably just using that tag until Lille got a new one made up. Lille liked to conserve both energy and money by reusing as much as possible.

"No way. I haven't even ordered my lunch." Amy rolled her eyes in my direction, then ordered Lille's special Ham-oneer, a double cheeseburger with a slice of fried ham on the top. It was pretty amazing. After the waitress left, she handed some folded papers to me. "That's a copy of both parking permits and the occupancy permit Paula filed a few years ago. Apparently, she moved from Bakerstown and he moved in just about a year ago."

I glanced over the information. Everything was pretty basic and information I already knew until they got to references. Paula had completed hers with friends and relatives. When she filled out the form for Ben, she'd put herself and a few people I'd met at the Senior Project. "The handwriting is the same, so Paula must have completed these."

"I agree. And from what I saw on Ben's application, the guy didn't have any friends or relatives in the state to put down on the page." Amy finished off the last tomato in two bites, then set the plate to the side of the table.

"Or Paula didn't know any of them." I considered this lack of information another clue. A clue I'd told Greg I wasn't going looking for, so how did I get him to ask the same question and get the same nonresponse? "It's curious, that's all."

"I could list many of Justin's friends and coworkers. A few of the phone numbers are in my contact list. So why, if they were living together, didn't Paula have this information?"

The not-Trixie dropped off our lunches and set down a variety of ketchups and sauces. "I'll be right back to refill your water glasses. But is there anything else I can get you?"

I glanced at the steaming au jus on my plate. "I'm good. What about you, Amy?"

"This is fine." Amy dismissed the girl without a look. "Are you going to give those papers to Greg?"

"I don't know." I didn't want to admit I'd just told him I wasn't investigating the murder. There had to be another way to get him the information. "It's complicated."

"Then I'll uncomplicate it. I made a second copy. I'll drop them off with Esmeralda this afternoon. It will give me a chance to get away from Marvin. That guy is driving me crazy."

As Amy went into all the current sins of her boss, my phone rang. Glancing at the display, I saw it was Sadie. "Hold that thought." I pointed to my phone. "Sadie's calling."

"Tell her I said hi." Amy dug into her burger as I answered the phone. "Hey, Sadie, what's happening?"

"Oh, Jill. I'm so glad I reached you. I don't know what to do. It's a complete mess." Sadie sounded like she was on the verge of tears.

"Calm down, Sadie. What's a mess?" I watched as Amy devoured three French fries at the same time.

"The house; someone broke into my house."

Chapter 14

I'd gotten my lunch to go and hurried over to Sadie's house after instructing her to stay outside and call 911 immediately. I'd been shocked to hear that she'd called me first, but then again, I knew my friend. She probably hadn't wanted to make a big deal out of the break-in if it wasn't a real problem. Sadie saw the best in everyone. Which was her greatest strength and one of her weaknesses.

Sometimes people weren't looking out for the best of humankind. Only what seemed to be the best for themselves. Greg called me jaded. I called Sadie naïve. We were both probably a little right and a little wrong.

I found her sitting outside her house on the front step, talking with Greg's other deputy, Tim. Tim had beat me there and had a South Cove police cruiser parked in Sadie's driveway, right behind the purple PT Cruiser she used for deliveries for her business, Pies on the Fly. When she saw me, she stood on shaky legs and waited for me to come closer so she could hug me.

"Oh, Jill. I feel so violated. How could someone do this to my lovely little house? Why?" She sobbed into my shoulder as I looked at Tim.

"Tell me what happened." I got Sadie back to a sitting position and handed her a pack of tissues I had in my tote for just such emergencies.

"I was out doing my deliveries for most of the morning. I finished baking around six and went inside to take a little nap. Then, about nine, I left to do my deliveries. I dropped Paula off at the church. She's been helping out Pastor Bill with some clerical work until she can go back to her own job." Sadie repeated the words like she'd studied them from rehearsing a play. "I got home just after twelve. I walked right in. Oh, Jill, what if he'd still been here?"

"He?" I glanced at Tim, who shrugged.

"Typically, it's a guy. And he'd have to be pretty strong to bust in the back door like that." He looked down at Sadie and put a hand on her shoulder. "I'll run up to Bakerstown Hardware and get you a new door and lock. I'll call in some buddies of mine and get it installed right after work."

"Oh, Tim, that would be so amazing. I'm not sure I'd feel safe in my own house if I couldn't lock the door." Sadie smiled up at the younger man with tear-filled eyes. "You are such a good man."

"Now you don't worry about anything. The crime lab should be here in a few minutes. Do you want to go somewhere with Jill until we have this place back to normal?" Tim was talking to Sadie but looking at me.

I nodded at his unspoken question. "Yes, let's go hang out at the shop for a while. I can get you some food from Diamond Lille's and we'll have lunch."

"That would be lovely. Maybe it would take my mind off what happened." Sadie stood, blowing her nose gently. She peered at my takeout bag. "It looks like you already have a lunch. I didn't disturb you when you were eating, did I?"

Before I could answer, she shook her head. "Of course, I did interrupt something. You were already at lunch, weren't you?"

"No worries. I was eating with Amy when you called. She had to get back to City Hall anyway." I glanced over at Sadie. She looked like she hadn't eaten yet. That I could fix. I couldn't do a lot of things, like run down a suspect, but I could feed my friend. "Tim doesn't need you here, so let's go hang at the shop. If he has a question, he can reach us there."

Sadie picked up her purse and started walking toward me. "Do you think I should call Nick at school? I don't want to worry him, and he has midterms coming up, so I'd rather not."

"You can tell him the next time he calls. Besides, by then, you'll have more information and you'll be stronger. He could probably hear your fear if you called now." I took Sadie's arm and lead her down the street toward Main. I would call Tim or Greg later to see when they thought Sadie could come back. And there was the issue of Paula. It was a bad time for a break-in. Of course, maybe there's no good time for a break-in. I felt Sadie pause, so I quickened my step toward the shop. "We really miss Nick at the shop. I know it's just part-time work until he gets out of school and a real job, but he's part of the CBM family now. And besides, he's very perceptive for his age."

"I raised a good boy." Sadie smiled, but the action looked strange on her pasty-white face. "I can't believe Tim is taking care of my door after work. He attends service with his fiancée at the church. Her name's Winn.

She's in my woman's bible study group. Very personable. She's getting a business degree over at the college."

I knew Sadie was chattering due to her nerves, but I was happy to learn more about Tim and his girlfriend. He'd been working for Greg for a while now and not once had I seen the guy out socially. And in a small town, that's saying a lot. Greg said he had a second job in security at Bakerstown College, so maybe that's where he'd met this Winn. I added in things like, "You don't say" and "You got that right." By the time we'd reached the shop, I could hear Sadie's nervousness leave her tone.

After sitting down at one of the tables, she took my arm. "Sorry I'm such a chatterbox today. I didn't even let you get a word in edgewise. I guess I'm more shook up than I wanted to admit."

"No problem. What can I get for you? My treat."

Sadie rattled off a drink and cookie order and took out her phone. "I need to talk to Pastor Bill and have him make arrangements for Paula. With all that's going on with her, she doesn't need my misfortune to deal with. I'll bring her back to my house tomorrow, after things are back to normal."

I walked over to the coffee bar, where Toby had already made Sadie's drink and poured me a cup of coffee. He paused at the dessert bar. "Tim called me and told me you were coming over. Can I call in a food order for Sadie?"

"Please. I don't think getting her on a sugar high is the best bet." I set my lunch into the small fridge under the coffee bar. "I'll figure out what she wants, and if you could run, I'll watch the shop."

"No problem." He handed me a plate with four cookies. "A few to keep you occupied. Tim says it's weird. According to what Sadie told him, there doesn't seem to be anything missing."

"Do you think maybe you were watching the wrong house last night?" Paula had to be the reason Sadie's house had been broken in to. Or something the thief thought Paula had at Sadie's. Unless the culprit was just looking for her double chocolate brownies, Sadie lived a pretty low-key lifestyle. I called it being a minimalist. She said she just didn't need a lot.

"Believe me, the thought had crossed my mind." He lowered his voice. "Do you know where Paula is right now? I think Greg is going to want to talk to her."

"The church. According to Sadie, she's working with Pastor Bill. But I think they're going to put her somewhere else tonight." I was glad Sadie wasn't bringing her back. And if I could talk her out of the woman coming back at all, I was going to try. But with most of life, some things were out of my control.

Toby followed me with the drinks as I took the cookies back to the table. "Sadie, give Toby your lunch order and he'll call it in and run to get it."

"Just get me the soup and sandwich special. Tuna on white, please." She patted Toby's arm. "Thank you so much for handling this. I could go myself..."

"But Jill won't let me." I smiled, finishing the sentence for her.

Sadie laughed. "You are a pretty intense person. I'd never want to get on your bad side."

"I have to take care of my friend, right? Besides, who will make these amazing cookies if you're not around?" I decided to see what she knew about the murder. "So, how's Paula?"

Toby shook his head as he walked away to call in the order. I thought I heard him mutter something like "Leave it to Jill." Or maybe it was "Leave it alone, Jill." But I ignored both directions and focused on Sadie.

"She's still shook up. Of course, the fact that her work friends are being just awful doesn't help. Can you believe they are telling people that Ben wanted to break up with her? According to Paula, they were making wedding plans. Sometimes people just want to gossip, you know." Sadie sipped her drink, and I saw some color come back into her face. "Anyway, she's starting to put her life together. The good thing was, they hadn't combined much of their financial lives. Which was for the best. Until marriage, you shouldn't deal with someone else's money problems. I guess Ben had a lot of debt Paula was worried about."

"That is a good thing." I just wanted to keep Sadie talking. Maybe something she said would bring to light a new lead away from the idea that Paula had killed her boyfriend. It was sad to say, but the fact that Sadie's house was hit might just give Greg the ammunition to convince the district attorney not to charge Paula.

At least that was the hope.

* * * *

Tim called at about five and said the lock had been replaced and Sadie could return to her home. Since Aunt Jackie had just come down and joined our group, Toby offered to walk Sadie home.

"Thank you for being such a good friend." Sadie hugged me. "I know you're concerned that having Paula with me isn't safe, but really, it's the right thing to do."

"Tomorrow. Not tonight, right?" I met her gaze. "If it's an issue of money, I'll pay the hotel bill for the rest of the week if it keeps people from breaking in to your house."

"Now, Jill, we don't know that's why the break-in occurred." Sadie laughed and looked at Toby for support. When he shook his head, she sighed. "Okay, so it's a strong possibility. And I'll leave her where she is tonight. I could use some sleep."

"Someone will be driving by a few times tonight just to make sure everything's okay. But if you even hear a squeak, you better call 911." Toby waited for Sadie to nod before turning to me. "Greg said to tell you that he would be home for dinner, but this development changes his plans."

"Now, you tell Greg he doesn't have to be ruining his evening just to check on me," Sadie protested.

I held up a hand. "Sadie, have you ever met my boyfriend? Me telling him something is like talking to a brick wall. Besides, I'd be worried if he didn't check on you. So don't ruin my sleep, okay?"

"You are as tenacious as you are beautiful." Sadie hugged me again. Then she put a hand on my aunt's shoulder. "You take care of yourself and this stubborn niece of yours. I'll see you tomorrow morning for your next delivery."

I watched them walk out of the shop, then turned to my aunt. "It's been a crazy couple of weeks around here."

"You could say that." Aunt Jackie sipped her coffee. "That woman is as sweet as the desserts she makes for us. Whoever broke into her house has to be as mean as a snake. Bad things shouldn't happen to people that good."

I was surprised at my aunt's words. She never had anything good to say about most people. She could find something to nitpick on with Mother Teresa. But I had to agree with her on Sadie. That girl was gold.

The door opened, and Pastor Bill came running in, looking wildly around the shop. "Where is she? Did she go to the hospital? Was she hurt?"

"If you're looking for Sadie, you just missed her. Toby walked her home." I watched his face as he processed the news.

"She didn't tell me about the break-in when she called to get Paula settled in a hotel. I thought she just needed some time alone. You know how hard she works at that bakery of hers. I found out from one of my parishioners, who called to see if Sadie was all right. I must have sounded like a fool." He ran his hands down his Dockers. "I ran all the way over here from the church when she said the police had told her that Sadie was at the coffee shop. I'm not sure I even said goodbye."

I tried to keep the smile off my face. I'd known my friend had been in love with Pastor Bill for over a year now. I just hadn't known his feelings before today. And maybe he hadn't either. "She's fine. A little shook up, but fine. I bet she would love to visit with you over dinner. Maybe you could take her to that beach club that opened a few weeks ago."

"That's a terrific idea." Pastor Bill turned toward the door, then paused and turned back. "Thank you so much for your assistance."

After he'd left, I looked at my aunt and we both started laughing.

"Well, if he doesn't follow up on his feelings for Sadie after this, he's a fool." My aunt poured the last drops of coffee into her cup. "Looks like we need a refill."

"I'll get it." I went back to the coffee bar and refilled the carafe. "It's been a busy day here. You want me to hang around for a while?"

"No, you go home and make that man of yours dinner. Sounds like he'll need the energy tonight." My aunt's hand covered what I knew was the heart necklace. Since I'd noticed her wearing it, she hadn't taken it off. She waved me away when I set down the carafe. "I'll just sit here a while more until we get a customer. By the way, Mary called, and we're going to the city on Saturday. I know you said you could cover, but if it's a problem, I can come back early."

"It's not a problem at all." I cleared the table of the extra coffee cups and plates. "Can I get you anything else before I leave?"

"I've got a book under the counter. Bring it to me and get out of here. I like quiet when I read."

I took the tray to the counter and put the dishes in the dishwasher. Then I grabbed my tote and her book. It was a historical romance, with one too many dukes on the cover. Regency England should have sunk into the sea from the sheer weight of the dukes authors had been writing into their books. I paused at the table. "Here you go. I really like this author's work."

"Just something that was lying around." My aunt's cheeks pinked. "Now go home."

"Yes, ma'am." I stepped out of the shop into the still-bright sunshine and smiled all the way home.

My phone rang as I was walking home. The caller ID showed the Senior Project. Maybe they had good news for me. "Hello?"

"Good, I caught you." A man spoke quickly into my ear. "This is Jill Gardner, right?"

"You're speaking to her. And you are?" Clearly not Denyse with my good news.

"I'm Earl Hess. I'm the executive director of the Senior Project. I was reviewing last week's intakes and found your file missing the intake form. I'm sure we must have sent you one by email. Have you returned it yet?"

"Actually, I've been a little busy." Which really meant, *I'm not filling out that form, now or ever.*

"It's important we follow protocol on all intakes. Please complete this tonight and I'll expect it in my email tomorrow when I come into the office."

I was about ready to tell him what he could do with the form and his email when I realized I was talking to dead air. He had told me what I was going to do and that was that. Too bad he didn't know me as well as Sadie did. She could have told him this was not the correct way to get me to do something. Of course, anyone who had spent over a day with me could have told him that his tactics wouldn't work. I tucked my phone back into my tote. "Screw protocol."

An elderly couple walking by me on the sidewalk sped up their steps, but as they passed, the woman gave me a thumbs-up. Apparently, I'd hit a button with her.

At least I was doing something right.

Chapter 15

Greg was already at the house peeling potatoes for French fries when I got home. Emma slapped her tail on the floor in welcome but stayed glued to her spot, where she could watch Greg. I put my tote on the sideboard and went to kiss him. "Now that's what I like to see, a man preparing the evening meal."

"With my trusty sidekick. I don't think Emma's left my side since I got home except for the few minutes she went outside to do her business." Greg leaned down and kissed me. "I decided I was going to take time for dinner. So I thought we could grill burgers to go with the fries. With all that's going on, I might be called out at any time."

"And you have to check on Sadie." I went to the fridge to grab a soda. Greg already had one sitting on the counter.

"I figured Toby would have alerted you." He set the final finished potato into a bowl with salt water and cleaned the peels out of the sink before joining me at the table. "I know the break-in must have something to do with the murder. When I talked to Paula this afternoon, she admitted to having a tablet that belonged to Ben. I guess he stored all their pictures on the thing. I've got it in the truck now, so after dinner, I'll be using the office to see if he had anything else stored there too."

I noticed he said "the office," not "my office." We were merging into a couple more and more every day. When Greg first moved in, he was hesitant to claim his own space. Now, less than a year into the arrangement, I was pretty sure my office was becoming his. Which was fine, since I rarely used it. I'd thought it would be a great idea, but most of the work I did at home was done at the kitchen table. The office was more of a well-decorated closet in which to store work stuff than an actual workplace.

"Sadie was shook up by the whole thing. I don't think she was this upset when she was being framed for murder a few years back." I settled back into the chair and took in my kitchen. I'd had someone try to break in to my house before, but with Emma on the job, they didn't get far. "Maybe she needs a dog."

"Maybe. Having someone say something about you that you know isn't true is one thing. Having someone in your house without your permission feels more personal. More of a violation." He glanced at his watch. "I think we have a few minutes before we need to get dinner started. Do you want to update me on your aunt? Anything new come up?"

"Actually, yes." I picked up the phone and dialed Harrold's number while Greg watched in confusion. "Operation Harrold is a go."

When the call was answered, his voice boomed over the speaker. "Well, if it isn't my second-favorite bookseller. What's going on, Jill?"

"I've gotten Aunt Jackie to agree to a city trip with Mary on Saturday. I'll call you from the shop as soon as they leave, but I think your project is a go." I smiled at Greg. "Let me know if you need anything."

"I'll handle things from here. But Jill, thank you. I don't know if this will melt her frozen heart, but I feel like I need to give this to her. And if the engagement is still off at the end of this, I just want you to know I was looking forward to calling you part of my family."

I said my goodbyes and set down the phone. Grabbing tissues, I wiped at my eyes. "That man is so sweet. My aunt is a fool."

"Sometimes it runs in the family." Greg patted my hand. "So what's Operation Harrold?"

I told Greg about Harrold's plan for the patio area and how he wanted it to be a surprise for my aunt. "Maybe, now that she knows this isn't Uncle Ted and Harrold makes the grand gesture, she'll break down and let him back into her life."

"And maybe not. Your aunt can be stubborn." Greg held up his hands. "But we don't have time to talk about that; let's get dinner started."

I stood, but he pulled me back down to the table. "What?"

"I wanted to ask you again if you'd found out anything about your aunt and this caller." Greg studied my face.

"No. Between hanging out with Sadie, working, and ignoring all the Senior Project emails and calls, I've been a little busy. But since you took her phone, he can't get a hold of her."

"And we didn't know she had already set up a meet for last weekend until you tracked her down. Sometimes your aunt doesn't show all her cards." He kissed my hand. "She's a lot like you in many ways. Why, are you having problems with the Senior Project?"

Now I did stand and get the burgers out of the fridge. Greg grabbed the seasonings and plugged in the deep fryer. We had this cooking thing down to a well-oiled machine. "I told the woman I met with that I didn't feel comfortable filling out the intake form because we were talking about breeches in security and information being used inappropriately. She seemed to understand, but everyone else there is making a big deal about protocol. I've had an email and a phone call from the administrator. I'm sure I'll get another one tomorrow when I don't follow his instructions."

"Well, if anyone can fight City Hall, it's you." He seasoned the burgers, then paused before going outside to start the grill. "Speaking of City Hall, I got a special delivery from your friend Amy this afternoon."

Crap. I tried to keep my voice steady as I took out a potato to slice it. "Oh, really? What did she have to say?"

"You're such a bad liar, and your friend isn't as sneaky as she thinks she is. Why were you looking at the parking and rental information for Paula and Ben?" Greg paused at the door. "Hold that thought and I'll come back and help you with the fries."

Well, our plan to sneak the information to Greg hadn't worked. Besides, it didn't tell anyone anything, except that Ben was a complete freeloader. And that didn't bode well for Paula's defense.

When Greg came back, I moved over so he could share the chopping block. "I'm not sure what I was looking for. Maybe some people who knew him better. He seems to have just appeared out of nowhere when he moved in with Paula."

"She says he picked her up in a country bar in Bakerstown. He went home with her that night and never left." Greg cut the potato into slices, then fries, and picked up a second potato before I was even done with the first one. "From where I stand, the woman is naïve. We're running his fingerprints and DNA now. I'm betting that Ben Penn isn't the name his mama gave him."

"If she finds out he lied to her—" I paused as Greg took the last potato out of the water and took my knife away from me. "She's going to be heartbroken."

"I'm thinking she's probably lucky to be alive. If she'd been home when the murder happened, she might have been killed too." Greg put the fries on a paper towel, then rinsed off the knives and cutting board. "Give me those burgers and you can start the fries."

I thought about Ben and what he could have been hiding from as I put the first batch of potatoes into the fryer. I got out a plate and covered it with paper towels, got my salt container out of the cabinet, and set the table. When Greg came back inside with the empty plate the burgers had been on, I leaned against the counter and watched him.

"Did you convince the district attorney not to press charges against Paula?"

Greg grabbed his soda. "I think so. He wasn't happy, but I explained that until we really know who this guy is, we can't know why he was killed. Can we stop talking about this for a while? I'd like to just eat dinner with my girlfriend and maybe play some catch with Emma."

"Can I ask one more question?"

He paused at the door. "Why not?"

"Why Paula? Was she just easy to fool?" I jiggled the fry basket, but they weren't done.

Greg shook his head. "That is one question I won't know the answer to until I know who Ben Penn was and what he was in to. The fact that Sadie's place was broken in to makes me think that whoever he was hiding from must have found him."

As I finished the fries and got the condiments out for the table, I thought about what Esmeralda had said. The scam that had been run on Jackie was a common one in her circle of thieves. Maybe when Ben moved in with Paula, that had been a con as well. Lonely women being preyed on for money. Well, Jackie wasn't lonely, but she had been vulnerable, especially when the guy pretended to be Uncle Ted. Paula, she'd been looking for love. And instead of finding a nice guy to spend her life with, she got taken.

There seemed to be more connecting lines to the two situations than I'd expected. But I'd told Greg I'd stop talking about the murder. And I couldn't bring up Jackie's connection without talking about the murder. Tomorrow would be soon enough to bring up the coincidences.

Right after dinner, Greg grabbed the leash. "Emma and I are going to run up to Sadie's to check in with her. Do you need anything?"

"No, I'm going to clean up the kitchen and then read for a while. See you when you get back."

I'd just gotten the kitchen cleaned when the phone rang. I checked the caller ID before answering, not wanting to talk to the head of the Senior Project again. "Hey, Sadie, Greg's on his way. Are you okay?"

"I'm fine. He just left. But I wanted to talk to you, and he had Emma in the truck, so I'm thinking he's on his way back, and we don't have much time." Even Sadie's cadence had sped up due to her urgency.

I sank into a chair. "What's up?"

"Paula called me in tears from the hotel. She says she thinks Greg is going to arrest her. Is that true?"

I knew Paula wasn't stupid. She had to have seen the signs. "Greg is still investigating. There's no need for her to get upset." Or hire an attorney yet.

"Jill, you know you can't lie to me. You have to convince Greg that Paula didn't do it. I know he doesn't like you investigating, but you're good at it. You always find the right person. You and Greg are like that couple in the movies who solved mysteries together."

"And I know when I'm being snowed. Seriously, Sadie. If I knew that Greg was going to charge Paula, I'd tell you." I hoped when we found Ben's real name, we'd also find his killer, because, right now, no matter how much I told Sadie she was wrong, Paula was the best bet.

I heard the sigh over the phone line. "I'm just so worried about her."

"I know." I heard a doorbell ring at Sadie's. "Are you expecting company?"

"No. I'm locked up tight. Let me just go get rid of them."

"Don't open the door. Look out your window and see who's there." I glanced out the doorway to my driveway, but Greg still wasn't back. And Sadie hadn't answered me. "Who is it?"

Sadie laughed, but I could hear the relief in her voice. "Pastor Bill."

"Is he alone? Can you see all around him?" I might be paranoid, but the preacher was as naïve as Sadie. Which probably made them a great couple.

"Yes, Jill, he's alone. Can I answer the door now?"

I paused, trying to be smart about this. After I'd gone through the mental exercise of ruling out our local Methodist preacher as a crazed killer, I responded. "Open the door, let him in, then lock the door after him. And tell me that you did."

"Yes, Mother." Sadie giggled. I heard the door open and then Sadie invited the pastor inside. Then I heard the locks click again and Sadie was back on the line. "We're back to DEFCON three. Doors locked. Only Pastor Bill entered the house when I opened the door. Unless our killer is invisible."

"Sue me for being careful." I went and sat on the couch, pulling over the comforter and moving my book closer. "Call me if you need something."

"Thanks Jill. I know you'll do your best."

I set the phone on the coffee table and tried to lose myself in the book. I kept hearing noises and thinking it was Greg. Finally, I gave up on the book and turned on the television. I had channel surfed most of the way around to the beginning without finding anything to watch when the front door opened and Emma bounded into the living room.

Greg came over and took the remote out of my hand. He keyed in a channel, then tossed the remote back onto the table. "Good, you were getting the TV set up for my game."

"Actually, I was trying to find a movie."

Greg pointed to the book. "I thought you wanted to read tonight."

Which translated into *I really want to watch this game.* I decided to take another tactic. "You took a while to get home. Sadie called, and Pastor Bill is at her house."

"Yeah, I know. I talked to him before he reached Sadie's. He's staying the night." Greg headed to the kitchen. "Do you need something to drink? I'm putting some popcorn into the microwave."

"We just ate dinner." I loved food, but even I couldn't eat anything else. Well, maybe some high-end chocolate. Or ice cream. There was always room for ice cream. I was pretty sure there wasn't any in the house because I hadn't put it on the grocery list when I ran out. But that wasn't the point. I wasn't hungry. "Wait, did you say Pastor Bill was staying the night at Sadie's?"

"Yes, and don't be spreading that around. He's already worried that someone will think the worst." Greg grinned as he brought his soda out to the couch and sat next to me. "He told me he was worried for her safety."

"I'm worried for their reputations." I curled up my legs beneath me. "Does this mean they have to get married?"

"Don't you start. The guy is a wreck. He's obviously in love with Sadie. I wouldn't doubt he will tell her about the way he feels tonight." Greg turned up the volume on the television.

"That would be nice. Sadie needs something good in her life. She's been all about raising Nick, and then about her business. I don't think she's even had a date, well, except for that train wreck with Dustin Austin after her husband died." I grabbed my book and scooted closer to Greg. "I'm glad you don't have to work tonight."

"I didn't say that. I do have to work. But now I don't have to run by Sadie's in a few hours. The pastor saved me a sleepless night. I just want to watch some of the game. Then I'm going to dig in to Ben's notebook. Let's hope I find something. I'm not sure how long I can hold off the dogs from pushing for Paula's arrest."

"But…"

He put a finger over my lips. "I feel the same way, but the evidence isn't supporting our feelings. Arguing with me isn't changing the facts."

He was right about that. The problem was, Sadie was counting on me to find the real killer. And, of course, Paula was innocent. But as I'd learned early in life, sometimes being innocent didn't keep you out of jail. I focused on the book and got lost in the story.

Greg moved me over about an hour later, and I used the interruption to go grab another soda and let Emma outside. When I got back to the living room, he was already in the office, working.

I set down the book, grabbed my notebook, and wrote down everything I knew about Ben. He'd shown up about a year ago and moved in with Paula almost immediately. The guy must have been charming at the beginning because she fell hard. He had a website advertising his computer and electronic skills, yet Paula paid all the bills. I wondered if Greg had looked at Paula's account to see if he'd been giving her money to help, but I could bet the answer was no. He had a lot of free time, so he hung around the Senior Project, where Paula worked, and helped with their computer systems. And people at the Senior Project had told Greg that he and Paula were having relationship issues. Yet from what she'd told me, she was still in love. So maybe the issues were one-sided. Maybe he'd taken on a new lover in all the spare time he seemed to have. And when he wouldn't leave Paula, she killed him. I tapped my pen on the notepad. Plausible. I wrote down a few questions, including where had he met the new woman? And why wouldn't he leave Paula?

I saw the light go out in the office, so I tucked my notebook back into my tote and picked up the book. Greg came out and kissed me on the forehead.

"I'm heading to bed. I'm beat."

I lightly grabbed his arm. "Did you find anything?"

"On the notebook? Yeah, but I'm not sure what I'm looking at. I'm going to have Tim and Toby take a look tomorrow."

I put on a bright smile. "Or I could look at it tonight? You know I like puzzles."

He tapped my nose. "Good try, Sherlock, but I've locked the tablet in the desk and hidden the key. Leave this one alone, okay?"

"I wasn't going to sneak in there to look." Although, technically, it wasn't sneaking if it was in my own house.

"Come to bed and leave it alone." Greg pulled me up out of the couch. "We need to get some sleep so I can have a fresh outlook on this in the morning. For Paula's sake."

I followed him upstairs, turning off lights as we went. He had known what to say to get me to agree. Saving Paula was mission number two. Mission number one was making sure no one was trying to hurt my aunt.

I felt like I was failing on both fronts.

Chapter 16

Typically, when the bell over the door at the shop rings, it makes me smile. I'm either going to sell a cup of coffee and share my love for the brew, or I get to sell a book and give the new owner a trip to another world. Wednesday morning, when the bell rang, I looked up and silently groaned.

Mayor Baylor and another man were coming into my shop. If he'd wanted coffee and treats for his meeting, he would have sent Amy. I was pretty sure the guy didn't read. So there was only one reason he was here: to talk to me.

Fake it till you make it. I turned on a hundred-dollar smile, "Good morning, gentlemen, what can I get for you this morning?"

The mayor's eyes darted over to the other man, who nodded. "Two large coffees to go, Jill. That would be great."

Okay, so I'd been wrong; there had been a coffee-related reason they'd come into the shop. "No problem."

As I poured the coffee, the men sat at the counter. Mayor Baylor handed me a twenty and I counted out his change, then gave them the coffees. I turned to refill my own cup. "Thanks a lot for your business. I'll be over on the couch reading if you need any refills."

He held up a hand. "Actually, Jill, there is one thing I wanted to ask you."

Uh-oh, here it comes. I took my cup back in front of them, keeping the coffee bar between us. "Sure. How can I help you?"

"Fred, Jill's our business-to-business council manager. She handles all the meetings for the business community here in South Cove. She's done an excellent job in the last five years of growing the group." Mayor Baylor nodded to the other man. "Jill, this is my campaign manager, Fred Mucke."

"Nice to meet you, Mr. Mucke." I held out a hand. I could be civilized too.

"Fred, please. I always think about my dad's pig farm in Illinois when I'm called Mr. Mucke." He sipped his coffee. "This is amazing. I can't believe I haven't been here before now. I'm always visiting South Cove to talk to Marvin for one reason or another."

"Thanks. We have it roasted especially for us. Well, and I provide the coffee for Diamond Lille's too. So if you're a coffee drinker here in South Cove, you're probably drinking my blend." I was chattering, but until I found out what they wanted to talk to me about, keeping my mind going was probably a good idea.

"Marvin tells me you're involved with our local police detective, Greg King?" Fred studied me, and now I thought I knew what this was about. They were feeling out the water, even though Greg had probably assured Marvin a million times that he wasn't interested in running for mayor.

I put on the smile again. "Yes. In fact, we're living together. I suppose a lot of couples do; it just makes more sense, with how high the prices for houses are this close to the coast. Rent or buy, it doesn't matter; you're going to be paying an arm or a leg, right? One of the reasons I'm renting out the building behind me. People need affordable housing. I'm lucky I inherited my house." Still chattering, but I wanted to watch the two men as they formulated what they wanted to ask me.

"Well, that's interesting." Fred glanced at Marvin, but when the mayor nodded, he turned his attention back to me. "We were wondering if you knew whether Greg was planning on setting up a political career. Many people in public service lean that way for their careers. It would be helpful if we knew who our opposition was for the early elections."

"I bet it would." I sipped my coffee.

When I didn't continue, Fred narrowed his eyes. "You know, this isn't a game. If he's filed papers, we will be notified. You might as well tell us now."

I set down my cup. "Why?"

Fred shook his head, obviously confused by my one-word response. "Why what?"

"Why do you think for the price of two cups of coffee I'd tell you anything about what Greg plans for his future career? Just because I'm his girlfriend? Honestly, you need to talk to Greg and see what he says. I'm not the boss of him, unlike other relationships I know." I aimed that statement directly to the mayor.

"We have asked Greg. He keeps saying he's not running." Marvin didn't wait for Fred to take the lead now.

"Then you have your answer. Look, I'd love to sit and chat, but I've got a book calling my name. Let me know if you need more coffee." With that, I took my cup and walked over to the couch.

Pretending to read, I kept them in my line of sight until they headed to the door a few minutes later, leaving their half-drunk coffee.

"Have a nice day," I called out as the bell over the door rang. Sometimes people confused me. Greg had told the mayor time and time again that he wasn't interested in the job, but for some reason, the guy didn't believe him. So they came to me.

Frustrated, I kicked off my flats and curled up my feet underneath me. This time, when I focused on the book, I didn't pretend to read.

Deek found me in the same position a few hours later. He glanced around the empty shop and then grabbed some coffee before joining me in the book area. "Busy day, huh?"

"No tour bus stops scheduled for the rest of the month. Everyone must be in New England watching the leaves fall." I stretched and set the book next to me. "How are classes going?"

"About the same. I hate to say this, but I think I'm getting bored with the student life." He grinned at the look of shock I must have been wearing. "Don't get all worried; I don't want to give up this plush job, but I may need some more hours starting in January when next semester comes. I've decided I'm going to write a book."

"Really? What about?" Now I was interested. As a reader, I loved authors, but I didn't want to be one. It seemed like a lot of work.

"High fantasy, but I think at the young adult level. We'll see. My mom is actually all in and says I can stay in the basement if I keep my job and show her forward progress on the novel." He grinned. "I may never have to move out."

"Everyone has to become an adult at some time in their lives." I studied the young man sitting across from me. He was our newest hire and had replaced Sasha when she went off to the city for a full-time internship for her last year of college. With Nick graduating soon, I would have had to hire another part-timer to cover his spot as soon as he got a real job in his field. This announcement worked in my favor. And Deek was amazing with the book clubs.

"Stop trying to wreck my dreams." He started to stand, then returned to his relaxed position. "And I have a message from my mom. She says there are several groups active in the same con you told me about. She's not sure if there is one in the area, but she confirmed with some friend of hers in the south that the people are out there. Does that help any?"

I nodded. I'd already determined that Jackie was being duped. And if there was a local group, Deek's mom would have known about it. I knew she was legit now in her business, but I had a good source that had told me that she'd grown up in the grifter life, like Esmeralda. "It does. I knew my uncle hadn't returned from the dead. So there was only one other explanation."

"I don't think you mean Spirit Cell Wireless." He sighed as he ran a hand over his blond dreadlocks. "Growing up with a mother who talks to the dead for a living wasn't the easiest thing. But I know she's not trying to steal from anyone. She really has a gift."

"I'm not a believer, but I know both your mom and Esmeralda give something to people they need. Hope, maybe. Or closure. Either way, it's not a bad thing." I slipped my shoes back on. I needed some time to think about Jackie's situation. Maybe it was all over and I just needed to get her a new cell phone. It irked me that someone could just get away with this and move on to their next victim, though. "I'm heading home. I've got a dog to take to the beach to run."

Deek followed me to the coffee bar, where I grabbed my tote. "Mom did say one more thing, but it's a little woo-woo."

"I'm always open to information, even if it's coming from a weird spot." I tucked a couple of books I'd set aside to take home into my tote. Maybe I'd hit Diamond Lille's for lunch again. That thing with the mayor had made me crave some comfort food.

Deek slipped on his apron and leaned on the counter to watch me. "She said things are more connected than you know."

"Like what?" My mind flashed to the discussion with the mayor and his bulldog, Fred. She couldn't mean that.

"She didn't say. In fact, she didn't seem to remember saying that. I asked her the same question and she waved me away like she does. It's a little creepy to watch."

I nodded. I'd seen Esmeralda do the same thing when she had an announcement from the other side. Even without believing in their talent, watching her have one of her visions was unsettling. "Thanks. I'll keep it in mind."

I passed by Diamond Lille's, thinking that maybe eating wasn't the best way to get rid of this dull ache I'd had in my head since that morning. I'd run, then I'd make myself a grilled cheese sandwich. Or a grilled tuna and cheese sandwich. Both sounded great right now.

Focused on the food I was about to devour, I strolled the rest of the way to my house. Once I'd changed, Emma and I went running. I was still thinking about the grilled tuna and cheese when I got home and saw Toby's truck in the driveway. He must have just gotten home from his night shift. I assumed the guy would be passed out in his apartment, but instead, he was sitting on my front porch, looking at his phone.

"Hey, Toby. I was just about to make lunch. You want some?" He looked drained.

He gave Emma a hug before standing. "I could use some grub. Thanks."

He followed me into the house and we got settled into the kitchen. "I'm thinking that you don't want coffee. You want a soda or tea, or maybe just water?"

"A soda will be fine. I wanted to let you know that no one came to the house last night, again. Greg wants me to stay out there one more night, but I don't think anyone's coming. Especially because they hit Sadie's house." He yawned as he opened the soda.

I quickly got out the cheese and butter and then set a box of cookies on the table. "You want a tuna and cheese melt or just grilled cheese?"

"Grilled cheese will be fine. I appreciate this. I ate some doughnuts at the station this morning, but I didn't stop for lunch before I came home." He took a couple of cookies. "Oh, and that tablet? It had a list of people and a whole bunch of stuff about them in a spreadsheet. Thousands of people. Where they lived, phone numbers, relatives' names. The weird thing is, the sheet was divided into 'active,' 'possible,' 'closed,' and 'pending.' And guess whose name was on the possible list?"

Still holding a butter knife, I turned around to see his face when he told me what I thought I already knew.

"I see you've guessed." He rubbed his face, like he could wipe away the tiredness that appeared to have wiped him out. "Your aunt's name was there, along with a ton of information about her. I think Ben was the con artist who was posing as your uncle."

I went back to working on the sandwiches. When I got one in the pan, I nodded. "That makes sense. The guy knew a lot about computers. He volunteered at the Senior Project."

"Greg suspects that's where he got the information. According to the people who work there, Ben had free rein with their servers and even set up their intake process." Toby studied me. "You don't look surprised."

"I'm not. I didn't know Ben was the guy behind the phone calls, but it makes sense why no one showed up or canceled the face-to-face meeting with Jackie last weekend. Ben was already dead by then." I finished Toby's sandwich and grabbed a plate and a single-serve bag of chips. I set the food in front of him, then joined him at the table. "You don't know how glad I am that this is all over. I've been so worried about Jackie."

"We still don't know who killed Ben, but there seems like there are at least a few motives. Hopefully, you and your aunt have an alibi for time of death?"

"You have to be kidding. We're not suspects, are we?"

Toby shrugged. "Probably not, but I'm sure Greg's going to have us interview every one of the people on that list. I think we're going to find a lot of people besides Paula who have some sort of motive to kill Ben. And most of those reasons will have a dollar sign in front of them. The guy kept a record of how much money he scammed, including the dates. It looks like this has been his main source of income for a while."

"More than a year?"

Toby polished off the sandwich and opened the bag of chips. "A lot more than a year. Why?"

"Because he just moved here and got tight with Paula. Which got him into their server. Where did he get the information about his marks before that?"

Toby pulled out his phone and keyed something.

"What are you doing?"

He stood and took his plate to the sink. "I just texted Greg your question. I don't think you'll see him home tonight. Way too many records to get through and people to call. Thanks for lunch."

I watched as he went out the back door and through the yard into the shed that was his apartment. The guy was beat. I was glad Greg got a good night's sleep last night because until this case was solved, he'd be up until all hours of the night. I made my own sandwich and, when it was done, opened the book I'd been reading earlier and got lost in the story. It might be seen as escaping, but right now, I didn't want to think about Ben or what he'd planned on stealing from my aunt.

A few hours later, my phone rang. "Hey, Greg, how's the case going?"

"Kind of blowing up over here. The good news is, we probably know why Ben was killed. The bad news is, not only is Paula still a suspect, so are a ton of people he scammed money from. One of the state guys is tracking his off-shore accounts. I think once we total it all up, we're going to find that Ben had quite a nest egg going. And a sugar mama in Paula to pay all the bills because he was claiming to be broke."

"Which is why Paula's still not off the list." I set my book next to me on the couch. "That girl can't catch a break."

"But you and your aunt are off the list. According to the time of death from Doc Ames, Jackie was manning the shop and you were with me.

I thought you'd like to know that so you didn't go running off to hide from the law."

Laughing, I stood and went to let Emma outside. "I don't hide from the law if I don't have a reason. Although a week in Mexico might be just what I need right now."

"Don't you dare take off while I'm in the middle of an investigation. I need a break too." He paused, and I could imagine him putting up his feet on his desk. "Look, the reason I called was to tell you I won't be home until late. Go ahead and eat. I'll order in something from Diamond Lille's."

"Toby said as much. By the way, he looks like crap. If you need me to cut his barista hours, just let me know. The guy looks like the walking dead."

Greg chuckled. "He swears he's fine. But I'll talk to him again tonight. I think he likes the extra money. He's been talking about buying a condo between here and Bakerstown."

"I thought he was holding out for a house with a backyard?" I heard voices in the background.

"Look, I've got to go. Don't wait up for me."

And with that, the phone went dead. I loved Greg's dedication to his work most of the time, but sometimes, I wished he had a normal, boring, nine-to-five job like an investment banker. Or a schoolteacher. Or maybe a mayor. Laughing at the thought of Mayor Baylor's reaction to that career change, I grabbed my book and went outside to sit on the swing. Emma came up and laid her head on my lap. It wasn't quite dinnertime yet. And I had a couple of chapters till the end of the book. Once that was done, I'd make a bowl of soup and see what movie I hadn't watched yet. Greg could only take so many romantic comedies before he insisted on a movie with more guns than people.

Chapter 17

The next morning, I was in the middle of my commuter rush when my cell rang. I ignored it and finished up the coffee order I was working on. I had three people in line with books in hand as well as a dire need for caffeine. Besides, it was too early to chat with anyone. I heard the beep about a phone message and then the shop's landline started ringing. I handed off the coffee and rang up the order before I picked up the phone. "That will be eight dollars and ten cents; charge? Coffee, Books, and More, this is Jill."

"Thank God I caught you." The man sounded like he needed a vat of coffee, not just a carryout order.

"What can I help you with?" I finished the transaction, then put a hand over the speaker as I asked the woman next in line for her order. As I started making the low-fat latte with a squirt of pumpkin spice, I focused on the phone call.

"I need you to fill out that intake form I sent you."

Frowning, I hit the button for the coffee to drip into the espresso cup. "Wait, is this the guy from the Senior Project?"

"Yes, Earl Hess. I need you to fill out that form as soon as possible."

I put the milk in the metal pitcher to whip and rolled my eyes. "Look, I've got a line of customers who need their coffee. Your form is going to have to wait."

The lady I was helping pulled out her wallet as I hung up the phone. "I hate pushy people. Sometimes they forget that what they're doing isn't an emergency unless they are performing brain surgery. My insurance agent always makes his annual policy checkup calls seem like they are life or death."

Laughing, I held up the whipped cream dispenser. The woman nodded, and I topped the drink off with a generous dab and a sprinkle of cinnamon. "I know. This isn't the first call I've gotten from this guy, but seriously, it's not even seven in the morning. Forms can wait until the coffee rush is over." And the rush was over right at seven thirty. I supposed most of my customers had at least a thirty-minute drive to their jobs, so once it got close to eight, they vanished. Unless it was Friday. Then the rush lasted through nine. This was one of the reasons I loved owning my own shop. I didn't have to check in at some arbitrary time. The needs of the customer dictated why I opened at six. I wanted my morning coffee, and I assumed they did too.

I sat down with a fresh cup of coffee and a slice of apple caramel cheesecake. I didn't know how Sadie made up these things, but I wasn't complaining. My breakfast was like eating a caramel apple at the fair. Or would be if the treat had died and come back as a cheesecake. I opened my laptop and scanned my emails. I had three new emails from the Senior Project. Two from the executive director and one from Denyse. I opened hers first.

Reading the message, I found that she hadn't found a connection between the Senior Project and my aunt. But she had found the date when my aunt's information had been added to their database: January 8 of this year. She asked to check again to make sure my aunt hadn't come in for an assessment but had forgotten to mention it.

As I looked at the timeline I'd pieced together of Ben's life, I thought I knew why her information was in their record. And it wasn't because she had received an assessment at the first of the year. For some reason, he'd merged information from another database into the Senior Project's files.

Why? That was the question. But Denyse had told me all she knew about the records, so it was time to let Earl Hess down. I wrote a short email explaining that I wasn't going to fill out the form because I'd decided not to go ahead with their counseling program. I thanked him and his staff for their time and wished them well. Hoping that would end the frantic contacts from the executive director, I focused my attention on the book order for the week.

I was so caught up in the process that I didn't realize Deek was already here until he refilled my empty coffee cup. He handed me a folded sheet of paper. "Can you order these as well? They're for my collection, so just one or maybe two copies. I hand-sell a lot of books I buy for myself."

"That's the joy of working for a bookstore. You know you're always free to grab an advance reading copy off the table in the back. You don't have to buy the books you're recommending." I glanced at the list and realized these were older, writing craft books.

"These are a little older than the books that are on the table." He winked at me. "I can't be a famous, wealthy author without studying at the feet of the masters, now can I?"

"Sure. By the way, can you work a longer shift tomorrow? Jackie's taking the day off to spend with Mary. Toby's swamped with this investigation, so it's just you and me. I hope I'm not messing up any of your plans." I didn't look at him while I was typing. If he said no, I'd just come back and work. I didn't have a personal life right now anyway. Not with Greg on a case.

"I told Trina I'd study with her, but if you don't mind her coming over here, Saturday nights are usually a little slow." He sat and sipped his coffee. "You know, we could have an open mic night on Saturdays so people can try out their work in front of other people."

"Jackie would never go for it." I shook my head. "Besides, I never got the draw. I don't want to be read a story, I want to read it. Alone, or sitting next to someone who's too busy with their own story to care that I'm lost."

"I don't want to comment on ages here, but it's really popular with the college set. And it would draw in more people. I'd be glad to work the later shift on Saturdays. It would make a long day, especially on book club days, but it's another way of marketing to a new demographic. Bookstores have to be thriving in this market. The coffee shop addition is smart, but we could change a few things."

"I'll put you on the agenda for the next staff meeting. You convince Jackie and I'll back you. But don't expect me to participate."

"Cool. I'm stoked at the idea and I promise, the rest of you will be too." He stood and headed back to the counter. "I'm taking over the helm. You want something else besides that coffee?"

I didn't really want to mention I'd already had cheesecake, a brownie, and a cookie. I was feeling like I needed some real food. "No, thank you. I'm going to finish up the book order, then head to Lille's for some grub."

"Okay. Thanks for the support, Boss."

As I finished up the last few items on the order, I watched Deek as he settled into his daily tasks. The guy was brilliant. He enjoyed working as a barista and he sold the heck out of books during his shifts. He had our profits up nearly 10 percent since I'd hired him. The book order done, I sent an email to our bookseller representative. I groaned when I saw another email from Earl Hess. The guy didn't give up. I took a breath. Maybe I was overthinking this. Maybe it was a routine note thanking me for looking at the agency and asking me to keep them in mind for possible future services. I opened the email and saw I'd been overly optimistic. The guy was practically screaming, using all caps to try to force me to complete the form. Did this kind of treatment work on anyone? I deleted the email before I could respond in an excessively nonpolite manner using words my mother wouldn't let me say.

I couldn't help it; deleting the email felt invigorating and exciting. Like I'd just turned off a bad television show or an over-the-top commercial for something I didn't need now and never would need.

This was a cause for celebration. It had been a sign that I was supposed to go to Lille's for lunch. I tucked everything in my tote. Then I waited for Deek to come out of the back room. When he finally appeared with two cheesecakes in hand, I waved. "I'm off. Call me if you need anything."

"Will do, Boss." He set down the cheesecakes and gave me a salute. "Enjoy your lunch and the rest of your day."

Walking outside, I saw Josh Thomas measuring the distance between the curb and the front of his building. I really didn't want to know what he was doing, so I sat at one of the café tables outside the shop and took a moment to call my aunt.

The phone rang and rang until I got the recording that the person with that number had not set up a voice mail yet. Aunt Jackie still had the burner phone. I called again. This time, when she didn't answer, I went around the building and headed up the stairs. Her car was in its spot. By the time I got to the door, my heart was racing. And not from the exercise. I knocked. "Aunt Jackie? Are you in there? Are you okay?"

No response. So I leaned my ear to the door. I could hear her television going. I knocked again. "Aunt Jackie?"

This time when I leaned my ear against the door I thought I heard something. I leaned in harder and almost fell on her when she opened the door.

"My lands, what on earth are you doing?" My aunt stared at me like I was a creature in the zoo. "Are you trying to give me a heart attack?"

I followed her into the apartment and closed the door behind me. "You didn't answer the phone."

"I was watching my soap and didn't recognize the number. So I figured whoever called would leave a message." She sat back on her recliner and paused the television, which was playing a commercial.

"You don't have your voice mail set up." I plopped onto the couch. "Where's your phone and I'll take care of that?"

"It's right there, under that magazine." My aunt sipped her coffee. "I don't like having a new phone. When will I get the old one back?"

"When the investigation is over." And if I had anything to do with it, maybe never. "Wait, why didn't you recognize my phone number? I've called you most every day for the last five years."

"On my phone, you show up as Jill. Not some string of numbers." She set down her cup. "Why are you here exactly? Do you need me to come in early? Did something happen to Deek?"

"No, Deek's downstairs working." I punched in numbers to have a generic voice mail account set up. "What passcode do you want?"

"One-two-three-four."

"You can't have that passcode. It's the first one they'll try if they're trying to get in to your voice mail." I stared at her. "Don't tell me you always use that code."

"Who exactly would want to get in to my voice mail besides you?" Aunt Jackie shook her head. "Okay, use one-zero-zero-seven."

"Will you remember it? It's not your birthday, so that's good." I keyed in the number twice, and when I finished doing that, I set up my name in her contacts list. Maybe next time she'd answer, but at least she wouldn't have the excuse.

"Of course I'll remember it." Her cheeks pinked. "I'm not forgetful."

I thought about the code. It wasn't Uncle Ted's birthday and it wasn't their anniversary, because that was in May. "Whose birthday is it?"

She unpaused the show and set the remote down on the coffee table.

I picked it up and set it on pause again. "Aunt Jackie?"

"Fine. It's Harrold's birthday, if you must know, Miss Nosy." She picked up the remote and tucked it next to her. "Why are you here again?"

"I was worried about you. I haven't heard from you in a few days." I leaned back, thinking about the significance of her using Harrold's birthday as her code. "You haven't heard from anyone claiming to be Uncle Ted again, have you?"

"I have a new number. Even if it was your uncle, he wouldn't know how to find me. I didn't tell him where I lived or worked." When I didn't respond, she sighed. "No, Jill, no one has contacted me in the last few days. And yes, I know the man who did isn't your uncle. There was something just off about his voice."

Maybe, or maybe not. Time to change the subject. "I talked to Deek and you're all clear for your day in the city with Mary."

"Good. She's looking forward to checking out a new art gallery." She looked at her watch. "If there's nothing else, I have a few things to do before I have to go to work."

I'd been dismissed. But at least she was all right. "Call me before you leave tomorrow. And when you get back. I'd like to know you're home."

"Yes, Mother." My aunt picked up the remote. "Anything else?"

"I hope you have a relaxing day." I moved toward the door. "Sorry for bursting in on you and interrupting your schedule. I was just worried."

As I closed the door, I heard her response. "I know."

No woman needs a man to complete her, but my aunt had been better with Harrold around. She'd been happier. They'd made plans to visit local sites and travel in the future. Now, she sat in her apartment with the hope of visiting the city with her friend once in a while. I really hoped Harrold's plan to win my aunt back would work because I knew she needed him. Probably more than she knew.

Diamond Lille's was swamped by the time I got there. Carrie waved me over to a table near the window. "Sorry, doll. I know you like your booth, but we've been slammed for a couple of hours. Maybe when it thins out, I can move you."

"I like this table." I glanced around the dining room. "I can see everyone who's here."

Carrie laughed. "You're always the optimist. What can I get you to drink? Vanilla milkshake?"

"Not today. Just some iced tea. And I think I'll have the stuffed meatloaf." I needed some comfort food after this morning. I realized I hadn't told my aunt about Ben's computer file on her. Maybe it was for the best. I could tell her after she got back from her day out.

"Mashed potatoes, brown gravy, and a salad with blue cheese on the side?" Carrie watched me.

"Perfect." I pulled out a book. Paranormal time travel with a sweet romance, as well as an epic battle scene. The author had pulled out all the stops. "Thanks, Carrie."

"That's what they pay me for, doll." Carrie patted my shoulder like she could sense my crappy mood and left me alone with my book.

Voices and noise from the crowded café surrounded me, but as I got deeper into the book, they faded away. Until I heard the name Earl Hess. I glanced up and saw Denyse Lindt sitting at a nearby table with the Senior Project receptionist. Keeping my eyes on the book, I tried to separate out their conversation.

"All I'm saying is that he's acting really weird. Haven't you noticed it?"

That must have been the receptionist. Denyse's voice was a few octaves lower.

"You don't know our esteemed leader very well. He's been strange since the board hired him two years ago. I swear, I've never met someone more stuck in the protocol of an agency. One of the reasons I liked working for the project was the rules were a lot less stringent. When I worked for the Department of Aging, we had to..."

"Here's your lunch." A plate hovered over my book.

I slipped my bookmark back into the book and moved it to the side. "Sorry. I was lost."

"Not anything new for you." Carrie set down the plate and then put a vanilla milkshake on the table. "Now, I know you told me no shake, but Tiny had already made this up when he saw you walk in. I'm not charging you for it, but he'll be hurt if you don't drink at least some of it."

No wonder I was always fighting off extra weight. My friends were all food pushers. Well, except for Amy. "Thanks, Carrie, it looks yummy."

By the time Carrie left my table, Denyse and the other woman were leaving. Apparently, they didn't like their boss any more than I did. But it was interesting that he'd only joined the group a couple of years ago. Interesting, but it probably didn't mean anything. I opened my book and held it with my left hand as I started eating. And then I got lost in the story once again.

Chapter 18

My phone rang as I was walking home from lunch. Glancing at the display, I saw it was from the funeral home. "Hey, Doc. What's going on?"

"Nothing much. In fact, it's kind of dead here." He paused, then, when I didn't laugh, explained the joke. "You know, because I work at the funeral home?"

"Oh, I got the joke. What's up?"

"I guess if you're not going to laugh at my humor, I'll just get to the point. Your uncle is absolutely dead."

Well, that was the answer I'd been looking for, but for just a second, I'd hoped that the story might just be different. "I assumed that would be your answer."

"Let me tell you how I know. I didn't do the autopsy or the burial, the other funeral home did; however, the doctor who pronounced him dead in the hospital is a good friend of mine. So I called him. He remembered your uncle very well. He said to send his good wishes to your aunt. It seems they played cards together back in the day."

The flash of memory made me smile. Aunt Jackie had her bridge group come every Friday night, even through my high school years. I'd be leaving the house to get to a football game or just hang out with my friends and her group would be coming in with bowls and plates filled with snacks. I always put away some of the better items for a snack when I got home.

"Jill? Are you still there?" Doc Ames's concerned voice pulled me out of the memory.

"I'm walking home. I must have hit a dead spot. Thank you so much for looking into this. I'm not sure that losing Uncle Ted a second time

will hurt more or less than dealing with the fact that someone was trying
to trick her."

"Your aunt is a strong woman. She can take the truth." I heard a bell
go off in the distance. "That's my tea. I've moved my microwave into my
office so I can warm up my drinks when I let them go cold without walking
all the way upstairs to the apartment."

"Have a good day, and thank you."

I put my phone back into my tote and tried to decide when I should tell
Aunt Jackie. If I waited to tell my aunt this part of the story until after she
got back from the city, she might be worried about it all the time she was
supposed to be relaxing. Or I could just call her tonight, so she could get
over being mad at the guy calling her before Saturday and actually have fun.

I decided to call her as soon as I got home.

Toby was getting into his truck when I walked up to the house.

"What's going on?" I paused at the doorway, my keys in my hand.

"Greg just called me in early. The good news is, the city has to feed
me because I'll be working more than eight hours. I love a free meal." He
waved as he pulled the truck out of the drive.

I greeted Emma when I opened the door. "Uncle Toby was just here
and said hello."

Emma woofed up at me. I grabbed the mail off the floor. I had a slot
in my door for a mailbox. Sometimes I loved it, but sometimes, I worried
Emma would change her pillow-chewing habit and eat my electric bill.
So far, it hadn't happened.

I put the mail on the table and let her out, then got myself a glass of
iced tea before sitting down to sort the mail. Most days it was a mixture
of bills, junk mail, and, since Greg moved in, a sports magazine.

Today was more of the same, except for a letter from the Senior Project
marked "urgent." I opened the envelope and wasn't surprised when an
intake form fell out along with the letter. Scanning it, I could see it was a
form letter for new clients prior to their appointment. Today, there was a
scratched line at the bottom.

MISS GARDNER, IT IS IMPORTANT FOR OUR FEDERAL GRANTS FOR US TO KEEP
TRACK OF THE TYPE OF PEOPLE WE ARE SERVING. PLEASE COMPLETE THE ENCLOSED
INTAKE FORM AND RETURN AS SOON AS POSSIBLE. EARL HESS.

That made sense. Grant reporting was an important part of any
nonprofit's accountability process, but with what had just happened to
my aunt, I wasn't going to fill this out now, later, or even if hell froze
over. I stood to throw it and the junk mail in the trash, then glanced at the

envelope again. My name, my address. But I hadn't given Denyse either. How had Earl Hess gotten it?

I set aside the letter and put the bills away in my office to pay another day. The magazine, I left on the table. It could wait there until Greg got home. I suspected he took them to work with him after he'd read them because he never had a stack sitting anywhere in the house. I knew Greg was probably going to be late again, but tonight, I'd stay up to wait for him.

The letter had me that spooked.

* * * *

Greg shook me awake. "Why didn't you go to bed?"

I rubbed my eyes and picked up the book that had fallen to the floor when I fell asleep. "I wanted to show you something."

"You could have shown me in the morning." He pulled me to my feet. "Can you stand while I let Emma out?"

"I'm awake. And I'll go with you to the kitchen. The thing I want to show you is in there." I hid a yawn behind the back of my hand as I followed.

After letting Emma outside, he held up the magazine. "This?"

"Yes, I wanted to make sure you got your sports scores." I reached past him and grabbed the letter. "This. I got this in the mail today. Not at the shop, but here, at the house."

He took the letter and read it. Frowning, he set it down and let Emma back in. "So you're refusing to fill out their form? It's probably a smart idea. I mean, especially with what we found out today. Ben may be dead, but we don't know if he was the only one with the leaked information."

"Yes, I'm refusing to give my info. But that's not the issue." I held up the envelope. "Look how it's addressed."

He took the envelope, read it again, then set it down. "Look, Jill, I'm beat. If there's something wrong with that address, I'm not seeing it. Maybe we should talk in the morning."

"There is nothing wrong with the address." I poked at the envelope with my finger. "And that's the problem."

"But if there's nothing wrong, why is that..." His face showed comprehension as he picked up the envelope again. "How did they get your home address?"

"I don't know. I gave Denyse my cell and my email address to send me information, but not my home address. Not with what was going on with Aunt Jackie." I shivered, even though it wasn't cold. "Tell me there's a logical explanation for this."

He pulled me into a hug. "There may be. Where's your laptop?"

"On the counter over there." I pointed to the shelving unit I used as my kitchen office storage. It saved me steps from walking to the office two rooms over.

He booted up the computer and went to a search screen. I watched as he typed in "Jill Gardner, South Cove, CA."

The hits that came up all were around the shop or mentions in Darla's articles for the local paper. I had a minilisting on the city council page as business liaison, but that listed my work email. Nothing had my home address on it.

"Well, isn't that interesting."

"If you think creepy is interesting. Did you really expect to find my home address on Google?" I rubbed my face.

"Actually, you'd be surprised at how often it works. But if it's not there, I think I'm going to go talk to Mr. Hess in the morning to find out where he got your address." He walked over to the counter and grabbed a sealable plastic bag. He used a napkin to put the letter and envelope into the bag.

"Isn't that overkill?" I nodded to the letter, now sealed in a bag on my kitchen table.

Greg locked the back door and turned off the kitchen light. "Not when you add in Ben's murder and your aunt's problem. I think we might have just gotten lucky. Let's go to bed. I've got an interview to schedule in the morning."

As we walked upstairs, I paused. "Is Toby still watching the empty house?"

"Yes, and Pastor Bill is still at Sadie's. He says he's there for the duration and is crafting a brief announcement to add to his sermon on Sunday. You should have seen Sadie's face turn beet red when he said that."

"You stopped by to see them? Is she all right?"

"Your friend is fine. They had a night of movies and popcorn last night, and tonight they were going to pull out the board games. She said having him over reminds her of the sleepovers she used to have as a teenager." Greg opened the bedroom door for me. "That time, the pastor blushed."

"You are so bad." I headed to the bathroom to get ready for bed, and by the time I got out, Greg was already asleep on his side. Emma was lying next to him, watching me. "Yes, you have to get down and sleep in your own bed. There's no room for all three of us."

When I snapped my fingers, she got down and I climbed in. I was asleep before I could think more about Sadie and Pastor Bill.

* * * *

The next morning, Greg and the letter were gone when I got up. By the time this case was over, he'd need a week to get caught up on sleep. I didn't have time for my normal run with Emma, so she pouted as I got ready for work. "You're just going to have to be mad at me," I told her as I was leaving. I couldn't even ask Toby to take her because he was burning the candle at both ends like Greg. Making a mental promise to Emma to run after work, I made my way into town.

Fall in South Cove is lovely. The stores all decorate in autumn colors, even though we didn't get the fall leaves like places north. And instead of frost, we got fog. The town seemed like a shot out of a Sherlock Holmes story as I moved my way through the empty streets. Diamond Lille's was open, her parking lot full. The bright lights shone out through the fog, and I could see people sitting at the tables nearest the window.

Which reminded me, I hadn't told Greg about Denyse's comment about Hess not being at the Senior Project for very long. I didn't think the fact she thought he was obsessed with rules was important, but as I texted the information, I added that as well.

I'd finished the text just as I reached the store. Looking up as I tucked the phone into my purse, I frowned. The lights were on in the store. I paused at the café tables and retrieved my phone.

"Do you need me to work?" Aunt Jackie asked, her voice still heavy with sleep.

"No. I need to ask you a question. Did you leave the lights on last night or did you already come down and open the store?" I knew the first answer would be no, but there was a chance.

"No and no." Now I could hear my aunt was wide awake. "I'll go down and check…"

"Do not leave your apartment. In fact, go check your doors and make sure they're locked and put chairs under them. I'm calling Greg."

"Okay. I'm going right now."

"I'm not hanging up until you check the rest of the apartment." I glanced upward and saw my aunt's bedroom light go on.

"I checked the closet and the bathroom. No boogeymen. Now I'm going into the kitchen and living room. Door on outside locked, and now a chair is blocking the door." She paused as she walked over to the other door. "Okay, the other door is locked. Where are you?"

"Outside the front door of the shop. I'm hanging up now and calling Greg. I'll call back in a minute." I dialed Greg's number and he picked up on the first ring.

"Hey, beautiful. I'm going to sneak out for some coffee later." He paused, and I jumped in.

"Did you see the lights on at the shop when you came in?"

"No, but the station is closer than the shop. I don't usually drive that way." Any humor that had been in his voice faded. "Why?"

"Because lights are on now and Aunt Jackie says she didn't leave them that way when she closed." I dug for my keys. "Just stay on the line with me. I'm opening the door now. She probably just forgot. She's had a lot of things on her mind."

"Jill, you stay right where you are. I'll be there in a couple of minutes."

I took a step toward the door. "Don't worry about it. I'm probably just sensitive after getting that letter."

"I told you to stay put. I'm almost there."

I turned around and saw Greg a few buildings down, crossing the street. The good thing about living in a small town was that no one was ever very far away. Typically, the only thing that made people late for meetings was leaving later than they needed to. Or doing one more thing at home. I waved and hung up my phone.

Between you and me, I was glad Greg had decided to come walk me through the shop. I expected to find I was right about my aunt being forgetful was the cause of the ruckus, but it didn't hurt to have the local police detective right there, just in case. I held out my keys and he took them and unlocked the door.

"Stay out here and keep your phone handy. If anyone runs out, call nine-one-one. If you hear something weird, stay out here and call nine-one-one. If you see anything but me waving you in, stay out here and call nine-one-one. Got it?"

"Hmmm, let me think. What was that number again?"

"Fine, I insulted you, but just stay out here, okay?" He gazed into my eyes and I nodded.

"I'll have my finger on the trigger." I watched as he unlocked the door and handed me back the keys. "Be careful," I whispered.

Greg nodded, and with a hand on his gun holster, opened the door and went inside. I watched as he went through the dining room, into the stacks, and then reappeared. He went into the back room, and it was a few minutes before I saw him come back and wave me inside. When I came in, I met him at the coffee bar, where he was pouring coffee into a to-go cup. We had one pot on a timer so I'd have coffee as soon as I opened.

"All clear. I went upstairs and cleared your aunt's hallway as well." He sipped his coffee as he walked over and studied the light switch. He picked up the phone and dialed. "Tim, can you come directly to Jill's coffee shop and take some prints for me?"

As Greg gave Tim directions to dust not only the light switch but the front and back door handles on the shop, I grabbed some paper to tape above the handles to keep customers from touching them. I kicked a doorstop into the front door so people could just walk in.

"Good idea." Greg nodded to the open door. "He'll be here in about fifteen, and once he's out of here, you can clean up the dust and get on with your day."

"Do you think she just forgot?" I glanced upward, like I could see the apartment through the floorboards.

Greg shrugged. "You both have been through a lot the last few weeks. Still, I'd rather not assume its stress. Just in case."

My phone rang and I jumped. "Crap, I forgot to call her back." I accepted the call. "Hey, Greg's here and everything is all right."

"Well, not everything. Have Greg come upstairs a minute."

I moved toward the back, then walked back to the door, kicking out the doorstop and locking it. "We'll be right up."

"You have a store to open."

"Don't argue with me. They can wait a few minutes for their coffee." I hung up and nodded to the back door. "Something's wrong upstairs."

He hurried past me and was at Jackie's door before I cleared the stairs. Jackie and Greg were watching me. "What's wrong?"

"Come this way." Jackie walked through the apartment and pointed to the open door to the patio. A red envelope was taped to the door with one word on the front: "Jackie."

Greg pulled out a pair of latex gloves and took the envelope off the door. Then he walked over to her small table and carefully opened the seal. "Get me a plastic bag, will you?"

My aunt went to a drawer and pulled out a couple of boxes, setting them next to Greg. "Not sure what size you need."

He smiled and picked two gallon bags. "This is fine."

My aunt took the boxes back, then came to watch as Greg slipped the envelope into a bag and then looked at the card. It appeared to be a Valentine's Day card. When he opened it, the signature was big on the bottom. Greg read the handwritten message aloud. "'I'm sorry I missed so many days. Love Ted.'"

"He's not dead." My aunt choked out the words.

I grabbed her arm. "Look at me. I was going to wait to tell you, but Doc Ames verified that Uncle Ted is dead. He knew his physician and called him. He said he personally declared him dead at the hospital. There's no mistake."

"Jackie, Jill's right. I've talked to the people at the county records department. The death certificate was misfiled. Your husband is dead. This is a hoax."

"So how did he know where I live?" My aunt sank into a chair. "I was so careful. I know you think I'm a silly old woman for believing, but I didn't give the man who called any information about where I lived or what I did."

Greg and I exchanged a look. Those were the exact questions I'd had of my letter from the Senior Project last night.

"We found a database on Ben Penn's tablet. We think he was involved in this scam." Greg put the card into the second envelope.

"But he's dead. How could he have placed this card?"

Greg took out a notebook. "When was the last time you exited the apartment from this door?"

"Yesterday evening. I watered all the plants. The card wasn't there at seven when I closed and relocked the door."

Greg looked at me. "Jill, why don't you go downstairs and open the shop? Tim will be showing up soon. I'll be down as soon as I ask a few more questions. Jackie, do you need me to go downstairs and get you a cup of coffee?"

"I'm fine, but if you're going to question me, can I go change into some clothes? I'm not used to entertaining people in my pajamas."

A smile flickered on Greg's face. "Of course."

"We can talk when you're done." I touched my aunt's arm. "If you need anything…"

She grimaced. "All I need is for this nightmare to be over. I'm so glad I'm going to the city tomorrow with Mary. I need a break."

As she walked away from me into her bedroom, I heard Greg mutter, "You're not the only one."

I kissed him, then hurried downstairs, hoping I wasn't making Tim—or worse, a customer—wait for their coffee.

Chapter 19

"Did someone break in?" a woman asked, glancing back at Tim, who was just finishing up the dusting on the door.

I handed her a large mocha. "I think 'tried to break in' is probably more accurate. South Cove Police is just very careful about property vandalism. I'm betting it was some kids out too late and causing problems."

"There was a shop in Bakerstown that was robbed just last week. It's such a shame."

As she left, Tim walked over and nodded to the back door. "I'll get the back door done and then I'm out of here. You can clean up the mess now. Boss still around?"

"He's upstairs talking to my aunt." I glanced toward the door. He should have been done a while ago. What exactly was he asking her? "Thanks, Tim."

"No problem. That's what we're here for, to serve and protect." He grinned as he crossed over to the office door. "I wouldn't turn down a cup of coffee and a piece of that cheesecake when I'm done, though. Probably against regulations, but I was rousted out of my apartment before I could grab some breakfast."

"Let me know what you want and it's yours. On the house." I glanced around the now-empty shop. "I'm going to go wash off that stuff and I'll be here as soon as you're ready."

"Winn's going to be so jealous. She loves coming here on Sundays to buy a book or two along with our second breakfast. We do like our treats." He disappeared into the back office.

I grabbed a bar towel and a bottle of spray cleaner. I cleaned up the door first and took the stop out from underneath so it could close. Then I cleaned the light fixture. I didn't know what they would find, but I assumed there would be way too many prints to try to separate out. Cleaning the door handle and the light switch wasn't on the list of daily tasks Jackie had on her many lists. I think it was on the Sunday list, which meant almost a full week of prints were on the door handle. Greg appeared from the back as I was putting away the cleaners.

"You were talking to her for a while."

He nodded and refilled his coffee cup, this time putting a lid on it. He leaned over and kissed me. "I already checked in with Tim. I'll see you tonight."

"Aren't you going to tell me what you talked about?" I watched as he strolled across the dining room.

"No, I'm not."

A few minutes later, Tim came out of the back room. "I'm done. Greg said coffee and cheesecake was fine, but if you don't mind, I'll take it to-go. I've got a report to write at the station."

I boxed up the cheesecake and poured his coffee. He didn't look at me while I got the order ready.

When I handed it to him, he smiled. "Thank you so much."

Then he left through the front door. I didn't even bother to ask him what he'd found. He was learning from the best, and if Greg didn't want him to talk, he wasn't going to talk.

The good news was, Greg thought he was coming home tonight. We might have a normal dinner for once. The bad news was, I didn't think he'd be any more talkative about what had happened in my shop that morning.

Deek came in at noon. I glanced at the schedule.

"I thought Toby had this shift?"

Deek washed his hands and put on an apron. "He called me last night and asked if I'd take it. He sounded beat."

"He's getting a lot of hours out of this investigation." I picked up my tote, ready to go home. "Remember, you're working a longer shift tomorrow. I'll see you then."

"No problem. I've already talked to Trina and she's excited about working here tomorrow night. She'll be so wired by the time we close, she won't sleep for days."

"I hope not." I gave him a quick salute. "The shop is in your hands."

"I'll be careful with it." He poured himself a cup of coffee and opened the newspaper. Hopefully, customers would start coming in sooner or later.

As I made my way home, I decided I was going to have to disappoint Emma on our afternoon run. All the excitement had worn me out. All I wanted to do was heat up some soup and cuddle up on the couch with a book.

When Greg came home, he brought dinner with him. Emma was at the door as soon as she could smell the chicken. In the bag from Diamond Lille's would be fried chicken, mashed potatoes and gravy, and a quart of coleslaw. My stomach grumbled as I followed him into the kitchen and pulled out plates and silverware. "Iced tea or soda?"

"Iced tea. I'm waiting for a call back from our friend Mr. Hess. He called in sick today, but he wasn't at his apartment, so I left a message on his cell to contact me as soon as possible." Greg washed his hands, then took the food out of the bags and set it on the table. "I asked Tessa, the receptionist, to check your name to see what address they have on you. It's the shop. She said your counselor, Denyse, sent you some pamphlets talking about how to prevent identify fraud with an elderly family member. She keyed it in yesterday after they looked up your coffee shop."

"That doesn't answer how they got my home address." I picked out a wing and a breast and put it on my plate as I waited for Greg to finish piling potatoes on his plate.

"No, it doesn't. But it does tell us how they guessed that your aunt lived above the shop. I know she thought she was being careful, but I'm sure she let drop that she was working for you and living in an apartment." He took a leg and a thigh and then finished the plate with some coleslaw. "The weird thing was, Tim didn't find any prints. I had him dust your aunt's doorways too. Nothing."

"Well, you can't expect to get clear ones with all the people we have coming in and out on a daily basis." I took a bite of the chicken. Juicy, crunchy, and perfect. Tiny, Lille's cook, knew how to fry a chicken. "This is so good."

"Yes, it is, but you aren't listening to me. I didn't say Tim couldn't separate out the prints. He didn't find any prints at all. The handles were wiped down. As was the wall plate on the light switch."

I set down the chicken and wiped my hands on a napkin. "I think I just lost my appetite. So someone *was* in the shop?"

"Looks that way. How, I'm not sure, but there appeared to be some scratches on the door handle in the back. Maybe someone picked the lock?"

"You know this means I have to sell the shop and move, right?" I looked longingly at the mashed potatoes.

"No, that's not what that means. I'm sure we'll find this guy. And I'm sure that they're tied in with the Senior Project staff. I'm not sure how yet.

But this Hess guy is looking more and more like my suspect." He took a big bite of the potatoes. "But if you don't want your half, I'm sure I can eat your food too."

"Get your grubby paws off my dinner." I picked up my fork. "How's my aunt? She blew me off when I wanted to talk to her after you left."

"She's scared and tough all at the same time. She knows this guy isn't her Ted, but there's a part that still wants to believe. She must have loved him a lot."

I nodded. "I didn't think she'd really fall again until I saw her with Harrold. And now this scam artist has ruined that as well."

"Well, I'm sure if something happened to me, you would be so grief-stricken you'd never look at another man until the day you died." He picked up the chicken leg and took a bite.

"Of course. Maybe not until the day I died, but I'm sure I'd be sad for at least a month. Maybe a week. What does this new love of mine look like? Does he surf? Maybe he's one of Justin's friends who has seen me from afar and has been in love with me since that day. I couldn't break his heart, right?"

"You're evil. That's all I have to say. I would give up on dating if something happened to you. But apparently, I'm the better man." He pointed his fork filled with mashed potatoes at me. "You should be more focused on the years without me."

"I would be. Especially if Geraldo could teach me how to surf. I would think of you every morning when we arrived at the beach." I took another bite. "Thanks for dinner; this is exactly what I needed."

"I figured. Remember that when Geraldo doesn't want to stop for lunch on your road trips." He held out the coleslaw container. "You done with this?"

"Go ahead. And if Geraldo isn't going to make time for meals, he's not my man." I was thinking about the shop break-in. "Maybe I should make new keys. I didn't change the locks when Sasha left. Not that I think Sasha is part of this, but maybe there are just too many keys out there."

"Wouldn't be a bad idea. I'll call a locksmith in out of Bakerstown for you if that's all right. They give us a deal if the order comes from the police." He took another leg out of the chicken box and seemed to inhale it.

"If they can come either in the morning or early afternoon, I'll be at the shop. Deek and I are splitting the day so Aunt Jackie can go into the city with Mary." I broke off a piece of the chicken and ate it. "Lille's chicken is so juicy, it's outrageous."

"And that's one of the reasons I brought it home. I know you've been fending for yourself for a few nights now." He leaned back in his chair. "I'm not stoked about your aunt leaving for the day. I'd rather she stick around town so I can watch out for her, but I guess no one will know where she and Mary are in the city."

"She has to go." I pointed the chicken I'd just taken off the bone at Greg. "It's important."

"Why?" He snatched the bite I'd let get too close and ate it.

"Hey."

"Sorry, not sorry." He grinned and pushed the box of chicken toward me. "There's more. So why does Jackie have to go to the city?"

"Because Harrold's coming over to finish the patio for her. He wants it to be a surprise."

Greg focused on his food, but I could hear the chuckle. "I forgot about Project Harrold."

"What?"

"Harrold has it bad for your aunt. I don't think he's going to let her get away with this coy act much longer."

"She's not playing coy. She had a stalker calling her and pretending to be her dead husband. That would mess with anyone's head."

Greg finished his plate, then took it to the sink to rinse and put it in the dishwasher. "You're right, of course, but it's fun to watch Harrold pursue your aunt. He's in to the courting routine. Are you done with this? I'll put it in the fridge so we can have a late-night snack."

"You have to go back?" I wasn't sure why I even phrased it as a question.

He shook his head. "I'm locking myself in the office and working on some reports. I need to figure out where Mr. Hess is hiding out so I can find him and convince him to confess."

"Is that all? You should be done in thirty minutes, an hour tops, right?"

He kissed me on the head as he grabbed the mashed potatoes off the table. "Your optimism is one of the reasons I love you. Knock when you're getting ready for bed. I'd like to say good night."

I finished my dinner and then cleaned up the rest of the kitchen. Bored, I decided to throw in a load of laundry. As I gathered up the clothes, I pulled everything out of Greg's discarded work jeans. A folded slip of paper fell on the floor. Curious, I opened it and found a phone number. And a name. Sherry.

I set his keys, his wallet, and the folded sheet of paper on his dresser. Then I picked it up again and looked. Was this ex-wife Sherry's number? Or some other Sherry? Was it about the case or just someone he knew? Why was I obsessing on this? Sometimes my investigative side took a bad turn.

Like the time I found out my husband had been cheating on me. I just kept gathering data before I finally caught them together. He'd tried to explain it away as a dinner meeting, but I'd already seen the graphic pictures they'd shared over text message. For months after that confrontation and during the divorce process, I'd questioned my sanity. Why had I gone looking for trouble?

But it hadn't mattered if I'd gone looking or not. The truth was the truth. And if Greg was seeing Sherry again, I'd know soon enough. Until then, I was going to leave Pandora's box closed. I took the basket filled with the laundry downstairs, then curled up on the couch. Turning on a DVD, I watched *Sleepless in Seattle* for the hundredth time.

Soul mates were meant to be, even if it took a while and a few cross-country flights to find the one. I glanced at the still-closed office door. I'd hoped I'd found mine.

And I knew my aunt had found her second one. Operation Harrold Wins Jackie Back was going to work. It had to work. All the best books and movies had a happily ever after. Real life should too.

Near the end of the movie, Greg came out with his coffee cup. He set it down on the coffee table and pulled me up into his arms. "You are the best girlfriend I've ever had."

"I'm the most patient one." It felt good standing there in his arms.

He laughed and tightened his grip. "I think I might call that characteristic stubborn, not patient. But that works too." He let me go and then picked up the cup. "Want something from the kitchen?"

"A bottle of water, please." I paused the movie. When he came back into the room and handed me my water, I held his hand for a second. "I washed your work jeans that were on the floor."

"Thank you. I meant to run a load after dinner and I forgot. Now you're really the best girlfriend I've ever had." He kissed me, making my heart flutter.

"Better than Sherry?"

"Honey, you passed that standard years ago." He stared into my eyes. "Something wrong, or does the romance have you weepy?"

"Nothing's wrong, I'm just feeling a little left out tonight. Let's go away when this case gets closed and play in the surf." I did love this guy, even if I had to spend a lot of evenings alone. I always had a good book by my side.

"I was thinking the exact same thing." He kissed me and then turned and disappeared into the office.

No scrap of paper was going to mess with my emotions. I turned back on the movie and enjoyed the awesomeness that was Tom Hanks as a single dad.

Chapter 20

Saturday morning, the coffee shop was buzzing. Deek's book clubs had just started new books, so several families had taken advantage of the beautiful fall weather to make the trip to South Cove to buy them, as well as get some coffee and cheesecake. I had most of the inside tables filled with groups, as well as all of the outside tables.

Between making coffee and dishing up treats, I was busy through the late morning. When Denyse from the Senior Project came up to the coffee bar, I'd just grabbed a cup of coffee and was sneaking bites out of a chocolate chip oatmeal cookie. I figured it counted as a breakfast food if you just looked at the oatmeal part.

"Jill, I didn't realize this place was such a popular spot. I should make plans to pop in for coffee on my way to work. I have a condo south of here." Denyse picked up one of the seasonal books I kept at the counter to tempt impulse shoppers. "'Fall on Highway 1.' What a great concept. I've always wanted to write a book. Are you an author too?"

"No, my love is reading. I think writing the book would strip all the magic away from the story for me." I set down my cup. "What can I get for you?"

"A large coffee to go. A girl has to watch her figure." She glanced over at the bookshelves. "You don't have any travel books, do you?"

"A whole section. My aunt curates those herself. She loves to travel, even though she's stayed closer to home the last few years." I poured the coffee and nodded toward the bookshelf. I waved away the plastic she offered to use to pay. "It's the one on the back wall behind the couch. Take this while you browse and pay me when you're ready to leave. That way, if you decide on a book, you only have to run your card once."

"Well, aren't you the trusting one." Denyse pulled out an envelope and handed it to me. "These are the fraud pamphlets I found. I didn't have your address because you didn't fill out the intake form, but I remembered you said something about running this place. So I took the chance I'd run into you or your aunt." She began to survey the shop again. "Do you think there are any books on South America? I hear the beaches down there are beautiful and not crowded yet."

"Thanks for these. I'll look them over when it slows down. I'm sure there are books on Mexico and Central America, but I bet you'll find what you need. My aunt loved traveling." I tucked the envelope under the counter.

"It must have been hard for her to curtail her adventures after the Ponzi scheme. There's a special place in the afterlife for people like that." Denyse took her coffee and wandered over to the travel section.

I watched her go. Something she'd said had bothered me. I couldn't put my finger on it. Maybe it was because it hit so close to home. I did feel bad that my aunt couldn't travel, even though I didn't know what I'd do with the shop without her. As much as I complained, she had saved my bacon several times because of her extensive knowledge.

"Miss Gardner?"

I turned to see a man with a tool belt and a clipboard waiting for me. Brad had come in earlier that morning from Bakerstown Lock and Key. He handed me four sets of keys. "I just finished up the apartment upstairs. Here are the keys for all four doors upstairs and down, but I'd consider setting up an actual security system. I don't install those, but I can send out a guy from our company who will give you an estimate of what it might cost."

"I'd love to see some information." I grabbed envelopes. "These two are for upstairs?"

He dug for some information on his clipboard. "Yeah, the ones on the left are for the back door, then the ones next to those are the inside door, and the others are for the two locks down here. The downstairs locks all have the same key."

I put one of each into an envelope, to put in the safe down here as an extra set. Then I made a set for Jackie. I put one on my key chain and one in my tote. I'd leave that one at home, just in case I needed it. Brad handed me a couple of flyers. "Thanks."

He pointed to one that was glossier and looked more expensive. "That one is the top of the line; we sell a lot of those. And the security company has the same special deal if the referral comes from your police department connection."

"Okay if I look at these later?" I held up the brochures. I didn't mean to rush the guy, but Denyse was already back with a couple of books to check out.

"No worries. I'll have the office send out an invoice for today's work." Brad turned and walked out the door as Denyse laid her books on the counter.

"You doing some remodeling?" She tilted her head to the exiting Brad.

I tucked away the security leaflets, but not before I caught her looking at them. "Just some updating. I've had the store for over five years now, thinking about making some changes."

"Well, security systems are a great purchase, especially with your aunt living upstairs." She pulled out her credit card. "You can never be too careful with the ones we love."

After she left, I started cleaning the coffee bar. It had been a crazy busy day, and Deek would be coming in soon to take over. I was ready for home and Emma and either a run or a nap. But something kept bothering me. I pulled out the security flyers. I'd want to talk to Jackie before investing this kind of money, but even if she didn't think the business could afford it, I was pulling the initial cost out of the Miss Emily fund.

Having the money my friend left to me in her will had made all the difference in my decision-making. Instead of having a bookstore on the brink of closing, I was able to hold on in the lean months and expand in the flush ones. And I'd been able to help several deserving students pay for some of their college classes. Denyse was right; putting in a security system to protect my one and only aunt—that was definitely money well spent.

Having that decision made and the coffee shop finally empty, I grabbed a cup of coffee and a few peanut butter bars and headed to the couch. Jill time.

My reading shift was interrupted a few times by random customers wanting a specialty coffee or someone heading to the beach needing something to read, but the rest of Saturday flowed easily. The universe must be making up for the craziness the morning had been. When Deek came in to replace me, I was just finishing up the book I'd started a few days before. I'd already picked out two more and they were in my tote along with the new keys, the fraud flyers, and the security ones. If Greg had a few minutes this weekend, I'd have him give me his impressions. One of the good things about living with a cop: he knew security.

"Hey, Boss Lady! My mom sends her love. And, well, this is going to sound strange, but she said to watch for the flowers tomorrow." He went to the coffee bar and put on his apron. "Not sure what that means, but there you go."

"Watch for the flowers? Crap." I knew what had been bothering me. I hadn't seen Harrold since he'd stopped in for coffee first thing this morning. He was probably up on the deck, dead of a heart attack. "I'll be right back."

I ran out the back door and looked up. Harrold was on the deck, along with Kyle, arranging the bench Kyle had painted. Kyle worked for Antiques by Thomas and had a flair for hand-painting wood furniture.

Kyle leaned over the railing. "Hey, Miss Gardner, it's looking good up here. Your aunt's going to be so excited."

Harrold slowly made his way down the stairs, holding on to the rail. "It's coming along nicely. Thank goodness Kyle took the day off to help me. He's such a good boy. I wish he liked model trains more than antiques. I'd steal him from Josh in a heartbeat."

"I heard that, old man." Josh came around the building with a flat of peonies. "I might not run fast, but I run faster than you do. The nursery dropped these off at the store."

"Sorry, Mr. Thomas. I told them to come to the back of the building." Kyle bounded down the stairs and took the flat from Josh. "I didn't mean to interrupt your day."

"No worries, Kyle." Josh put his hand over his eyes and took in the process on the deck. He reached out and patted Harrold on the back. "You've done a good job. She's going to love it."

Harrold put his arm around Josh and my eyes bugged out. "I hope so. You know Jackie can be a little particular in her likes and dislikes."

"Don't I know it." Josh grinned at him. Then he looked at me. "How are you today, Miss Gardner?"

"Fine; thanks for asking." I couldn't think of anything else to say.

"Well, I better get back to the shop before the customers steal me blind." He nodded to Harrold. "Come see me next week and let me know how the reveal goes."

"I will. I'll bring Lille's cinnamon rolls if you have coffee."

Josh took another glance at the patio. "I'll have my pot brewed by eight."

I waited for Josh to return to the front of the building. He'd lost a lot of weight and no longer wore the black suits that made him look like a funeral director. When he turned the corner to go into his shop, I turned to Harrold. "What was that all about?"

"What?" He glanced at the flowers Kyle still held. "Those will work nicely. Take them up and I'll be right there."

"Sure, Mr. Snider." Kyle bounded back up the stairs with as much or more energy as when he came down.

"You and Josh are friends now?" I whispered the question.

Harrold laughed and put a hand on my shoulder. "Josh came over to talk to me when Jackie broke the engagement. He wanted to express his condolences, because he knew what it felt like. I think he was looking for me to bash Jackie, but instead, I invited him in for coffee. We've been meeting up at least once a week since then. He's a good guy."

"Mr. Thomas is the best. He's just a little cautious around people," Kyle called from the patio.

"And there you go." Harrold started walking toward the stairs, then stopped. "Where is my head? I didn't ask you if you needed anything. Don't tell me that Jackie is on her way back already. We need at least another hour to get that last flat planted and everything cleaned."

"No, I was just checking to see if *you* needed anything. Can I bring you some water or a treat?"

Harrold shook his head. "We're good. I brought a cooler filled with waters and those sugary sodas the kid's so fond of. Lille brought us out lunch about an hour ago."

"Okay, then. If you need anything, I'll leave the back door open. Just come on in through the office. Either Deek or I will be tending the shop."

I left the two men working on a landscaping project for my aunt, who didn't seem to realize what she had in her hands. A man who was smitten and willing to do anything for her. As I walked through the office door out into the dining room, Fred Mucke waved me over to where he stood, talking to Deek.

"There she is. I'm so glad I caught you, Miss Gardner. I was afraid you might have gone home for the night." He took my arm when I reached them and walked me over to the book shelves.

I wanted to shake him off, but I knew if I did, the fact that I was impolite to the his henchman would be an issue the next time I saw Mayor Baylor. And I did still like my job as the business representative to the city council. When we reached the sitting area, I sat in the wing-back chair, instead of the couch where Fred had been leading me. He frowned, then sat.

"What can I help you with, Mr. Mucke?"

He smiled a little. "Direct and to the point. Marvin said you were like that. Anyway, I'll do my best to copy your communication style. Like I said, I'm so glad I found you. I'm not sure I could have gathered up the courage to come again."

I felt my eyes narrow as I studied him. "The courage to tell me what? I've already told you and the mayor that Greg isn't running in the primary."

"And Mayor Baylor respects your honesty. I'm not here about the election." Fred looked around nervously, but besides Deek, who I knew was watching the two of us very closely, the shop was empty. "I'm afraid this is a personal matter."

Alarm bells went off in my head, but I wanted to hear him out. "What do you want to say?"

Fred took a deep breath, then spoke. "I'm afraid I saw Greg in a compromising position this morning with a woman I think he called Sherry."

"Sherry's his ex-wife. If she was there, she was probably trying to get money out of him." If this guy thought he could make me jealous just by mentioning Sherry's name, he was so out of his league. I'd already blown all my gaskets when Sherry tried to get Greg back. And he'd assured me that the sun would turn to ice before he left me for her. Although there was the issue of Sherry's phone number in Greg's pants pocket. But I shook off the doubt. If I was worried, Greg would be the person I talked about this with, not some stranger. I stood. "If that's all, I have a business to run."

"It's not the first time I've seen them together. I mean, rumors must be all over City Hall about their midday trysts. I even hear he's bringing her into his office after-hours." He waved me back into my seat. "I don't want to hurt you; I just thought you should know. Especially because you were so nice to Marvin."

"If causing a rift between Greg and me was the purpose of your visit, you failed. Greg would no more cheat on me than dishonor his job. He's a good, kind, and thoughtful man. And you should be afraid of him as an opponent. Anyone with half a brain would vote him into the mayor's chair if he'd just run." I pointed to the door. "This is my store and I choose who we will serve. You have just become the first person banned from Coffee, Books, and More." I took a breath to try to calm down my shaking hands. "Do I have to ask Deek to escort you or will you leave now?"

"You're going to regret this." Fred stepped toward me, and all of a sudden, a flash of electric-blue hair moved in between us.

"I think Jill asked you kindly to leave. I won't be so nice if you're not moving toward that door by the time I count to five." Deek held the baseball bat Aunt Jackie had bought five years ago to keep behind the counter. I didn't think it even had been moved from the shelf where she'd put it since. Now he tapped it in his hand. "One, two, three…"

"Fine, I'm out of here." He stomped out of the shop like a child who had been told he couldn't have candy. "I'll never try to be the hero again. Apparently, you like being cheated on."

The shop was dead silent after he left the room. Deek set down the bat on the table. "Man, I'm glad he left. I've never hit a person with a baseball bat. At least not intentionally."

When I didn't answer, he sank into the couch. "Look, he was just trying to get under your skin. You know Greg wouldn't do anything to hurt you."

"I know that." But it didn't explain the piece of paper I'd picked up off the floor. Could Fred have planted it? Or was it really Sherry's number with a perfectly good explanation? "I knew he was lying when he said everyone at City Hall had been gossiping about it. If it was true, Amy would have told me. Well, after she kicked Greg's butt."

"It's good to have friends." Deek fidgeted. "I don't know protocol here. Do you need a hug? I feel like I do and the guy wasn't even in my face."

"I'm good. But I think I'm going to walk home." I looked around the empty shop. "Unless you think you'll need me?"

He twirled the baseball bat. "I think I'm good. But why would the guy try to mess with you like that? Any clue?"

"He's the campaign manager for the mayor. My thought is they're really concerned about Greg running. Which he isn't. But after this? He just might." I tried to settle myself. I hated conflict. That was why Greg and I got along so well. We kept things out in the open so there wasn't any. Well, unless I was sticking my nose in one of his murder investigations. "I don't understand politics, and after today, I don't want to. If Aunt Jackie comes back from the city before you close up, give her the envelope under the cash register."

"Works for me. Do I need a new key to close up with?" He followed me to the coffee bar and replaced the bat onto its storage shelf. Thank God Jackie planned for any future event, even when the possibility was slim to none. But I wasn't sure I was going to tell her about today.

"Yes. OMG, yes. I totally forgot." I grabbed the closing key, which we kept on a South Cove key chain in the cash register. I replaced the key and put it back in the drawer. We only used it when someone besides Aunt Jackie or me closed or opened the shop. That way we didn't have to make keys for all the employees. "Seriously, I need to get my head in the game. With everything that's going on, I'm losing it."

"Stress makes people miss things. Then they get more stressed when they realize they missed something." Deek refilled his coffee cup. "Do I need to do anything with the guys out in the back?"

Leave it to Deek to notice everything. The guy was amazing. "See if they want something in about an hour. They should be done soon, or at least I hope so. I don't think Jackie was planning on staying in the city late."

"It's a nice thing the train dude is doing for her. I hope she takes him back." He sipped his coffee, but I noticed a little tremor in his hand. He grinned when he realized I had seen it. "I have to admit, this was a pretty exciting day. I'll be fine as long as the guy doesn't come back. Then I'm just calling the local law enforcement number and letting your boy toy kick his butt."

"Great plan." I grabbed my tote and rechecked what keys I had. I needed my own keys to the apartment and the shop, which I would give to Jackie if she came home late. I needed to run to Bakerstown and have more keys made. If Denyse hadn't interrupted me, I would have had Brad make me another set of everything.

"Boss Lady? Are you all right? You look like you just saw a ghost." Deek studied my face.

"What? Oh, no, I'm fine. I was thinking that I need to get some duplicates made." Well, I hadn't been exactly, but whatever I *had* been thinking about had disappeared. I knew I needed the keys. "See you tomorrow."

"Are you coming in?"

Typically, I took Sundays off, but I hadn't talked to Jackie about her shift, which I should know, she'd be here. "I might pop in. If Jackie doesn't want to cover the register during your book club."

"See you when I see you. Get home safe, okay?" Concern filled his voice.

"I'm calling Greg as soon as I hit the street, so I'll be fine. Do you want me to call when I get home?"

His face brightened. "Would you? That would be great, so I don't worry. That guy's aura was black as night. And I know you're still shaken up, I can see that without my superpower."

"Okay, Mom. I'll call." Smiling as I left the shop, I realized Deek had not only filled the gap at the shop when Sasha left but also become part of our little family. Even though his blond dreadlocks, now with electric blue edges, hadn't come from my side of the family tree.

Chapter 21

As I walked home through South Cove, trying to let the afternoon sun and the ocean breezes calm me, I dialed Greg. He picked up on the first ring.

"What's happening? Are you on your way home?" He sounded warm and loving, and the words almost made me tear up. Yep, the incident had shaken me more than I wanted to admit to either Deek or myself.

Trying to keep my voice steady, I told him about the incident. Afterward, his side of the line was quiet. "Greg, did I lose you?"

"No, I'm here. I'm just trying to fight off the urge to go kick down the mayor's door and ask him what game he's playing here. You know I would never do that to you. Not here at the station, not anywhere."

I blinked back the tears. "I know you wouldn't, because if Amy found out, she'd take care of my busy work. Then I'd dump all your worldly possessions in the yard and Emma and I would roast marshmallows over the bonfire."

"Sounds like you've given this some thought." He chuckled; then his tone got serious. "I know Marvin hates me, but this is above and beyond his usual tactics. You don't think this is about the mayoral race, do you?"

"I think that's exactly what it's about. The guy is scared of you. And he thought if I got mad enough, maybe that would upset your plans to run." I waved at a local artist, who was sitting outside his shop, drawing. I decided to put it all out there. "Greg, there is one thing. When I dumped out your pockets so I could wash your jeans, I found a slip of paper with Sherry's number on it."

"I saw that on top of my wallet and shield. I was going to ask you about it. I thought you put it there."

"I did put it there, but it came out of your pocket." I let the implication hang.

"Jill, I haven't talked to Sherry in months. Pat stopped me a few days ago and let it drop that Sherry was in New York on a shopping trip for the store. Of course she's been there for months, and Pat's getting a little fed up with her excuses."

"Running a business is hard on your own." I felt for Pat's situation. As Sherry's best friend, she'd gone into the Vintage Duds consignment store thinking she had a partner. But Sherry was all about the flash. "So she wasn't at the station last week and she couldn't have given you her number."

"Pat will tell you the same thing." He sighed. "I hate that I have to defend myself against this. But I know you deserve the whole truth. I had my shield and wallet on my desk a few days ago when the mayor pulled me into a meeting about the case. He said he needed an update. Maybe this Fred guy planted it. That's the only explanation I can think of. He probably counted on you finding it and then upped the game when it didn't change anything."

"The guy is slime. That's all I have to say. I told him he was banned from the coffee shop. It kind of felt good. I've never banned anyone before."

"Do you need me to come home? I'm working a lead on trying to track down this administrator from the Senior Project. More and more, I'm thinking he's the one. Tim talked to his last employer, and I know you're going to be shocked, but they had a data leak in the months before the guy left."

"All I can say is, I feel a lot better now that the locks have been changed." I put my house key into the front door lock and turned it. "Look, I'm home and Emma's going to go crazy in a minute, so I'll talk to you later. Just don't beat up the mayor, okay?"

"I won't. I don't think." He paused. "I love you, Jill."

"Are you coming home for dinner?"

"Signs all point to the affirmative. Unless…"

I finished his sentence. "Unless you find Earl Hess. I know the drill. I love you too."

As I had foretold, Emma went crazy as soon as I opened the door. What can I say? I was surrounded by love today. Well, except for the crazy at the shop. I pulled out food for lunch and decided to eat in front of the television to catch up on some of my shows.

Emma nudged me a few episodes later, and I paused the show and went to let her out. Glancing at the clock, I realized I hadn't called my aunt yet. Or planned anything for dinner. I took out a packet of frozen hamburger for tacos to defrost in the microwave, then dialed her number.

"Hello?" Mary's voice came through the speaker.

"Hey, Mary. Is Jackie around? I needed to chat with her for a minute." I bet she was in the bathroom. My aunt didn't think it was polite to take the phone into the restroom, and when someone did at a public place, she made sure to point out that flaw.

"She's right here, but she's driving. Tell me what you need to say and I'll relay it."

"Or she could just wait five minutes and I'll be at the apartment," Jackie said. "Unless you change your mind about me taking you to the house. I can drive an extra couple of blocks, you know."

"You do so much already. I need to finish out my steps because we didn't hit the museum today. I'm short about two thousand. And you know I don't like to break a streak," Mary responded.

"Wait, you're already in South Cove? I didn't expect you here until late." I sent up a silent prayer that Harrold and Kyle had finished and left. Jackie hated surprises, and she could be a little crabby when she first discovered a change.

"Jackie wasn't feeling it, so we came home after lunch," Mary explained.

"You said you were tired too. Don't blame this all on me," Aunt Jackie huffed. "Someone is in my parking spot. Wait, is that Harrold? What is he doing here, and why is he lifting that box? He knows better. He's going to throw out his back again."

"I'll be right there. Don't let her go crazy."

"Why would she go crazy?" Mary asked.

Instead of answering, I hung up and threw my phone into my tote. Because Harrold was still there and Jackie had come home, the only parking I would have was a possible street spot, but it was Saturday night, and with the bar across the street, I knew it was impossible. I let Emma back in and started running into town.

Greg was driving down the road the opposite way, but when he saw me, he made a U-turn, then stopped in front of me, opening the passenger door. "Get in. Where are we going?"

"Back to the shop. Aunt Jackie's home and Harrold hasn't left yet." I climbed in and slammed the door. "You'll probably have to park in the alley. I don't think there's going to be a spot out front."

"I can park anywhere I want; I'm the head of police here." He took off, just a little above the speed limit. "So, do you want to tell me why I'm flying back into town? Harrold and your aunt have seen each other since the breakup, right?"

"They have, but he landscaped her patio today. She's going to be mad." I leaned forward and pointed to the left turn that would take us to the alley that ran behind the shop. "Turn there."

"Yes Jill, I know where to turn." He slowed his speed, and when we came up on the shop, a group was standing around the bottom of the stairs.

I looked up and saw Jackie on the new patio. She sank onto the bench while I watched. Greg parked and I jumped out of the car and ran up to Mary and Harrold. Kyle was still there, watching Jackie's reaction, and so was Deek. "How's she taking it?"

"She hasn't said a word since I told her what I did." Harrold looked down on me in concern. "Do you think she's all right? Jackie is never this quiet. Maybe we should call for an ambulance?"

I shook my head. "Let me go talk to her. She won't hit me."

Everyone moved aside and I had a clear path up the stairs. When I got there, she was sitting with her eyes closed. "Aunt Jackie? Are you okay?"

I heard the sniff first; then she took a tissue out of her purse and wiped her nose. "I'm fine. That stupid man, he is so stubborn."

"Harrold?"

"Of course Harrold. Did you think I meant the crazy man who has been stalking me?" A tiny smile curved her lips. "Did you know we talked about this? About making this patio a place we could watch the sunset? It was one time. He mentioned it one time, and I'd told him a different time about how lovely Kyle's hand-painting was on the woodwork."

I watched as she touched a row of flowers on the end table. Kyle had covered the top with flowers and then made pretty rows on the back of the shelves. The whole thing was covered with a heavy coating of shellac to keep it waterproof. "It's lovely. Everything is so bright and pretty."

Jackie swallowed hard. "I know." She looked at me and the tears flowed. "I'm so sorry I hurt him. How can I ever make it up to him?"

"I think saying thank you would be a great start. He's about to call an ambulance because he thinks you had a stroke or something." I waved Harrold up the stairs as I handed her an envelope. "Here are your new keys. I had the locks changed while you were out."

"You were both busy today. And all I did was wander through art galleries." She smiled as she took the envelope. "Thank you, Jill. I may not say it much, but I appreciate all you do for me."

Now I was speechless, but Harrold was already standing by the door, so I just reached over and kissed her on the cheek. As I passed Harrold, I patted his arm. "Good luck."

When I got to the bottom of the stairs, I nodded to the back door of the shop. "Let's take this inside."

"I need to get home to Bill. I told him we were in town already, and now he's probably thinking I'm lost." Mary kissed me on the cheek. "Thank you for suggesting this outing. We had a lot of fun and we talked. I know she's been under a lot of stress, but she knows now not to keep things like this from me. I mean, what are best friends for if we can't talk about when our dead husbands start calling."

I laughed as I watched her walk between the buildings and to the street. Deek shrugged. "All I have to do is lock the back door and I'm out of here. I have a date tonight with Trina."

"Then lock up and go. I'll ride home with Greg." I looked around because he wasn't standing with us. Then I saw him on his phone over by Harrold's truck. "Or maybe walk home."

Deek paused. "I can drive you home. I'm going that way anyway."

"No worries. I'll hang here until Greg's done with his call. Go get ready for your date. And thanks for stepping in today. I appreciate how well you've melded with this job and our crazy crew."

"You all are fun. At my last summer job, I made milk bottles all by myself. Longest eight hours I've ever experienced. Four bottles, label, put in a bag. Four more bottles, label—well, you get my drift. This doesn't even seem like work." He waved and went through the back door. When I turned back around, Greg was walking toward me.

"You've got to go."

He nodded. "I can drop you off, though. I'm heading to the highway."

"Is it about Ben's murder?" I followed him to the truck and snuck a peek at Harrold and Jackie, who were now sitting together and watching the sky. Maybe she would let him back in. Especially after Mary had given her such a bad time.

"They found Earl Hess tied up in an empty house. It was for sale, and the Realtor and his clients got quite a shock when they opened the garage." He started the truck, but before he put it in gear, he glanced upward to the patio. "They look good together."

"I just hope she comes to her senses and tells him everything. She finally told Mary." I shut my door and put on my seat belt. Even with such a short ride, you never knew what was in store for you around the corner. Besides, Greg drove fast. "Maybe I could come with you."

"Good try, but I'm thinking not. I'll have Toby grab some burgers on the way out. Make sure you eat."

"I'm making tacos. I'll eat." As crazy as today had been, maybe it had ended with one good thing. My aunt and Harrold back together. All I could do was hope.

I was frying up the now-defrosted hamburger when a knock came at the front door. I turned off the pan and Emma and I went to answer it. Emma barked once, then sat. A response she usually had for my aunt. I didn't look out the window, just opened the door. It wasn't my aunt.

Sadie and Pastor Bill stood on my porch. I noticed he had his hand on my friend's back in a very personal way. "Hey, I didn't expect to see you two today."

Sadie opened the screen and they walked in. She handed me a box. "We brought you cookies."

Now Emma's reaction made sense. She had smelled the cookies and figured whoever was at the door needed to be let inside. "I was just starting dinner. Can you stay?"

She shook her head. "Actually, Bill is taking me out tonight. We just came from seeing Paula, and I wanted you and Greg to hear what she had to say."

"He's not here. Come into the kitchen. I can at least get you something to drink while we talk."

Sadie looked up at Pastor Bill, and the smile he gave her melted my heart. Cupid must be taking up residence in South Cove, because love was definitely in the air today. "We have time for one cup."

"Great; follow me." I turned to Pastor Bill as we walked to the kitchen. "I don't think I've had you over to the house before."

"No, but I came here many times to visit with its previous owner, Emily. You've made the place shine with youth and life. She would be proud." He pulled out a chair for Sadie. "Now you just need to add some little feet to the mix."

"Oh, we don't need another dog. Emma's quite enough." I turned away to grab cups and wipe away the tears that the mention of my friend Emily had brought.

Sadie's laugh tinkled through the room. "Jill, he wasn't talking about another dog. He was hinting, poorly, that you and Greg needed to get married and start having kids."

I almost dropped the cup I was setting in front of Pastor Bill. "Oh, well, I don't think we're ready yet..."

"Don't let him mess with you. That decision is between you and Greg, not anyone else." Sadie stood and grabbed the coffeepot. She filled the cups and set napkins in front of each person. Then she opened the box of cookies. "Sit down and let me tell you what Paula said."

Sugar, flour, butter, and a bit of almond filled the room. I took one and bit into it before I set the other half on the napkin. "These are heavenly."

Sadie blushed. "Thanks. So, we went to see Paula today. She got the other half of this cookie batch. Anyway, she broke down crying and told me that she'd snooped on Ben's computer and found love letters to another woman. I guess they were pretty graphic about what he wanted to do to her, so Paula felt like she couldn't tell us. Like we'd think differently of her just because the guy was a big, fat cheater."

"Men like him break down a woman's confidence and they feel like it's their fault." Pastor Bill squeezed Sadie's shoulder. "I hate to admit it, but sometimes men aren't the partners and companions God created them for. I mean, this guy lived off Paula for a full year. She paid all the bills. He kept saying he'd have a big paycheck soon. That they'd be in fat city then."

"From his self-employment?"

Sadie shook her head. "Paula said he only put up the web page. He never took on a job, from what she could find. Why would you even spend the money on designing a web page if you weren't going to do the work?"

"Good question." I finished my cookie and grabbed another.

Pastor Bill looked at his watch. "If we're going to make our reservation, we'd better get going."

As they stood, I thought of another question. "Did Paula get this girl's name?"

"She did. She said it was Dee." Sadie hugged me, and I watched them climb into Pastor Bill's older sedan. He held the door open for her, then waved at me before getting in himself. And then they were gone.

I wrote down everything they'd said in my notebook. As soon as I saw Greg, or he called, I'd tell him about the mystery woman. With Earl Hess found, maybe this Dee would be another lead.

I was just finishing the hamburger when a thought hit me. Dee. Denyse. Could it be the same person? Could that be why Ben was hanging out at the Senior Project, because he was sleeping with Denyse too? I picked up the phone and called Jackie's burner phone. No answer.

I put the hamburger in the oven on low, then grabbed Emma's leash. I needed to make sure Jackie hadn't talked to a Dee at the Project and to warn her to stay away from Denyse until Greg could clear her. And I didn't like that she wasn't picking up her phone. "Want to go for a ride with me?"

Chapter 22

Pulling in next to Jackie's car, I rolled down the windows for Emma. I pointed to the patio. "You stay here and I'll be right up there."

Emma made three circles and then lay down on the passenger seat. She was used to waiting for me. I never took her out when it was too hot, but we got a lot of cool days where she could go with me. I rubbed her head before I left. "Don't be sad; after dinner we'll go to the beach for a walk."

Her ears perked up, but she didn't lift her head. I was being punished.

Laughing, I locked the doors of the Jeep and ran up to Jackie's. A quick stop and I'd be back making tacos in less than ten minutes. My stomach growled in protest. It was almost seven now and I hadn't eaten any lunch. The almond cookies were letting me down.

I knocked on the door. No answer. I called out, "Aunt Jackie, I need to talk to you."

I waited; still no answer. Maybe she'd gone to dinner with Harrold. I could only hope. I called her phone again and heard the ring inside the apartment. And she'd left her phone behind. Great. My aunt seriously didn't understand the concept of keeping a phone on you at all times. When the voice mail answered, I left a quick message. "Call me as soon as you get home. I need to talk something out with you."

As I ended the call, I turned to go down the stairs, but I heard a crash. Fear exploded in me. She was inside but unable to get to the door. Was it a heart attack? Or a stroke? I dug for my keys and dialed 911 at the same time. If she was just asleep, I could call back. The operator answered on the first ring.

"Send someone to the apartment above 123 Main Street, the coffee shop in South Cove. I heard a crash, and my aunt's elderly."

"Is she hurt?" the operator asked.

I dug for my keys one-handed. "I don't know, I'm not in the apartment yet."

"Well, before we send out an ambulance, let's see what's going on with your aunt. Let me know when you're in the apartment. I'll stay on the line." The operator's calm voice wasn't helping the situation.

"Just send an ambulance."

"I'm not going to do that. Now, are you in the apartment yet?"

I tried to put the key in the lock, and my aunt answered the door. "What's going on out here?"

"Are you all right?" I scanned her, looking for signs of pain or a stroke. My aunt sighed. "Jill, I'm fine. I just dropped my teapot."

"From what I'm hearing of the conversation, you don't need an ambulance?" the operator interrupted.

"I guess not. Sorry for the bother."

"I'm glad it turned out okay," the operator replied and then hung up on me.

"I need to get ready for dinner. Harrold's coming by in a while and taking me for steak." Jackie started to close the door.

"Wait. All I needed to say was, I think there's something wrong with Denyse and the Senior Project. So stay away from that place, okay?"

My aunt nodded and tried to close the door again. "I understand, Jill."

I turned to leave when the door flew open again.

"Is something wrong?" I asked my aunt.

As I watched, she was pulled back into the apartment. "I was going to let you go, but now I need to know what you think you know about me." Denyse appeared at the door with a handgun. "Come on in and let's have a little chat."

I resisted the urge to glance back down at my Jeep and my dog. Hopefully, someone would find her before she got tired of waiting and jumped out the window, or worse, chewed up my seats. I walked inside the apartment and heard the door slam behind me. All thoughts of Emma flew out of my head. This must be what prisoners felt when the cage doors closed. I took my aunt's hand. "Are you really all right?"

"She's fine, or will be if you follow my instructions," Denyse said. "Go over to the couch and sit down. I need to be able to see your hands at all times."

I walked my aunt over to the couch and we sat, but not before I felt her hand tremble in mine. Aunt Jackie was scared, not something I'd seen often. "So I'm in here. What do you want? Money? We don't keep much on-site on the weekends. Deek did a drop at the bank after he closed the shop. It's protocol. We don't want to be robbed or seen as an easy place to rob."

"Which is why you changed the locks?" Denyse challenged. "Or was there another reason?"

"Jackie has been getting calls from a blackmailer. Changing the locks is supposed to keep out the riffraff, but I guess even that didn't work." My tone was flat, but I could feel my anger seeping through the words.

"Cute. But don't get all high and mighty with me. I'm here to help. Don't you remember our slogan?" Denyse leaned forward. "Moving here was the worst decision I've made for a while. It didn't help when that moron followed me."

"Are you talking about Earl or Ben?"

The twitch in her cheek told me I'd hit the spot with my guess. I rolled my shoulders. "Or maybe both."

"Ben was supposed to be working the Atlanta area. Earl, I set up in Des Moines. But neither one of them could deal with being alone. You can't overfish an area or the fish realize what's going on and you get caught. I told them both to stay put, but they're men. What can you expect?" She narrowed her eyes. "I came here today to try to determine if you were putting things together yet. Your aunt should have stayed put in the city. She never would have been picked up as a mark again if she'd stayed put. It's hard to keep track of the sheep you've already fleeced."

"I was just a sheep to you? That man—he pretended to be my dead husband. Don't you have any feelings at all?" my aunt barked out at Denyse. Apparently, she was tired of letting everything go.

"Like I said, the idiots targeted you a second time. If they had been coordinating with me, I would have seen the duplications. Neither one of them were detail people."

"Were? Is Earl dead too?" I knew he was alive and probably singing like a canary. That was what happened when the woman you loved left you tied up in a hot garage. Loyalty got tested.

"You're awful chatty. Are you expecting your white knight to come save you?" Denyse peered at me. "What are you expecting to happen here? If you'd just kept your nose out of it, I would have been gone tomorrow and your aunt would have lived through this. Now, she's going to have a heart attack and you're going to die trying to save her. Maybe a fall down the stairs. We'll start inside, and if that doesn't work, we'll move to the outside staircase."

"Don't you have things all planned out? I'm taking this isn't your first rodeo."

When she didn't answer, I pushed. "Seriously, you're going to kill us anyway, why not brag a little?

"Stand up." She waved the gun at me.

"What?" Now I was completely confused.

"Stand up and take off your shirt. Let me see if you're bugged."

I raised my eyebrows. "Paranoid much?"

"Are you going to stand up or do I shoot your aunt in the foot? That will really hurt, and if she already has arthritis, it's going to bother her the rest of her life." Denyse turned the gun toward Jackie's foot.

"Fine, but I think you're just getting your jollies." I stood and pulled off the South Cove Rocks T-shirt I'd been wearing all day. I slowly spun around. "Satisfied?"

"It makes me feel better, yes. I can't be too careful with you. Rumor around town is you like solving murder cases. Is that to get one-up on your boyfriend? Or is he just dumb as dirt?"

I wanted to respond, tell her that Greg was one of the smartest men I'd ever met, but it was clear the woman had a thing about being better than the men in her life. I pulled my shirt back on and sat. "I just like figuring out puzzles. But I didn't realize you were involved in both Ben's murder and my aunt's phone stalker until I walked into the apartment."

"Really? I thought you'd figured it out today, in the shop. You looked a little off when I left. What had you concerned then?" Denyse leaned forward, watching me.

"I was thinking about Ben and his other woman. You know, the nurse at the nursing home?" I wanted to get her angry. Maybe she would make a mistake.

"That tramp? Who can account for where a man wants to take a drink?" She bit her lip. "Maybe I should have killed him then. That would have saved me some aggravation."

"I should have figured out your involvement." I mentally slapped myself. Denyse had mentioned Jackie's being in a Ponzi scheme. I'd never told her what happened, just that she was victimized before. That was what had been bothering me. But when Fred came and told me about Greg, that had distracted me. "Actually, it was something Greg told me. That someone at the Senior Project had said that Paula and Ben were breaking up. And then Paula admitted she'd found your love letters to her boyfriend. What? Had he broken off your relationship so you shot him?"

"Like he'd choose that weak dishrag he was using as a place to stay over me." Denyse looked almost offended. "No, he died because he was stupid. And because he threatened to turn me in if I didn't increase his cut. Greedy little traitor."

A knock came on the back door.

"Just be quiet," Denyse whispered, her dark eyes showing her fury. "What is this, Grand Freaking Central?"

The knocking continued. "Oh, Jackie, it's Harrold. I'm here to take you to dinner and celebrate our new engagement. Don't even pretend not to be home. I'm not going anywhere, not again."

Denyse closed her eyes, her teeth gritted together. "Okay, let's move to the door. Jackie, you'd better convince him to leave better than you did this one."

"If you hadn't dropped the gun and made a noise, she would have gone away." Aunt Jackie rose slowly, and I followed suit.

Our group of three moved over to the door, and when Jackie opened it, Harrold's voice boomed into the room. "You'll never get rid of me again. Not after all that we've been through."

I watched as Harrold quickly took Jackie's arm, pulling her out onto the patio. I realized then that we were being rescued. I pushed the door shut after her and felt the gun in my side.

"What do you think you're doing?" Denyse shouted at me.

Before I could answer, I heard the crack of the other door and dropped to the floor. Denyse spun around, but not quickly enough, as Greg, Toby, and Tim had already come through the door and Toby had the hand holding the gun above her head. Tim was on the other side, with the left arm behind her back. I heard her scream in frustration, but I watched as Greg calmly took the gun out of her hand.

"Cuff her and put her in the back of the squad car. Tim, you keep watch, and Toby, you go let Emma out of Jill's car before she rips open the door." Greg kneeled next to me. "Why am I always rescuing you?"

"Because you love me?" I let him pull me off the floor and into a standing position. "How on earth did you know what was going on?"

"Harrold. He came by to pick up Jackie and saw Emma in the car. She was going crazy, trying to get out and up to the patio. Harrold went up the stairs onto the patio and listened for a few minutes at the open kitchen window." Greg pointed to the window, where the breeze was making the curtains fly. "He thought maybe you and Jackie were fighting about this whole stalker thing, but when he realized Denyse was inside, he came back down and called me."

"Is Emma all right?"

The back door opened and Emma flew inside. She was pulling Toby by the leash and stopped in front of me. She jumped up, put her feet on my chest, and gave me several doggy kisses.

"Somehow she knew you were in trouble." Greg stroked her head and then snapped for her to get down.

I knelt to be at her level and rubbed behind her ears. "I told her we'd go walking after dinner. I guess I took too long to get back to the car."

* * * *

Emma and I were sitting in Greg's office, waiting for him to finish up so we could go home. He didn't want me alone after what had just happened. He'd promised me that we'd be on the road in less than fifteen minutes and had me call in an order to Diamond Lille's that he'd stop to pick up and then meet me at home. With all that had happened, I didn't mind waiting for him to follow me there.

Harrold and my aunt had decided to go to dinner anyway, which proved how much they really wanted some time together. I wasn't going to complain. The fact that they were finally talking again made me smile. I was deep into the book I'd had tucked into my tote. It was a historical mystery by one of the top women in the mystery world. I had loved all her books, and this new one was even better than the last.

"Miss Gardner. I'm so glad you're all right." Mayor Baylor stood in the doorway.

Emma growled, and he took a step back.

"Thank you, but I'm not speaking to you right now." I grabbed Emma's collar. "You and your manager's cheap trick didn't work. And Greg's told you several times, he's not running."

"I don't understand. What cheap trick?"

I set down the book and studied his face. Marvin looked truly confused. "You didn't send Fred to talk to me?"

"Fred said he needed to work on the survey metrics. I haven't seen him since Wednesday." He stepped closer, but Emma's low growl made him pause. "Seriously, what is going on? I know you were at your aunt's apartment when Greg apprehended the killer. That's all I know."

"Fred came to see me today to tell me that Greg was having an affair with Sherry."

Marvin shook his head. "His ex-wife Sherry? Like that would happen."

"Well, Fred planted Sherry's number on Greg and told me it was all over the City Hall gossip chain." I watched his face as it turned from confusion to anger.

"Believe me, if your boyfriend was stepping out on you here in the building, your friend would have put a stop to it before anyone could have told you." He shook his head. "I can't believe Fred did that. I mean, I've had to pull him back before, but he never did anything this underhanded."

"Well, Deek witnessed the entire conversation if you don't believe me." I stroked Emma's head, trying to calm her down. "And please don't bring him to my coffee shop; he's been banned for life."

"I don't need a witness. You misunderstood me. I'm sorry this happened and I'll deal with Fred. He won't bother you again." He turned his attention to Greg, who had walked in at the end of the conversation. "Again, let me express my apologies for his actions."

"He's lucky I was too busy finding a killer today because if I'd seen him, I would have had to arrest myself for assault because I was going to beat the crap out of him." Greg moved around the mayor, sat next to me, and took my hand.

"Fred will not be in the building again." Mayor Baylor nodded. "I'm not sure what's going to happen with our relationship, but he won't be here again."

Greg and Marvin locked gazes, and after a few minutes, Greg nodded. "We need to go. Our dinner's waiting for us."

As I walked out of the office to my Jeep, I leaned closer. "What was that last stare down about?"

"It's a guy thing. But Marvin knows if his guard dog ever does anything like this again, I'll take care of it." He opened my door and motioned Emma into my Jeep. Then he held it for me. "Go home. I'll be right behind you."

As I climbed into the car, I kissed him. "Don't forget my milkshake."

Chapter 23

We'd finished dinner and were sitting outside on the front porch watching the sun set. The show seemed brighter and more beautiful, probably because of what we'd gone through. I took a sip of my beer. "So, you never told me about Earl. Denyse said he was part of her crew, but did he explain why she'd tied him up in that garage? It seems like she had to know someone would find the guy."

"She didn't think the house was on the market until next Wednesday. I guess the Realtor jumped the gun and wanted to show it to a prospective buyer." He rubbed his thumb over my hand.

"Wait, she owned the house? Why was she selling?"

"Her owning the house is a little iffy. Toby called and talked to the woman in the nursing home who actually owned it, and she thought Denyse was helping her sell it. She was a client of the Senior Project and said she signed a power of attorney last week. The Realtor told Tim that Denyse had a quitclaim deed, not a power of attorney."

"So she was stealing a house from an elderly woman in a nursing home? That's unbelievable."

"I think it gets worse. I'm going to try to track down where this group was living before to see if we can get them on multiple fraud charges. Of course, there's the actual murder charge, which Denyse says Earl did."

I interrupted. "And Earl's blaming Denyse."

"Yep, you got it." He finished his beer. "The bad thing is, the Senior Project may not come back from this kind of bad press. I hope Paula's ready to be the executive director, because she and this Tessa seem to be the only two who weren't involved."

I thought about all the people like my aunt who had their life savings stolen by people who should have been helping them. "I hope they are able to keep the place going. Any way to measure how much data got leaked?" "According to Earl, Denyse was building her group. He thought it was just the three of them. But I think the guy is trying to make it seem like less of an issue. Like they were just a little guilty."

Harrold's little Smart car turned into the driveway. Greg stood to greet them. "Looks like we have visitors."

"I'm just glad they're talking again." I finished my beer.

As Harrold and Aunt Jackie walked up the pathway, Emma's tail beat on the wood floor of the porch.

"Good evening, children." Harrold handed Greg a box. "We thought we'd bring you two dessert."

Even though I'd finished my milkshake, I wasn't going to say no to a dessert. "Great. Can I get you coffee?"

"No, we're on our way back to Jackie's to pack an overnight bag. With the door broken, I'd feel more comfortable if she stayed with me for a few days." He grinned. "But that's not what we came to tell you. Jackie, do you want to say it?"

My aunt came over and sat by me on the swing. "I've asked Harrold to marry me and he's said yes. I figured because I was the one who messed up the last engagement, I needed to be the one to start the new one."

"I was totally blindsided." Harrold grinned. "And flummoxed when she asked. The only thing that ruined the moment was she didn't buy me a ring."

My aunt patted my hand. "Don't you believe him. He jumped at the chance to marry me."

"Congratulations. Again." I kissed her on the cheek, and Greg shook Harrold's hand. Then Harrold gave me a hug, and I whispered in his ear, "Welcome back to the family."

As the men talked about the events of the day, I saw Jackie take off the silver heart necklace she'd been wearing for weeks. She dropped it in my hand and closed my fingers around it. "What are you doing?"

"Your Uncle Ted gave that to me on our first-month anniversary. I've held tight to it and his memory for a long time. But now, I want to see where my life with Harrold will go. I want you to have this. I don't have a lot of jewelry to pass on to you, but this necklace has my heart as well as your uncle's. I hope you treasure it as I did."

I looked at the silver heart and tears filled my eyes. "Thank you, Aunt Jackie. I love it already."

My phone buzzed with an incoming message. I was going to ignore it, but my aunt picked it up from the swing where I'd set it when we came outside. "You'd better check this. It might be Deek trying to call off tomorrow. I swear, that kid doesn't have an ounce of responsibility in him."

"You know that's not true, and tomorrow is his book club. There is no way he'd call it off." But after she gave me another glare, I opened the message and read it. "It's from Amy. She's decided to have a joint bachelor and bachelorette party in Vegas. Do we want to come?"

Greg grinned. "Justin must have learned from the conference snafu."

"What does that mean?" My aunt pulled her phone out of her purse as it was buzzing as well. "I got the same message."

"It means, we're going to Vegas, baby!" Greg slapped Harrold on the back and my aunt and I shared a look.

It didn't really matter what we thought. Amy was the bride, and we were there to support her. So we were going to Vegas.

"We may have to shut down the store," Jackie said. "Especially if both of us will be out of state."

"I think the store can manage without us for a weekend." I started to put away my phone, but another text came through.

HOW ARE THE TABLE DECORATIONS GOING?

This time, I turned off my phone and set it down. I could answer her tomorrow. Then I watched the end of the sunset surrounded by the people I loved. All was back to normal and good with the world. As it should be on a late fall evening in South Cove.

Dear readers—If you follow me on Facebook (at LynnCahoon, Author), you know I love trying new recipes. I got this one during a cooking class held at a local grocery store. Several of my friends tried it, but reported so-so results. Definitely not the way the cookies tasted during the class. As I reviewed the recipe, I found the original recipe had too much flour listed. Changing it up, I got the perfect cookie.

I hope the recipe works for you as well. Jill would love these cookies.

Lynn

Easy Almond Cookies
Preheat oven to 350 degrees.

Cream the following:
3 tbsp butter, softened
1 cup firmly packed brown sugar
Add in:
1 egg
½ tsp almond extract
Mix the following dry ingredients in a small bowl:
1 cup flour
½ tsp cinnamon
¼ tsp baking soda
¼ tsp salt
Mix the wet and dry ingredients, then add:
½ cup almond slivers

Form the dough into small balls. Roll in 2 tbsp sugar, then put on greased (with spray oil) or parchment-papered cookie sheets. Bake for 10 minutes, cool on baking sheet for 2 minutes, then transfer to a wire rack.

Makes about 2½ dozen, depending on the size of your cookie balls.

Welcome back to South Cove!

Make sure you've read all the books in the series
Available now from Lyrical Underground
And don't miss Lynn's other mystery series
The Farm-to-Fork Mysteries
And The Cat Latimer Mysteries
Available now from
Lyrical Underground
And
Kensington Books

About the Author

Lynn Cahoon is the award-winning author of several New York Times and USA Today best-selling cozy mystery series. The Tourist Trap series is set in central coastal California with six holiday novellas releasing in 2018-2019. She also pens the Cat Latimer series available in mass market paperback. Her newest series, the Farm to Fork mystery series, released in 2018. She lives in a small town like the ones she loves to write about with her husband and two fur babies.

Sign up for her newsletter at www.lynncahoon.com

Guidebook to Murder

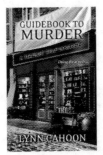

In the gentle coastal town of South Cove, California, all Jill Gardner wants is to keep her store—Coffee, Books, and More—open and running. So why is she caught up in the business of murder?

When Jill's elderly friend, Miss Emily, calls in a fit of pique, she already knows the city council is trying to force Emily to sell her dilapidated old house. But Emily's gumption goes for naught when she dies unexpectedly and leaves the house to Jill—along with all of her problems…and her enemies. Convinced her friend was murdered, Jill is finding the list of suspects longer than the list of repairs needed on the house. But Jill is determined to uncover the culprit—especially if it gets her closer to South Cove's finest, Detective Greg King. Problem is, the killer knows she's on the case—and is determined to close the book on Jill permanently…

Mission to Murder

**In the California coastal town of South Cove, history is one of its many
tourist attractions—until it becomes deadly...**

Jill Gardner, proprietor of Coffee, Books, and More, has discovered that
the old stone wall on her property might be a centuries-old mission worthy
of being declared a landmark. But Craig Morgan, the obnoxious owner of
South Cove's most popular tourist spot, The Castle, makes it his business to
contest her claim. When Morgan is found murdered at The Castle shortly
after a heated argument with Jill, even her detective boyfriend has to ask
her for an alibi. Jill decides she must find the real murderer to clear her
name. But when the killer comes for her, she'll need to jump from historic
preservation to self-preservation...

If The Shoe Kills

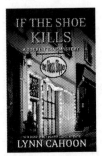

The tourist town of South Cove, California, is a lovely place to spend the holidays. But this year, shop owner Jill Gardner discovers there's no place like home for homicide...

As owner of Coffee, Books, and More, Jill Gardner looks forward to the hustle and bustle of holiday shoppers. But when the mayor ropes her into being liaison for a new work program, 'tis the season to be wary. Local businesses are afraid the interns will be delinquents, punks, or worse. For Jill, nothing's worse than Ted Hendricks—the jerk who runs the program. After a few run-ins, Jill's ready to kill the guy. That, however, turns out to be unnecessary when she finds Ted in his car—dead as a doornail. Detective Greg King assumes it's a suicide; Jill thinks it's murder. And if the holidays weren't stressful enough, a spoiled blonde wants to sue the city for breaking her heel. Jill has to act fast to solve this mess—before the other shoe drops...

Dressed to Kill

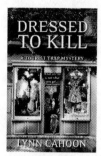

Jill Gardner is not particularly thrilled to be portraying a twenties flapper for the dinner theater murder mystery. Though it is for charity...

Of course everyone is expecting a "dead" body at the dress rehearsal... but this one isn't acting! It turns out the main suspect is the late actor's conniving girlfriend Sherry...who also happens to be the ex-wife of Jill's main squeeze. Sherry is definitely a master manipulator...but is she a killer? Jill may discover the truth only when the curtain comes up on the final act...and by then, it may be far too late.

Killer Run

Jill has somehow been talked into sponsoring a 5k race along the beautiful California coast. The race is a fundraiser for the local preservation society—but not everyone is feeling so charitable...

The day of the race, everyone hits the ground running...until a local business owner stumbles over a very stationary body. The deceased is the vicious wife of the husband-and-wife team hired to promote the event—and the husband turns to Jill for help in clearing his name. But did he do it? Jill will have to be very careful, because this killer is ready to put her out of the running...forever!

Murder on Wheels

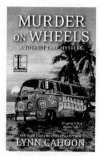

The food truck craze has reached the charming coastal town of South Cove, California, but before Jill Gardner can sample the eats, she has to shift gears and put the brakes on a killer...

Now that Kacey Austin has got her new gluten-free dessert truck up and running, there's no curbing her enthusiasm—not even when someone vandalizes the vehicle and steals her recipes. But when Kacey turns up dead on the beach and Jill's best friend Sadie becomes the prime suspect, Jill needs to step on it to serve the real killer some just desserts.

Tea Cups and Carnage

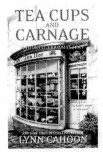

The quaint coastal town of South Cove, California, is all abuzz about the opening of a new specialty shop, Tea Hee. But as Coffee, Books, and More owner Jill Gardner is about to find out, there's nothing cozy about murder...

Shop owner Kathi Corbin says she came to South Cove to get away from her estranged family. But is she telling the truth? And did a sinister someone from her past follow her to South Cove? When a woman claiming to be Kathi's sister starts making waves and a dead body is found in a local motel, Jill must step in to clear Kathi's name—without getting herself in hot water.

Hospitality and Homicide

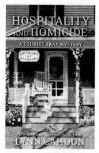

A visit to the serene coastal town of South Cove, California, could make anybody feel refreshed and inspired. But as Jill Gardner—owner of Coffee, Books, and More—discovers, some folks won't live to tell about it...

Mystery author Nathan Pike checked into South Cove Bed & Breakfast to compose a compelling novel, not commit murder. But things get real when a rival B&B owner ends up exactly like the victim in his draft—undeniably dead. As Nathan prepares to complete his magnum opus behind bars, Jill's the only one who can prove his innocence and deconstruct the plot of a twisted killer!

Killer Party

For a gang of old college buddies, the quaint resort town of South Cove, California, is the perfect spot for a no-holds-barred bachelor party. But for Jill Gardner—owner of Coffee, Books, and More—this stag party is going to be murder...

After a few months of living with her boyfriend Greg, Jill is still getting used to sharing such close quarters, but she's got no hesitation about joining him for a weekend at South Cove's most luxurious resort. While Greg and his college pals celebrate their buddy's upcoming wedding, Jill intends to pamper herself in style. But when the groom is found floating facedown in the pool, Jill must find the killer fast, or she might not have a boyfriend to come home to any more...

Printed in the United States
by Baker & Taylor Publisher Services